Property of
the State

Books by Bill Cameron

The Skin Kadash Series
Lost Dog
Chasing Smoke
Day One
County Line

The Legend of Joey Series
Property of the State

Property of the State

Book 1 of The Legend of Joey

Bill Cameron

The Poisoned Pencil

An imprint of Poisoned Pen Press

Copyright © 2016 by Bill Cameron

First Edition 2016

10 9 8 7 6 5 4 3 2 1

Library of Congress Catalog Card Number: 2015949434

ISBN: 9781929345229   Trade Paperback
      9781929345236   E-book

The Poisoned Pencil
An imprint of Poisoned Pen Press
6962 E. First Ave., Ste. 103
Scottsdale, AZ 85251
www.thepoisonedpencil.com
info@thepoisonedpencil.com

Printed in the United States of America

To Alison Dasho

1.0

In life, at least for me...

1.1: Surfing the Plan

"Joseph. Don't sit down." I'm barely through the door of Moylan's sixth period Trigonometry dungeon but he's already on my ass. "You're required in the office."

My therapist says I should count to ten before I open my mouth. With Moylan, I seldom make it past one. "My name isn't Joseph."

"You're avoiding the issue."

Everyone is pointedly ignoring us. "The issue is my name *isn't* Joseph. Why is that so fucking hard to remember?"

"I won't tolerate such language. That's a referral."

"A referral for who?"

The man has a face like a clenched fist. "I will not debate you. The matter is closed." He puffs up, in case I missed the part where he's being an autocratic douchenozzle. "Report to the office, Joseph."

Fine.

I drag my pack through the middling busy corridor, aware my shirt is stuck to my back. Only two weeks into the school year and the AC is tits up—with the Oregon summer lingering beyond all reason. I dodge people working the equation on the Prove It board outside Moylan's room. Others gather in study groups—or to gossip—in every free corner. At my old schools, people would be in class, but at Katz Learning Annex, the schedule is more guideline than rule. The hallway chatter is loud enough to loosen teeth.

When I turn the corner to the main hall, I see Trisha Lee sitting on the floor outside the library, a book open on her lap. One hand fiddles with one of her big braids looping across her shoulders. She looks up as I pass. Her eyebrows form twin question marks.

"Cooper summons," I tell her. "No idea."

She frowns like she knows something I don't. "Text me later?"

"Sure."

I see way too much of Mr. Cooper—or, as he likes to say, "Gary Cooper…no relation." No relation to who? Wait, don't ask, because if you do you get the *Encyclopedia Bigwhuptica* entry on the life and times of some actor who's been dead since before color.

He waits for me in the outer office, cool and relaxed in his suit and tie despite the heat. He's tall, and one of those people who likes to stand too close. I'd have to tilt my head back to make eye contact, so I don't bother. "Right this way, Joey." At least he knows my name. He gestures me through the door to his corral, as he likes to call it. The hinges could use a spritz of WD-40.

I have no idea why I'm here. My only involvement in the Drama of the Day was as a witness. Duncan Fox and one of his minions were slap-fighting in the hall at the end of lunch period—some kind of impromptu celebration. They were both laughing, though Duncan had that edge, which told me he was playing to win. He even tried to drag me into the ruckus—"Yo, Getchie, you missed the show. Gotta settle for the after party."

I moved back as he swung wide and wild, unaware of Philip Huntzel coming out of the bathroom behind him. Elbow to face, nothing but net. Philip's nose exploded.

At that exact second Mrs. Huntzel came charging up the hall.

Normally, your mother isn't there to rescue you in high school, but Mrs. Huntzel volunteers in the office. All day. *Every* day. Don't get me wrong. I like Mrs. Huntzel. She hired me to clean stately Huntzel Manor, and she pays in cash. Keeps me in coffee, cell service, and carpentry supplies. But it wouldn't be such a bad thing if she gave Philip a little air.

Cooper has me sit down on one of the two wooden guest chairs, then drops into his own leather throne. Because of Mr. Cooper, I know what pomade is. I can smell it from across the desk. The office is decorated like a chain restaurant, Western-themed. Lassoes and riding gear adorn the walls around a framed photo of Cooper on a horse. The nameplate on his desk has a six-pointed sheriff's badge engraved next to his name. Subtle.

"I'm disappointed in you."

So, not Duncan and Philip. I hold my backpack in my lap, gaze up at the smoke detector, waiting for the red light to blink. At least his office is quiet.

"A serious matter has been brought to my attention. Obviously, I want to hear your side."

Uh-huh. When they tell you, *Anything you say can and will be used against you,* they are not kidding. Even if what you say is completely innocent, they will twist it into a reason to screw you over.

There's a knock on the door. Cooper calls out, "Come on in."

After the way Cooper greeted me, I'm not surprised to see my caseworker. Mrs. Petty last came to this office in the spring, the day I tried to dislocate Duncan's jaw. A misunderstanding.

Mrs. Petty is about the size of your thumb, but don't get any ideas. Her miniature torso is shaped like the Tasmanian Devil, her short hair fits like a helmet over her dark scalp, and when she's riled her eyes flash like lasers. In a fight between Mrs. Petty and a rabid pit bull, the safe bet's on her. I've seen her stare down torqued-up tweakers three times her size.

Cooper is all sorrowful smiles and apologies. "Sorry you had to come in, Mrs. Petty."

"It's no problem. Joey and I are overdue for a check-in anyway." She sits down in the empty seat next to me, pats my hand. "Aren't we, Joey?"

I see my therapist more often, but Mrs. Petty sits in on sessions once every month or two. I don't feel neglected.

Cooper folds his hands on the desktop. I refuse to meet his eyes. "I called Mrs. Petty in because I felt it was important she be here to discuss the current situation."

"Discuss the current situation" is code for "we're about to take a dump in your hat." My legs twitch, ready to bolt. Except I'd have to go through Mrs. Petty.

"Joey, you understand the laptop Katz provides you is for academic use only."

They issued the laptops on the first day of school. There was all kinds of fuss about what the nitwit underpowered machines were for. ChalkChat, so-called "collaborative education software" for getting assignments and messaging our teachers, came pre-installed. Annoying, but whatever. Wayne Bobbitt, my alleged foster father, insists on having my login, so I've been careful about what I do on the computer.

Cooper makes a church with his hands. "I've received reports from the school IT department that you've used your computer to visit inappropriate websites."

I Spock one eyebrow. Though they deny wiretapping us, everyone knows better. Jeff Somers even worked up a hack to block the spyware, makes it look like the computer is asleep while you're doing...whatever. But so far, all I've used the machine for is ChalkChat, JSTOR, and word processing.

Except, apparently not.

I could deny it, but what would be the point? You can't win. There's no defense, because even if you can somehow prove they're wrong, they punish you for making them look bad.

I still haven't said anything. Cooper is getting impatient, but Mrs. Petty has known me longer. She leans across the arm of her chair. "Joey, this is a serious matter. Your place here at Katz is not guaranteed."

Cooper nods. "According to your Individualized Education Plan—"

"I'm pretty sure my IEP doesn't mention porn."

It's a guess, but dead-on based on their expressions. Cooper sits back and looks at Mrs. Petty. Gravity has taken charge of the corners of her mouth. Cooper lifts one hand and turns it over.

"Semantic games aren't the way to go here. This is your third strike."

Apparently Moylan's referral already made its way up the chain of command.

"You remember what we told you the last time you were in this room."

My eyes find the smoke detector again. "Why do you think we take our metaphor for the end of mercy from baseball? Why not football? I'd have another down to shape up. Or in hoops, I'd have two fouls to give."

"Joey—"

"Of course, if we were talking soccer, I'd already have a

couple of yellow cards, so maybe I should be glad we went with baseball."

"Joey Getchie!"

I've pissed them off, but this situation was going wrong before I opened my mouth. I settle back in my chair. I wonder if Mrs. Huntzel will get home from the emergency room with Philip anytime soon. Doesn't matter, since I have a key and the alarm code. Tuesday is living room and library day, dust and vacuum. Takes two hours, because every surface is covered with knickknacks. The living room alone has more square footage than the entire Bobbitt hovel.

"Joey?" Mrs. Petty's voice is calm, as always. I realize I'm staring at the photo of Mr. Cooper. He looks more at home in the saddle than he does behind his desk. I turn to Mrs. Petty.

"What?"

"The computer?"

"What about it?"

They exchange a look. I've missed something.

"No laptop, one month. You need to hand it over."

In my arms, my backpack gathers sudden weight.

"But I need it." My tongue feels like it's glued to the roof of my mouth. "I have—"

"You can do any assignments that require a computer in the school lab." Cooper frowns. "There's no need to make this difficult."

Yes, there is. "I left it at the Boobies."

"Joey." Mrs. Petty says I'm being childish when I call them the Boobies. She doesn't have to live with them. "Why don't you open your backpack, just to make sure?"

Everyone in the room is already sure.

Wayne "reviews" my work every night, which is when I figure he watches the porn. It would never occur to him the

7

school is watching too. I might try explaining that to Mrs. Petty and Cooper, but *no matter what you say…*As heat boils off my head and puddles around me, I slide the laptop out of my pack.

Cooper waits, his lips compressing, then reaches across his desk and gestures impatiently. When I don't move, Mrs. Petty grabs the computer and hands it to him. He sets it on the credenza behind him. I offer him the power cord too, but he's on a roll and ignores me. "If you perform up to expectations, you may earn the computer back early."

Time off for good behavior. Cold comfort.

I set the cord on his desk. The laptop won't turn on unless it's plugged in. If Cooper, or someone from IT, decides to find out why and opens the battery compartment, getting expelled will be the least of my problems.

Fuck. Me.

I wonder how far I can get on foot. "That's it?"

They exchange another look. Mrs. Petty reaches for my hand, but I pull away. It takes everything I've got not to stare over Cooper's shoulder at my laptop. At my doom.

"Then I guess we're done."

1.2: The Boobies

"You're lucky you're not on your way to Madison."

Mrs. Petty threatening me with a transfer to an actual high school is weaksauce compared to making me ride in her forty-year-old Impala shitwagon. She can barely see over the steering wheel.

"Cooper likes having my GPA on the books. He's got budget meetings coming up."

"Joey, you're not as smart as you think."

I simmer for a minute.

"Fine. Cooper's budget has nothing to do with it. I get another chance because I'm a sad little orphan."

Her lips go two-dimensional, then she lets out a long, slow breath. "You get another chance because there are people—like me—who believe in you. Despite how difficult you make it."

In January, I plan to apply for early graduation. The last two summers, my various foster oppressors kept me out of trouble by packing me off to summer school. Sucked, but as a result I'll meet the requirements by the end of second semester; senior year would be a waste of my time. Mrs. Petty and Cooper will push back, but the guidelines are clear. I'll have the classes, the credits, the GPA. And once I have my diploma, I'll file for emancipation. Only sixteen and I have issues—according to everyone—so emancipation will be tough. But if the court won't grant it, I'm gone anyway. I can't handle living with the Bobbitts much longer. I'm way past ready to jump off the Services to Children and Families hamster wheel too.

Not that Mrs. Petty needs to know any of this. No point in giving her a head start on plotting against me.

I close my eyes. The interior of the car smells like burning metal. She keeps talking, but I don't listen. It's the usual speech. *One of these days you'll come to understand how hard we are all working on your behalf....Not just me, or your teachers, or Mr. Cooper, the Bobbitts too....It isn't nice the way you talk about them....You're lucky you're not living in a group home. Wayne and Anita took you in when your care options were paper-thin....blah blah blah...*

The car stops and I look up. We're at the Boobie Hatch.

"I'm supposed to be at work. Today is living room and library." A man's gotta have priorities.

"I left a message on Mrs. Huntzel's cell phone. You can catch up tomorrow."

It doesn't work like that. I have a schedule. Monday is dining room, conservatory, and foyer; the foyer floor has to be waxed and buffed, and the dining room can seat twenty-four, so it takes a while. Tuesday: living room and library. Thursday, I do the upstairs public areas and the finished parts of the basement. Friday, I clean Mrs. Huntzel's office and scrub the kitchen floor, catch up on anything outstanding. Saturday mornings, there's outside—anything the yard service doesn't take care of. Wednesday—tomorrow—is therapy. I'd miss that in a heartbeat, but Reid would come unglued if I skipped. So would Mrs. Petty, if she thought through the implications of what she just said.

"Come along, Joey."

Wayne waits for us on the porch, shoulders straight and hands behind his back. Parade rest, so he tells me.

This visit is scheduled.

The temptation to flee is strong, but the thought of Mrs. Petty stalking me through backyards and over fences like a miniature Terminator stops me. I follow her up the steps.

"Thank you for coming, Hedda." Wayne talks like this is his idea, but I know who calls the shots here. I look at Mrs. Petty. She doesn't seem to care.

"Will Anita be joining us?"

His face twists into a crazed scowl. I suppose he's trying to show concern, but to me he looks like he's having a hemorrhoid flare-up. "She has a doctor's appointment, I'm afraid."

"How is she doing?"

"It's been tough, as you know."

Anita used to drive a forklift at this big home improvement warehouse down in Clackamas. Stacks of plywood, pallets of lawn fertilizer, barrels of paint. One day in June, she got the forks jammed in the beams of a high pallet rack. Rather than call for help, she climbed the lift mast to see if she could free the forks herself. Thirteen vertical feet below, the concrete floor brought her to an abrupt stop. Now, three months later, she's in a lawsuit with her company and—near as I can tell—addicted to oxycodone.

But we're not allowed to talk about that.

Wayne leads us inside. It's a small house on the flats east of Mount Tabor between Eighty-second Avenue and I-205. The design is Lego Modern, but the construction is Rain-Soaked Cardboard. Every blocky edge is soft and frayed, the corners all dark with mildew. In the living room, a sprung couch is centered on the big boxy TV, old-def. As usual, Wayne is watching cable snooze. He's all about the news, while Anita lives for reality TV. *Who Wants To Be A Kardashian Towel Boy?* and *I Can't Stop Giving Birth!* compete with *Headline News* and roundtable shout fests. For me, it doesn't matter what's on. It's all noise.

One direction, the dining table is piled high with overflow from Wayne's office—he's some kind of insurance guy. Home way too much, which is all I need to know. The air is stale and smells of creamed chipped beef—Wayne's favorite meal. The other way, a short hallway under the stairs leads to the Bobbitt bedroom—*shudder*. One can only hope they don't actually mate.

The only thing the house has going for it is the second floor. Since her accident, Anita can't manage the steep stairway, so I only have to deal with personal space invasions from Wayne. He's bad enough, but at least he doesn't steal my money to buy dope. Excuse me. *Medication.*

"So what's the problem this time?"

Wayne used to be in the Marines, but all that's left of those days is his sharp voice. The rest of him is as soft as the couch where he spends most of his waking hours.

Mrs. Petty heads for the stairs. "Just a spot-check. How is Joey doing?"

"His grades are satisfactory. I wish I could say the same about his attitude."

Goes both ways, Wayne. He and I follow her up. Spot-check means a room search. She wants to know what I'm hiding.

My room—a narrow brown cell with a sloped ceiling—is spotless. Not much to mess up. There are no pictures or posters on the walls, no books except a student dictionary, an ancient encyclopedia set, and a Bible I've never opened. The twin bed is made to Wayne's Marine Corps standards, the itchy olive drab blanket taut across the thin mattress. The dresser is steel-framed pressboard. Socks rolled in the top drawer, shorts folded in the second. Shirts and pants below. I have a few items hanging in the shallow closet. The desktop holds only a Tensor lamp and a mug filled with pencils. I'm pretty sure Wayne comes in and sharpens them when I'm gone.

Mrs. Petty flicks the Tensor lamp on and off, then glances in the closet and pulls open my dresser drawers.

Wayne folds his arms and makes his drill sergeant face. "I check the drawers and closet for food every day."

She and I both know stashing food is so nine years ago. She throws him a side eye he doesn't catch, then kneels to tap along the baseboards. When she hears a hollow spot, she looks back at me and pulls a Leatherman tool from her pocket, opens the flathead screwdriver. She slips the head into a narrow gap between the wall and the top of the baseboard. A two-foot section clatters onto the bare wood floor. Wayne draws a breath.

Behind the baseboard, I've cut away the drywall to reveal a shallow space framed with thin slats of pine. The wall studs are on sixteen-inch centers, making the space a little more than a foot wide, three inches deep, and four inches high—as big as I could make it and still hide it behind the baseboard.

Mrs. Petty stands up. "Empty. Should I be pleased, or keep looking?"

This particular hidey-hole is a gimme. I've never used it. There are a couple of others in the room, one pretty easy to find if she wants to, one I hope she'll miss.

"A sneak." A vein stands out on Wayne's forehead.

Mrs. Petty seems less concerned. "How long has this been here, Joey?"

I shrug. She knows better than to ask me questions like that. She turns to Wayne. "I see it as a good sign. At least it's not stuffed with chocolate." I've never hoarded candy, as she knows. I look out the barred window—for security, allegedly. The key hangs on a hook on the wall, but as soon as Mrs. Petty leaves, Wayne will retrieve it. He doesn't want me sneaking out at night. Or, apparently, escaping if the house ever catches fire. A shadow pressure of fear constricts my chest at the thought. I shove it down again and focus on the smoke detector on the ceiling above the window.

Mrs. Petty spends a few minutes tapping the walls without finding anything of interest. I'm not surprised when she unplugs the Tensor light and tries it in the one unused outlet in the room, just as she isn't surprised when the light doesn't work. She uses her screwdriver to remove the faceplate. The plug assembly, unwired, swings out on hinges. The space behind it is much smaller than the space behind the baseboard, an ordinary PVC electrical box. Mrs. Petty reaches inside and pulls out a USB thumb drive.

"What's this?"

She waves the seemingly innocuous object at me. Like I'd tell her what's actually on it.

"Wayne's collection of Internet porn?"

This is how I end up in trouble. But sometimes, a smart-assed remark is worth the look on their faces, no matter the blowback afterward.

1.3: Oh, My Nose

Mrs. Petty pockets the thumb drive, but I'm not worried. She won't find the hidden script Somers created to fake out the prying eyes of Katz IT. It's designed to auto-load on mount—but only if the spyware is present. Otherwise, all you see is a boobs-and-bullets game demo he put there to give the witless something to fret about.

Her gaze drips with disappointment. Story of my life. "Joey, I think I'll sit in with you and Reid tomorrow." Oh good. A tag team. She eases past Wayne and heads down the stairs. His own parting shot features flecks of spit. "Clean this trash heap." He doesn't slam the door on his way out. Not quite.

People say there are reasons I find myself in these situations. In the typical rundown, Mrs. Petty—or my therapist, Reid—will bring up my father, Orville, and my sister, Laura, dead when the house burned down. They might mention my mother, Eva, last seen tearing off in the family pickup around the time the fire broke out. Maybe they'll remind me I nearly died myself. A neighbor pulled me out of the burning house just as the first fire truck arrived.

The thing is, it all happened over ten years ago. I've been property of the state longer than I was in parental custody. I try to tell them: I barely remember what Laura looked like. As for Orville and Eva, well—I have a clearer picture of the back of my own head. If you ask me, post-traumatic stress disorder is just psychobabble used to control people who won't act the way the world thinks they should.

I rub my hands on my pants and glare at the security bars. Where I came from doesn't matter. Where I'm going even less. Right now, all that matters is Wayne and the next ten minutes.

I move to the door, crack it open. I can hear murmuring down below. Mrs. Petty is probably pointing out the ways things could be worse, maybe sharing an anonymous horror story about one of her other cases. *This situation with the computer,* she'll say, *it's perfectly normal. Boys like to look at explicit sexual imagery.*

So do middle-aged ex-Marines, but I doubt Wayne will cop to using my laptop to find spanking material.

I close the door and regard the trash heap. I vacuumed and dusted before school, a daily requirement. During her search, Mrs. Petty didn't make much of a mess, but I return the lamp to the desk and close up the hidey-holes. Just for giggles, I stick the window key inside the outlet compartment. Since she showed him exactly where to look, Wayne will get a cheap thrill when he finds it. If I'm lucky, he'll think she sussed out all my hides.

When everything is in order, I sit on the bed. Wayne's meltdowns follow a standard arc. Thunder, stomping, foaming. Once his heart rate passes one hundred sixty, he'll suck air until he can breathe again and then send me to bed. The Bobbitts aren't allowed to not feed me—regular mealtimes are part of my treatment plan. But Wayne's definition of a meal is pretty loose. I'll be lucky to get a couple of Kraft Singles on toast and a glass of milk.

But when Wayne opens the door, I can see something is off. His face is the color of his beloved chipped beef. Beads of sweat gleam in his crew cut. "What did you say to her?"

There's no good answer to a question like that. Wayne's pupils bounce side to side, as if he can't decide which of my eyes he wants to gouge out first.

"I asked you a question." His voice has a crazy wobble. He takes a step, then another until he's standing over me. White goo collects at the corners of his mouth. A vein thumps at his temple.

"What did you *say* to her?"

"I didn't have to say anything. We could both hear you fapping as we drove up."

Prolly shoulda have counted to ten.

Wayne picks me up, two-handed, and throws me against the wall. I don't have time to be surprised. The whole house seems to shake as I bounce off sheetrock and pitch face-forward into the corner of the desk.

A shatter of light blinds me. I fall sideways and crack the back of my head against the desk chair. Sickening waves roll from my gut to my throat. I'm not sure what I'm seeing at first. A scarlet glimmer through broken glass. Spilled paint splashed across the floor. Feels like something is trying to get at my brain through my sinus cavity. I reach for the edge of desk—anything solid. Then I see Wayne.

He looks glassy-eyed and ghost white. Something I've never seen before.

I put my hand to my face, touch gore. The pain hits and I fall back against the desk. Maybe I make a sound. Darkness threatens at the edge of my vision, fog the color of smoke. I blink back tears. I have to breathe through my mouth. The air tastes like metal.

"Wha'd you do t'me?" I'm not sure he can understand me. Even inside my head, the words sound like I'm talking through a wad of half-chewed paper.

Wayne backs up to the bed. He starts to tremble. A stain darkens his khakis at the crotch and down the inside of his legs.

The weird panic I feel at the sight of Wayne pissing himself is almost worse than the pain. All I want to do is get away. I stumble to the doorway, catch myself and somehow think to grab my backpack. I almost fall down the stairs, find my feet at the bottom. Leave a bloody handprint on the wall next to the front door.

When I step out onto the porch, I nearly collide with Anita.

Anita is Wayne's opposite, a broomstick with scarecrow hair and eyes like the undead. She's as tall as me, but not even half as wide. Now she's leaning on her cane, her face flushed from the three-step climb from the front walk. Nothing in her expression suggests anything is amiss. Even her voice is flat.

"Joey, what happened to you?"

"Wayne peed his pants."

She's baffled, as usual. "What are you saying?"

"He *pissed* himself." I lurch past her down the steps. The sun hangs over Mount Tabor, but overhead the sky has gone cloudy and dark. Anita taps her cane on the porch, pretending to be blind maybe. "Where's Wayne? Have you made supper?" I never make supper. Wayne doesn't like me around sharp things.

"I'm outta here." Probably unintelligible, but whatever. Somewhere in the back of my mind, I think this may be the last time I will ever talk to Anita. I take one last look at the house. Wayne peers back from my bedroom window, hands gripping the bars that keep me in at night.

As the rain begins to fall, I run.

1.4: Zombie Apocalypse

All I can think to do is put distance between me and the Boobie Hatch. At best, I'm looking at a long, grim night ahead. At worst, Mrs. Petty tracks me down and dumps me in some stack-'em-and-rack-'em warehouse where everyone sleeps in triple-bunked cots and fetal alcohol savages issue beat-downs out of boredom. If I was schizoaffective or borderline personality disorder I might score a room in a country club like the Parry Center, but—my luck—I'm not even on the autism spectrum.

The situation outside isn't much better. Whacked out hobos will throw down over a doorway or a dry spot beneath an overpass. Downtown, pimps troll runaways for mouths to add to their blowjob squads. I might ride the MAX until it stops running. Warm and dry, but I'd risk getting rolled by rail thugs, if I'm not booted by a transit cop first. In the shelters—assuming I could score a bed—it's beat-downs or worse, all over again.

For all that, I prefer my chances outdoors. Wayne will already have his story worked out—"He attacked me. All I did was push him away to protect myself." I'll take a hobo over the system any day of the week—at least you can sometimes cut a deal with the hobo.

I pause next to a rusty Camaro to hork bloody snot into the gutter. In this neighborhood no one will notice—domestic bloodlettings are as common as feral cats. Rain falls onto my neck out of a sky more blue than gray. The rainbow will be behind me, but I'm in no mood for fucking rainbows. I can hardly breathe, my face feels like someone drove a spike through it, and my options are for shit. Except: keep moving.

At Eight-second Avenue, a bug-eyed kid in the backseat of a passing minivan takes a break from his in-flight movie to gape and point. The van drives on, but a hooker on the corner finishes his thought. "What in hell happen' to you?" Half a block later, I catch my reflection in the window of a discount cigarette shop.

I look like zombie apocalypse, phase two.

There's a McDonald's on the next block where I sometimes stop on my way to school. I don't get but two steps through the door before an assistant manager scoots out from behind the counter. He's waving twig arms and shaking his head. His neck is four sizes too small for his collar.

"You hooligans aren't welcome here."

Hooligans? "I just want to wash my hands and face."

"Bathrooms are for customers only."

"Fine. I'll have a vanilla shake." I pull a tangle of singles from my pocket so he knows I can pay.

For a second his Adam's apple quakes, like maybe he works on commission. But then his eyes go hard. "Get out, before I call the police."

I need to get cleaned up and under cover until I can figure out how to keep my long-term plans on track. Cops I do *not* need.

There are other places along Stark Street—a pizza joint, a few restaurants, a coffee shop—but I have no reason to expect a warmer welcome in any of them. Marcy would let me clean up at Uncommon Cup, the café where I feed my caffeine jones, but UC's on the far side of Mount Tabor and way down Hawthorne. Thirty blocks—and me bleeding the whole way.

Then I have a thought: the Huntzels are half as far as Uncommon Cup, on the west slope of Mount Tabor Park. Mrs. Huntzel won't cover for me with Mrs. Petty, but if I'm lucky I can get there before the APB goes out. She'll let me wash up, maybe loan me some of Philip's clothes. When she asks what happened, I can tell her I was jumped by hooligans.

The Huntzel house is a castle, the kind of place where magazine-ad teens live in shows on the CW. The view alone— of the Hawthorne and Belmont districts and all the way to downtown Portland—screams money. Not that the Huntzels are flashy. Mrs. Huntzel may drive a Beamer—the 740i, her one indulgence—but she gets her hair done at SuperCuts. Mr. Huntzel drives an old Toyota and dresses like a Walmart greeter. And Philip dresses like *me*. Still, things stand out, and not just the BMW. Everything in the house is oversized, an exercise in excess, from the slate roof to the baby-grand piano in the basement rec room—a twenty-by-forty chamber also home to ping pong and pool tables, a fireplace big enough to roast a pig, and a half dozen dead animal heads on the walls. And that's just the daylight end of the basement.

Hell, there are thirty-two smoke detectors in the house. And people wonder why I need a week to clean.

I approach from the rear. Caliban—a freak show mutt who adopted the Huntzels, or maybe just Huntzel Manor—greets me outside the laurel hedge that forms the boundary between park and backyard. From the front, Caliban looks like a dust mop on stilts. The full three-hundred-sixty-view is even more absurd: a lion reimagined by *The Biggest Loser*. Mrs. Huntzel said she thinks he's half-Pomeranian, half-greyhound, half-pit bull. I don't *even* want to know how that happened.

When he sees me, he charges up the hill, tongue flapping. I flinch in anticipation of the tackle, but he barrels past and spins, then hip-checks me.

"Watch it, dog." I rub his shaggy head and continue down to the hedge gate. The rain has stopped and sun shines through broken clouds. I cross to the veranda, peering through windows. No sign of life. At the side door, I knock and wait. The air feels dense, or maybe the pressure is all inside my head. If it was right after school, I'd go in—except for days when I ride with them, I often beat the Huntzels here. But it's past five. I feel weird arriving so late.

When no one comes, I make for the front door. Caliban pads along behind. The doorbell is a freaking gong: you can hear it anywhere in the house.

Nothing.

"Where is everyone, dog? Still at the hospital?"

Caliban wags his tail, which I take as a yes.

My head is about to fall off and gore has glued my shirt to my chest. Any minute, carrion birds will start circling. "They won't mind if I go in and clean up, will they?" Another wag. I'm surprised he can understand me. In my ears, my voice sounds like a swarm of bees. Not that it matters. I'm talking myself into what might be viewed as trespassing should someone get pissy about it. Small fries, if Cooper tries to start my laptop.

"I'm going in. Cover me."

Wag.

I use my key at the side door and step into a mud room with openings to the front hallway, the south stairs, and the kitchen.

"Hello? Anyone home?" I punch in the alarm code on the panel inside the butler's pantry. On the long center island in the kitchen there's a Rite-Aid bag—Vicodin for Philip. They've been here and left again, if the silence is any indication. Knowing Mrs. Huntzel, she took Philip for ice cream.

Caliban follows me to the downstairs bathroom. The face looking out of the mirror sends a wave of nausea through me. Blood crusts my neck and shirt, and still oozes from a swollen gash near my right nostril. I soak a towel with cold water, hold it against my nose. After a minute—or an hour—the nausea subsides enough that I can rinse. When I finish, my face pulses in time with my heartbeat and my shirt is drenched, but the reflection in the mirror is slightly less harrowing. I hide the gash behind a *Star Wars* bandage from the cabinet over the sink.

I wipe up and put the towels in to soak in the laundry room, then return to the kitchen to see if anyone has come home. The house is a tomb, the only sound the ticking of the grandfather clock in the front hall. The crackle of the Rite-Aid bag in my hand is louder.

Anita swears by OxyContin, but she won't turn up her nose at Vicodin. I've never had either. The dull, red ache in my head tells me there's a first time for everything. I quickly dry-swallow a pill and return the bottle to the bag. Hopefully Philip won't count.

I close my eyes and lean against the counter. Caliban sits patiently as I await the bliss state which seems to define Anita's existence. There's a metallic taste in the back of my throat and a throbbing between my eyes.

Anita is a moron. Or I am.

I open my eyes. Through the window I can see all the way to the West Hills. Money.

"This sucks, dog. Let's go find some dry clothes." He wags his tail.

Philip's room is a minefield of empty cereal bowls and

paperback science-fiction novels. My cleaning duties don't include personal areas, thank God. His Book is on top of the tangled wad of blankets and pillows at the head of the bed. That tells me all I need to know about how bad his nose is. He never goes anywhere without his Book, a three-ring binder filled with page after page of notation on every chess game he's ever played.

Rooting through his dresser for something to wear, I'm surprised by a folder under his socks. It's filled with clippings from grocery store tabloids, all pictures of Bianca Santavenere. Weird. I would not have pegged Philip for an obsession with the used-to-be teen star now best known for stunting wardrobe malfunctions to get on TMZ. I remember her mostly because Maddie, my first foster mother, used to watch reruns of Bianca's show while us kids cleaned house. It was one of those teen drama-fests—lots of expensive clothing, crying jags, and "we have to talk" moments. But Bianca is ancient now, like forty-something.

Philip, dude...seriously?

I snag a sweatshirt with the words *Symphonica d'Italia* on the front, whatever that means. A pair of gym shorts completes the ensemble. Back in the laundry room, I strip to my underwear. Clothes join the towels in the washing machine, heavy-duty cycle.

As I pull on Philip's sweatshirt, a wave of dizziness comes over me. I shake my head. Mistake. Woozy, I drag my backpack to the rec room. I'm thinking I should start cleaning—good way to explain my presence. But my arms and legs feel like mud. I need to sit down for a few minutes first. Catch my breath, maybe check messages. Mrs. Petty will have something to say even if I have no intention of calling her back.

The oversized sectional couch is softer than I remember. My phone rests in my hand, ignored, as I melt into the upholstery and peer at the moose head hanging over the mantle. A quarter-inch layer of dust coats the broad antlers. I can't believe I let it get so bad. I make a mental note for Thursday, rec room day. The other heads—bighorn sheep, a couple of pronghorns, a Thomson's gazelle—will need dusting too.

Caliban scootches up beside me and I scratch behind his ears. "You gonna back me up, dog?" His fur is a tangle of twigs and mud. "I could say I was coming over to take care of my Tuesday schedule and you knocked my ass down the hill."

Wag.

"I agree. A Caliban-tackle face-plant is way more plausible than hooligans."

1.5: Lay Low

A voice jerks me out of a slow-motion dream. I'm running from Wayne, running from Anita's forklift, from Mrs. Petty's Impala—all to a soundtrack of feverish violin music. Cooper is asking me why my laptop won't boot up. I blink and suppress a groan. The light through the French doors is thin and watery.

"Philip! How many times have I told you to wait until you have a full load before you do laundry?"

Mrs. Huntzel's voice. Close, but not too close. The laundry room is at the far end of the basement, but sound echoes strangely against the old stone foundation. I can't hear Philip's response, but I can guess, based on Mrs. Huntzel's next words. "Don't tell me you didn't do laundry. I'm putting it in the dryer as we speak."

Sorry, Philip.

Gingerly, I explore my face with my fingers. It's mushy and tender at the point where my nose struck the corner of the desk, but the Vicodin must have done its job—I feel okay. Not great, since I'm pretty sure a family of mice have taken up residence in my sinus cavity. But not terrible.

I sit up, dig my cell phone from under my hip where it slipped while I dozed. No messages, which surprises me. Mrs. Petty should have been burning microwaves.

Sooner or later I'll have to try to walk back Wayne's stream of bullshit about what happened, but if she's in no hurry, neither am I. Between Wayne and my laptop, the system will reboot my life sooner or later, regardless of my busted-to-hell face. I could be looking at a lockdown farm.

I can handle getting yanked from Wayne and Anita's. I can even handle a group home. But if they pull me from Katz, I'll probably have to kiss early graduation good-bye.

One lousy school year. That's all I need.

But at the moment, I have a bigger problem. According to the clock on the cell phone display, it's a little before seven.

In the morning.

"Shit."

Caliban, conked out beside me, lifts his head. His tail thumps the couch.

"Shhh." I put my hand out and get a lick.

Sleeping over wasn't the idea. Whatever Mrs. Huntzel might think of me coming to work late due to a Mrs. Petty after-school intervention, I can't believe she'll be happy to learn I camped out for the night.

Behind me, through the rec room door I can see across the slate-floored landing to the doorway that leads into the utility part of basement. A long hallway runs past the vault—of course Huntzel Manor has a frickin' vault—and storage rooms to the laundry room tucked under the south staircase.

The main stairs lead to the front hall—risky. There's a passage past the laundry room into the garage cellar, but the only door out that way faces the kitchen. A skinny spiral staircase in the corner of the rec room climbs through the living room and up to the library on the second floor, but that takes me back to the main parts of the house. The French doors leading to the lower veranda aren't an option. They'll set off a security system alert as soon as I open them. And I don't have a key to the small door next to the fireplace. Not sure anyone does.

My best bet is to lay low and wait for everyone to leave. First bell is in less than half an hour. Mrs. Huntzel never misses first bell. Twenty minutes, tops, and I can let myself out. No one has to know I was ever here.

I hunker down on the couch.

Caliban noses my hand. He wants to play.

"Shoo, dog."

Disappointed, he jumps down and trots off. He leaves a patch of leaf fragments and dried mud on the couch cushion. Something else to clean on Thursday. His ticking footsteps fade as he heads out the door.

I thumb through the menus on my phone, trying to decide whether to text Trisha, when Mrs. Huntzel passes on the other side of the French doors. Because of the slope, the lower veranda sits in a little bowl accessible only from the rec room or down narrow steps from the upper veranda. She's dressed for school in one of her gray suits. Her hair, copper fading to steel, is brushed back from her face. As I watch, she pulls a pack of cigarettes from her jacket pocket, lights up with an expert flick of a Zippo. Through the door, I can hear the sharp, metallic clack as she closes the lighter.

Her gaze uphill, she folds her arms across her chest, the cigarette between the first two fingers of her right hand. Smoke rises past her ear until she raises her hand to take a drag. When she turns, her expression is dark and troubled. As she exhales, her lips curve into a sharp frown.

At that instant, my cell phone chirps in my hand, a text message:

joey, so sorry about teh news. txt me. <3

Trisha. Talk about timing.

Mrs. Huntzel looks over her shoulder. Through the windows, her eyes seem to meet mine. I press back into the couch cushions, paralyzed, as her eyebrows narrow.

Half the house is uninhabited, but I manage to hide in the one room with an unobstructed view from outside. Better options are accessible via the spiral staircase not ten feet away: the library, one of the guest rooms, hell, even Kristina's room. Philip's older sister, no one enters her forbidden chamber. When I ask Philip about her, he bristles. *She's horrible....* *Nobody wants her here.... She left, isn't coming back.* I could hide in her room for a month if I had to.

Mrs. Huntzel moves closer to the window. She takes another drag, shoots smoke through her nose. One hand goes to her temple to adjust a strand of hair. I'm half a second from diving over the back of the couch when I realize she's looking at her own reflection. She closes her eyes and shakes her head, then lets out a long, smoky breath. She's just turning away when Caliban appears, wiggling his bony ass. His appearance seems to startle her. The cigarette falls from her hand and rolls off the edge of the veranda.

My spark of anxiety about the fallen butt doesn't have time to flash as Mrs. Huntzel bends over to greet the homely mutt. "How on earth do you get in here?" She sounds exasperated even as she runs her hand through the dog's mane. No one knows how Caliban comes or goes. One of my first jobs for the Huntzels was checking the laurel hedge for dog-sized openings. Nuthin'. After that, they gave in to the inevitable and semi-adopted him, even allowing food and water dishes in the mudroom. "Come on. I have to get Philip to school."

A moment later, she's gone.

1.6: Worse Than I Thought

I have no idea how Katz Learning Annex came to exist. It's a Portland Public Schools magnet, like some hippies staged a sit-in back in the dark ages and no one noticed they never left. For one thing, Katz doesn't give out normal grades. You either Meet Course Criteria, Exceed Course Criteria, or Underperform—MEU, the Katz Meow, they call it. Vomit. If you underperform, you can appeal to a committee and half the time, talk your way into at least an *M*. According to legend, Yancy Krokos once pushed three *U*s to *E*s with the help of a PowerPoint presentation and a scorching guitar solo.

Katz is the kind of place where you're as likely to hear Russian, Mandarin, or Japanese as English. A lot of classes are open attendance, which means you only have to show up for tests. Friday afternoons are early release. Half your day you might work on your own, which can mean almost anything—Sketch Echols spent a month photographing "texture" around the building for some kind of art project. Denise Grover wrote a thriller about Rosalind Franklin and the discovery of DNA for her life-science requirement. The system is so loose some people skate all trimester, then blast through twelve weeks of coursework in a long weekend fueled by cupcakes and Monster drinks.

But show up late for Day Prep—what normal schools call homeroom—and Cooper ropes you into the corral for a stern lecture about responsibility. Six minutes or sixty makes no difference. I'm already late, so I stop for coffee.

Uncommon Cup is medium busy, the tail-end of rush hour, but Marcy has my order ready when I get to the front of the line.

"Double shot with two lumps, J-dawg."

She hands me a miniature cup on a saucer, the raw sugar nuggets on the side along with a tiny spoon. "Thanks, Marcy. Can I get a couple of chocolate donuts?"

"Sure. What happened to your face?"

"Narwhal attack."

"Just when you thought it was safe to go back in the water."

When I turn around, I nearly collide with Trisha. "Jo-o-o-oey." She draws the word out, like she's pronouncing it for the first time. "Did you get my text?"

"Yeah. I figured I'd see you at school."

"I didn't think you'd show."

Why wouldn't I? I never miss. Whatever Mrs. Petty's plans, I'm not going to make things easy by skipping. More to the point, how would Trisha know anything was up? Cooper can be a pain in the ass, but at least he gets confidentiality. "I'm just running late."

"Your clothes are wet."

"The dryer cycle wasn't finished."

"You want to sit down?"

"Um…" I don't…I do. I don't know what I want to do. I'm not surprised Trisha is here. She's got the Katz Meow dialed in, knows exactly when to show up for class and when to dance the Monster Shuffle. A café offsite is the perfect setting to

---

compose sestinas or read the latest Jacqueline Woodson novel. "For a minute, maybe."

She leads me to a table next to a big fish tank built into the wall. Trisha's round eyes are shimmering amber. Her mouth is shaped like a heart. When she talks to you she stands with her heels together and her hands clasped beneath her breasts. It's hard not to stare.

But that isn't why I like her. I like her because she doesn't treat me like I'm a bug in a jar even though I only own three changes of clothing and live with strangers. A foster herself, she made me on my first day at Katz. The difference is she's been in her placement for years. Her foster parents, the Voglers, seem to like her.

Now, as the fish flit around in the tank beside us, she inspects my face. "You look like Philip."

"It's nothing. I fell."

"On what? A claw hammer?"

"My desk."

"Didn't you go to the hospital?"

"Of course I went to the hospital."

She looks unconvinced. Not that I blame her. "What?"

"It's just…They gave Philip a fancy protective mask. You got a poorly applied Yoda Band-Aid."

"Awesome, my Band-Aid is."

"Okay. Whatever." She shakes her head. "I guess we know what living in the big house on the hill buys you at the emergency room." The scorn in her voice is impossible to miss—Trisha doesn't like Philip. She watches the fish for a moment. "I'm still in shock about what's happening."

It takes me a second to realize she's shifted gears. Not even Trisha would be shocked by Mrs. Petty pulling me out of Katz. Especially if she knew what was inside the battery compartment of my laptop.

"Did I miss something?"

"Where on earth have you been?"

Hiding out at Philip's is not a response that will score me any points. "Nowhere."

"You don't know about Duncan?"

"What about him?"

She studies me for a long time. I can't read her expression. "He's in a coma. They don't know if he's going to make it."

"Wait."

"That's why I texted you, dipshit." Her lips purse. "You know, Joey, every once in a while you're allowed to communicate with other human beings."

I break one of my donuts into pieces on a napkin. "What happened?"

"No one knows. After he blew up Philip's nose yesterday, he left school. They found him on Forty-ninth. Some woman walked out her front door around one-thirty and saw him in the middle of the street in a puddle of blood."

In the fish tank, bubbles emerge from a plastic treasure chest.

"I don't understand what kind of person runs over someone and then drives away."

I pulverize the second donut.

"Everyone's gone crazy at school. No one's getting anything done. When I left, so many people were jammed in the office asking questions, I think Mrs. An was going to lose it."

"Wasn't Mrs. Huntzel helping?" She may be a volunteer, but Mrs. Huntzel has better attendance than Cooper.

"I didn't see her." Trisha makes a face, and I regret the question.

One day near the end of last school year, Trisha stopped to chat while I waited next to the BMW for Philip and Mrs. Huntzel. Trisha bent down to peer through the windshield at the leather seats. "Must be nice," she said.

"What?" I said.

"Fancy car, mansion, houseboy. And all this free time to shadow her precious princeling around school too? What's that about?" She smirked at me, then raised up suddenly.

"I won't be judged by the likes of you." Mrs. Huntzel had materialized behind us, Philip on her heels. "Step away from the car."

Trisha's expression went dark but she didn't move until Philip pushed past. He barely touched her, but Trisha wasn't having it. "Hey, watch it!"

"You heard my mother, graham cracker."

Leave it to Philip to come up with a goofball burn that made no sense. Trisha seemed to get it, though. She threw him a glare hot enough to melt steel. He ignored her and got in the car. Mrs. Huntzel looked at me. "Are you coming, Joey?" All I could do was look at Trisha apologetically and climb into the backseat.

My employment situation is a topic Trisha and I don't discuss.

In the tank, the fish suddenly scatter, a cue. "I gotta get going."

"You could come over."

I shake my head. "I can't." It's bad enough I'm late.

"It's okay, Joey. Mom and Dad are both at work."

Trisha and I spent some time together over the summer: coffee, movies, even a couple of poetry readings. But the only time I was at her house was in August, the day I built her hidey-hole. Ever since, Trisha has been trying to get me to come back. She doesn't understand why I won't. Thinks it's the house, which smells like dying flowers and bug spray. I've never told her about how Mr. Vogler fronted me in his driveway as I left and said if I returned, he'd speak with Mrs. Petty about my interference. "We're trying to help Trisha move past all this. You know how it is, Joey." I didn't, not really. *All this? Interference?* His voice was friendly, but I caught the undertone of threat. Mr. Vogler has been around the foster system for eons. If he wanted to, he would know exactly how to wreck my Plan. Get me kicked out of Katz, or worse.

"I only meant to get breakfast."

She reaches across the table and grabs my hand. We sit there, Trisha stroking my palm with her thumb. Her amber eyes capture me, and in that moment I feel like I could lose a day just looking into them. Neither of us has touched our coffee. My donuts lie in ruins.

"The fish are like us." She looks at the tank. "They're always moving, but they can't get away."

I wonder if she has a plan, or if she's like every other foster I know. Waiting for the next bucket of shit to spill into her life. A lot of kids in her situation—long-term placements— are adopted. That the Voglers haven't made the arrangement permanent probably means something.

"I could show you what I hid in the space you built for me." Her gaze returns to me, liquid and disconcerting. Like the way she looked at me when I showed her how to secure the finial at the peak of her headboard, concealing the hollow space I'd augered out inside.

I look away. "Keep it secret. Even from me."

"Joey." She draws my name out again. "No one expects you to go to school today. Everyone knows you're Duncan's friend."

Right.

In the last twenty-four hours, I've been pegged with Wayne's smut addiction, got my face smashed for pointing it out, witnessed the pervo piss his pants, and learned Duncan Fox got run down in the street. Yet somehow Trisha Lee is what knocks me off balance.

"I'm sorry." I need to stay at Katz to keep The Plan on track. "I gotta get to school."

0.7: Private Lunchroom

I'm not much of a chess player. Hell, I don't even *like* chess.

Yet when I came to Katz, first thing I did was join the Chess Club. I went to the meetings after school twice a week. Played every day at lunch. According to club rules you had to log a minimum of six games a week (Sunday off for good behavior). The serious players managed a lot more. Philip often played four games at once. During my brief tenure with the club, he whipped my ass at least twice a week while defending his position as first board against all comers.

But it was worth it, because membership in Chess Club got you something no one else at Katz had.

Access to the private lunchroom.

Katz is the ninth school I've attended. Freshman year alone, I moved three times. One morning, a week into the school year, I opened the bathroom door to find my foster father dead on the toilet. Heart attack. The dude did like his bacon. A situation like that means emergency placement—wherever there's a spot. I found myself twenty miles away—Lents to Forest Grove—with nothing but the few things I could stuff into my suitcase.

Six weeks later Mrs. Petty put me in what she thought would be a more permanent home. Northeast this time,

Parkrose. New neighborhood, new parents. New school. The
one good thing to come out of that placement was my foster
dad introduced me to carpentry. Mr. Rieske was a cabinetmaker—had a workshop out back bigger than the house. Gave
me my first hammer. But come Valentine's Day, my one decent
placement ended when he drove into the concrete divider at
the Gateway exit on I-84. Mrs. Rieske's neck was broken by
the steering wheel. He bled out before EMTs could arrive.
Lucky me, I was at the house with two other fosters and a
sitter. Next day, I found myself in North Portland, sharing a
bedroom with a bald kid who masturbated to a photo album
filled with snapshots of—I think—his biological parents. At
least I got to stay at Parkrose High School. The long bus ride
each way was a welcome escape from the mess at the house.

Except, fuck, the noise, noise, *noise*. Trisha says I'm the
Grinch, but I honestly don't understand how everyone else
deals with the freaking noise. Since most of my placements
have been in multi-kid households, I move from chaos to
cacophony. At home, it's TV, shouting, fapping, weeping. At
school, it's lockers slamming, heels clacking and squeaking
against tile floors, and unending jabber. Always the jabber. In
the hallways, the bathrooms, under our desks during lockdown
drill. No one ever…shuts…*up*. The cafeteria is the worst. So
when I learned about the private dining room, I was ready to
commit to a life of chessery, or whatever you call it.

By February of my sophomore year, the Katz Learning
Annex was something of a last resort for me.

I'd just been kicked out of Central Catholic for calling a
staff member a dried-up hag in desperate need of a lay. How
was I supposed to know she was a nun? She looked like an
English teacher. The distinction was lost on the principal and
my foster parents. Ciao, Natrones. Hello, Boobies.

Normally, I'd go to whatever school was in my foster home's neighborhood. Central Catholic was a special case, a setting where I would be "both challenged and strictly supervised." Fail. With Katz, Mrs. Petty wanted to try something new, and somehow had the muscle to walk me past the usual application process. Maybe they had a Sad Lil' Orphan exception.

We started in Cooper's corral, where I got the standard sales pitch. Something about diversity and intellectual freedom. I didn't listen. "Alternative educational setting" is just a fancy way of saying "you're on your own, sucker." Fine. Sold. Now where am I going to sleep tonight?

But nothing is ever simple. "The Katz philosophy is based on a foundation of empowerment through critical thinking, but critical thinking requires an informed mind." I had to take the tour.

As Mr. Cooper led Mrs. Petty and me through the halls, he rattled off empowering factoids. The school—mystery of mysteries—had classrooms, a library, a media center, and computer lab. Even a gym—an echoey, faintly rancid chamber not much bigger than a classroom. Sports aren't really a thing at Katz. There are no extracurricular athletics, so the facilities are only the minimum necessary to meet state PE requirements. Cooper sounded apologetic, as if he secretly wished Katz had a shot at the state basketball championship.

"We do compete in a number of areas. Our forensics squad is active, and the chess team did very well last year."

Whatever. I was more interested in the locations of the fire extinguisher cabinets and alarm switches.

As he yapped, I stared sightlessly into the cafeteria, or, as Cooper called it, the Commons, "where students relax and refresh over the midday meal." I happened to be watching as a girl with amber eyes exited the food line and slipped on a puddle of spilled milk. She caught herself—wipeout averted—but I might have reacted when her gaze met mine. Maybe my jaw dropped as Cooper happened to mention the Chess Club, because suddenly he got the idea that I gave a rat's ass.

"You should come meet the team."

Please. But he marched us across the Commons into the narrow hallway which led to the gym. For a second I thought he was taking us back there, but then he stopped at a closed door and swung it wide. Inside, nine or ten kids sat at small square tables eating lunch and playing chess. Cooper spoke to a stout, sandy-haired kid at a far table. "Duncan, we have a new student considering Katz. He's interested in the club."

I wasn't, but I *was* interested in the room. Small, lots of natural light, two smoke detectors, and—best of all—*quiet*. Katz isn't a big school, but the Commons thrummed with typical, toothaching din. In the calm of this hidden chamber, my powers of critical thinking felt instant empowerment.

"What's the story here?"

It was my first question of the visit, which not only inspired a giddy fit in Cooper, but even got Mrs. Petty's attention.

"This room was the instructors' lounge in the days before Katz was Katz. Since ours is a student-oriented program, we felt it was more appropriate to resource the space for student activities. The chess club holds daily practice here during lunch."

Duncan, clearly not thrilled by the interruption, stood. Cooper introduced him as club president.

"You play?"

"Sure."

"You any good?"

Now that was a question. I didn't know. Maddie taught me to play when I was six years old. She used chess as a way for the children to earn privileges and develop our little pea-brains. A game got me a half-hour of PlayStation or TV. After I learned the moves, the stakes went up. Win a game to earn full-hour, but lose and get nothing. The woman was nuts. Mad Maddie, the older fosters called her. Still, I picked up some chess basics. Even beat her a few times before my stash of half-rotten mac-and-cheese in the back of my closet earned me a new placement.

Duncan inspected me. Easy to guess what he saw. No family, Walmart knock-offs. An Other. Duncan Fox was well-fed, well-clothed, cocky. His teeth gleamed inside their Invisalign braces. His hair had never been cut in the kitchen.

I looked him in the eye and answered his question. "Good enough to beat your ass."

We both knew I wasn't talking about chess. But Mr. Cooper clapped me on the shoulder and suggested I sit down for a game while he and Mrs. Petty went off to talk details.

The others came around to watch. A change of pace, I suppose. Duncan won in minutes. Then he stood up and brushed me off with a wave of his hand. "We don't need you."

But one of the others shook his head. "You can't stop him from joining." Philip Huntzel, who chewed carrots as he watched the game, open-mouthed and intense. His teeth were bigger than his eyes and he had a high-pitched, buzzy voice. Elf features straight out of *The Hobbit*. Aspergers was my guess. Reid hates it when I diagnose people almost as much as I hate it when he diagnoses me.

Duncan grumbled something about how they could do without the deadweight, but Philip shrugged.

"Read the bylaws."

Anywhere else, Philip would be lucky to be merely ignored. In the Katz chess room, he was Jesus. Later, I'd learn he went undefeated his freshman year in tournament play until the

41

state championship. This year, as a sophomore, he's expected to win it all. Not sure what he saw in me then. Maybe another weirdo. Or maybe it was part of some rivalry with Duncan. When he spoke, Duncan backed down, but I could see the bottled-up rage behind Duncan's eyes. None of my business.

Besides, I was focused on the lunchtime peace and quiet before me, all for the low, low price of a game of chess.

Things were looking up.

1.8: The Rapist

"Joey, your interest in sexual imagery is normal."

Wednesday, four p.m., and we're back to the porn.

Now it's Reid Brooks, my therapist. This is his opening, the first words out of his mouth after the empty pleasantries. We only have twenty-eight minutes together, so he likes to get right on it. But calmly. Once I said, "Therapist is just the rapist with a college degree." I thought I was being hilarious. His response: "Plus I bill insurance." Nothing ruffles Reid. If I jumped on his desk and hooted like a monkey, he'd offer me a banana.

His office is in an old brick building on Belmont about five blocks from Katz. Third floor, quiet, good light. In addition to his desk, there's a tall bookshelf, two leather chairs, a low table with a box of tissues, a credenza full of games and toys. Each of the four walls has a clock on it, presumably so he can track the time from any direction without looking like he's clock-watching.

"You're uncomfortable. I get that. This is an uncomfortable topic to discuss with adults."

I examine the books on his shelves. *Abuse and Neglect: A 21st-Century Reconsideration…Clinical Approaches To*

Attachment Disorder...DSM-V. I doubt Reid has trouble falling asleep at night, but I wouldn't want his nightmares.

"Do you have a girlfriend?"

My mind flashes to Trisha. For a moment. "No."

"What were you just thinking about?"

"I was thinking how creepy your books are."

He doesn't sigh. Mrs. Petty would, but he simply gazes at me.

"Mrs. Petty says you implied Wayne was the one who used your laptop inappropriately."

"I never mentioned my laptop."

He gives me the Look. The *You're Avoiding the Issue* look. Him and Moylan.

I say nothing. *Never admit to anything*—something I learned the last time I was falsely accused.

"You know what I mean, Joey."

"It was a joke, Dr. Brooks." I smile, but he knows better. He doesn't ask me not to call him doctor, even though he doesn't like it. He has a wall of framed degrees, but not one of them is for doctor of anything. Master of Social Work and Master of Clinical Psychology are the two biggies, but there are plenty more. Reid went to school for a long time. It's one of the reasons I don't say much to him. The man knows his shit.

"Mr. Cooper suggested a review of your IEP."

An Individualized Education Program isn't supposed to be about behavior. It's meant to be about accommodations for students with learning disabilities. But they always shovel behavior stuff in there. *When the velocity of Joey exceeds X, the school reacts with force Y to knock his ass back into a lower-energy orbit.* Officially the IEP is intended to address my lapses into what Reid calls dissociative fugue. He says it means I lose awareness of myself and my surroundings. I say boring shit is boring.

But right now, I'm not bored. Because I didn't expect Reid to open with the porn. You ask me, events have advanced beyond the browser history on my Katz laptop.

When I first sat down, Reid had asked about my nose, but I could tell he wasn't really interested.

"Botched trepanation."

He made a wincy face, muttered something about how I should be more careful. Then, "Oh, Mrs. Petty called. Something came up, so she won't be joining us today. But she briefed me on what happened."

Here it comes, I'd thought. Mrs. Petty decided to let Reid break the bad news to me. New school. New placement. Medication, maybe. Juvenile detention also a possibility. Except he went right to the porn. No Wayne, no where was I all night? No secret laptop compartment.

Porn.

I don't get it.

These are the facts as I understand them:

Wayne chucked me face-first into furniture after I suggested he masturbates loud enough to be heard over the engine of an old-school muscle car.

I fled the Boobie Hatch and haven't returned.

There is no three.

"Why don't you tell me about school today."

"It was just school."

"We both know better than that."

"You mean Duncan?"

"You're his friend."

People keep saying that. Trisha over donut crumbs, Harley May Jones when she stopped me outside her classroom to say she understood why I skipped Day Prep. Even Mr. Cooper, who marched me into the corral after the assembly. "I know

45

you're his friend." Why do they think that? Because we still talk to each other after the Fight of the Century? The favored myth seems to be we're rivals who found brotherhood on the field of combat. That it's détente, not friendship, is a fact which eludes most observers.

"Did you talk about the accident?"

"Did who—?" I remember where I am. "Sure. Some."

"Joey." The Look.

I sigh. It's 4:12. Not even half done.

"The police don't know anything. Duncan hasn't regained consciousness. No witnesses have come forward. At the assembly, some cop asked us to call a number if we knew anything. He said it would be confidential." I can't keep the derision out of my tone.

"Sounds like you don't believe that."

"You know how you can tell a cop is lying?"

"His lips are moving?"

I don't want to reward him, so I stare out the window. The afternoon sun stings my eyes.

"Not all cops are Sergeant Yearling, Joey."

"Yes, they are."

Zachariah Yearling was my foster oppressor when I was eleven, a cop they dumped me with after the aptly named Quittners dropped out of the system. There was a wife, too, a beige woman I remember only as *The Missus*—dead now. Sergeant Yearling was the one who taught me about cops.

Reid's lips pooch out. Normally, he would challenge me, but today he's got other things on his mind.

"Where were you when it happened?"

"They found him during fifth period."

"Which is…?"

"Directed Inquiry." Harley May is both the Katz official hippie and my DI advisor so I got a double-dip of her wet-eyed concern today.

"That meets in the library, right?"

No, but he knows that. He's fishing. "I didn't see it happen, Reid."

He folds his hands and smiles. "I don't think you did."

At the assembly, in addition to Cooper and the cop, Harley May gave a little speech about honoring our feelings for Duncan. One-on-one counseling with a district grief specialist would be available for those who wanted it, or we were free to talk with her any time. Harley May is one of the school guidance counselors. The budget only allows one-point-five, so she has to double up as teacher a couple periods a day. Definitely not a nun. She dresses like she's twenty-two, but her purple hair has gray roots.

"Joey, we both know I don't need to explain to you the goal of these sessions."

"No."

"Why don't you tell me what you think we're trying to accomplish here."

This is one of Reid's techniques. We run through it every month or so, usually when I'm being difficult. I don't mind, because it's easy and uses up time.

"Our goal is to redirect my destructive impulses into productive behaviors. We focus on the positive benefits of honest communication, and the constructive expression of feelings. You encourage me to open up about my needs so we can find appropriate ways to meet them, and discourage my habit of sabotaging my progress with poor decision-making."

"You express yourself well when you want to."

I was reciting from memory. "It's a gift."

47

He smiles again. "So use that gift now. How do you feel about what happened to Duncan?"

A more important question is why haven't the Boobies called out the Marines?

Wayne wouldn't come looking for me himself. Not the Boobie style. And Anita couldn't if she wanted to. But they would let Mrs. Petty know, and probably the police. *Teen runaway! Be on the lookout!* Not that cops give two craps about runaways, but if I got picked up in a sweep, my name would be flagged in the computer.

If Wayne hasn't called Mrs. Petty, it's not because he's afraid of what I'll say. History always works against me; all he needs is a plausible yarn. "The boy went mad!" Whatever he's come up with, we all know I'm in a final straw situation. My days as ward of the Boobies will end. Except Wayne apparently has decided not to rat me out.

Only one reason I can think of why he might want me around.

Money.

I don't know what a foster parent stipend brings in. Enough to cover my food and day-to-day needs, allegedly. Not that the Boobies spend much. I eat subsidized breakfast and lunch at school. I pay for double shots and my cell phone out of my Huntzel income. Hell, I even bought my last pair of shoes. How much can creamed chipped beef and toast cost?

"Joey?"

Reid is talking. "Sorry. What?"

"We were discussing Duncan."

"What about him?"

"Where'd you go just now?"

"I'm sitting right here."

The Look. "How about Duncan? Are you worried about him?"

A lose-lose question. If I say no, a checkmark goes in one column. Mrs. Petty's oversight tightens, maybe I find myself in a compassion development group: eight weeks of sitting around a table with cat burners and Dexter-wannabes. If I say yes, Reid will want to explore my feelings.

I stand mute.

Reid waits a moment. Someone out in the hallway is crying. A voice makes comforting sounds. A door closes and it's quiet again, except for the faint rumble of a bus in the street outside. I sniff and for the first time since last night don't taste blood. I can even smell a little bit now: furniture polish. All I want to do is keep my head down. Show up at school. Graduate early. Escape. Is that too much to ask?

Apparently.

"Joey, do you know when you get to stop coming here every Wednesday?"

"When I turn eighteen?"

"It can be sooner than that."

I don't say anything. This is an old ritual too.

"When you prove you're capable of trust, we're done."

"Nothing's ever that easy."

"Joey, if that was easy, you'd have been out of here years ago."

I glance at the clock. 4:19. Not enough time to get cornered. "I hope he's…okay." I *do* hope he's okay. Doesn't mean I want to share on the subject.

Reid nods. "Let's talk about that."

Nine minutes later, I step out onto Belmont, bemused. The sun is dropping fast toward the West Hills, the chill pushed by a cold breeze out of the Gorge. All I can do is catch the next bus heading east. I get off just short of I-205, walk the last few blocks to the Boobie Hatch. I can feel my pace slow as I near the house, but then I let out a long relieved breath. Both cars are gone. All I want to do is slip inside, snarf some cold chipped beef, and go to bed. Tomorrow morning is soon enough to face the Reckoning of the Boobies.

But when I get to the door, my key doesn't work.

That bastard changed the locks.

1.9: Housework

When I ring the bell this time, Mrs. Huntzel comes to the door.

"Joey." Not a greeting, a statement of fact. "It's Wednesday."

"Well, yesterday got messed up, so I thought I would catch up today. I know it's late, but I had my thing after school." I don't use the word therapy with anyone but Reid and Mrs. Petty.

"Oh." She smiles like she's not sure what to make of my arrival, but then she turns and waves me in past her. I cross through the mudroom into the kitchen. Bread, deli meat, and vegetables are spread across the center island.

"Are you hungry? I'm making a sandwich. You should have one."

"I have a lot to do."

"Nonsense. You and Philip are exactly alike; you never eat enough." She puts her hand to her forehead like she's checking for a fever, then offers me that smile again. "Go. Sit. Do you prefer mustard or mayonnaise?"

"Mustard, I guess." I don't really care. But I haven't eaten since lunch. I shuffle over to the nook where Philip eats his breakfast, slump into one of the chairs. I'm tired, not in the mood to work. But that's not why I'm here anyway. The job is just my way into the house.

Mrs. Huntzel busies herself at the counter, knife blade tapping the chopping block as she slices tomatoes. Outside, I watch Caliban climb the hill above the laurel hedge. Off on adventures. My phone vibrates in my pocket. My first thought is Mrs. Petty, catching up at last. But when I check, it's Trisha.

how was schl? call if u want.

I'm trying to decide how to respond when Mrs. Huntzel sets a plate down in front of me. Artisan bread, aged cheddar, fresh greens, paper-thin tomatoes, and what would be a week's ration of smoked turkey if Wayne was doling it out. Kettle chips on the side.

"Do you want something to drink?"

"Just water. Thanks."

"I'll get you some milk."

She pours milk for both of us and joins me at the table. But rather than eat, she stares out the window. Her eyelids are heavy and her breath whistles through her nose. For a second she reminds me of a girl I knew a few years back: a compulsive shoplifter who would cut herself every time she got caught. You meet all kinds in the system, and you get used to most of it after a while. But cutters always freaked me out. When I bite into the sandwich—mayo, not mustard—my chewing roars in my ears. I follow Mrs. Huntzel's gaze. Sunlight plays through the trees up the slope above the hedge. She seems to be watching the dance of light and shadow. At the Boobie Hatch, the TV would be on full volume in the background.

"Where's Philip?" Breaking the silence.

"Did you see him today?"

"Just for a minute." The only class we share is Trigonometry—Philip is a grade behind me, and miles ahead in math brains. But Moylan doesn't allow chatter. Philip sat alone at the back of the Commons during the assembly. He was wearing the plastic mask Trisha told me about. I thought about going to talk to him, but people kept interrupting me until finally Cooper called for quiet. Afterward, he clonked into Trisha as he raced from the room, sent her phone flying. His fault from where I was sitting, but he called her a clumsy zebretta—whatever the hell that means—then bolted. There was no sign of him during lunch.

"You've been hurt as well."

"I fell."

That's good enough for her. Philip looks worse, but maybe it's the mask.

"You should be careful."

"Me and Philip both."

Her lips press together as if she wants to blame Duncan for my face too, but can't work her way around his coma. She shakes her head at last, and glances toward the door. "Philip went up to bed." I wonder if he's looking at his pictures of Bianca Santavenere. "I appreciate your company for supper. Mr. Huntzel is away again."

She still doesn't eat. Something is on her mind, but the last thing I want her to do is tell me about it. Nothing good ever comes of knowing other people's secrets. I finger my chips. The tension in the kitchen could crack teeth.

I say, "I noticed the heads in the basement need dusting."

"They do?"

"I can take care of it tomorrow, maybe."

"Whatever you think is best." She picks up her milk at last and drains the glass. Then she stands and pushes her fingers into her eyes. "You'll excuse me. It's been a long day."

God only knows what made it so long; she wasn't at school for the first time in the history of forever. She pads out to the main hall and is gone, leaving me alone with two sandwiches and a double helping of chips.

My sandwich and chips are down before the soft echo of her footsteps fade. Then I wrap her sandwich and put it in the fridge, pour her chips back into the bag. Rinse our plates and glasses, stick them in the dishwasher. And listen. The house is dead quiet. The thing I like best about Huntzel Manor. Time to get to work.

Tuesday on Wednesday: living room and library, dust and vacuum. I note my start time on the clipboard in the mudroom. The vacuum cleaner and other cleaning supplies are kept in a storage room in the basement next to the boiler room. It would be a hassle if not for the one-man elevator that goes from basement to second floor, up the middle of the spiral staircase. I start in the library because when you dust, you start at the top and work your way down. Maddie the Mad Chess Woman drilled that lesson into me in first grade.

It's a big job, but I've been doing it since April. I've never broken any of the ceramic figurines on display in the living room: poodles and fat-cheeked girls wearing poofy dresses. The library is easier, even though I have to use a stepladder to get at the highest bookshelves. I work alone, the way I like it. Feels weird to run the vacuum cleaner with the house so dark and empty, different from the afternoons when Philip or Mrs. Huntzel might wander through. I try to hurry, but it still takes me more than two hours—longer than usual, probably because my face is pounding the whole time. Mrs. Huntzel won't question the time. She never does.

I'm rolling the vacuum cleaner onto the lift on the first floor when Philip appears at the top of the spiral stairs. The transparent plastic of his mask warps his elf face. "Why are you here?"

"Just catching up from yesterday."

Mrs. Huntzel views me as Philip's protector, someone to look out for him when she's not around. Philip hates it, even if he does seem less jumpy when he knows I'm nearby. All it took was me knocking Duncan sideways one day to make a friend, I guess. Reid would ask me how I feel about that.

But something is different now. When Philip reaches the first floor, he stops. "Your face is grotesque."

"At least I don't have to wear that terrifying mask."

I can't read his expression, but there's something vaguely hostile in his stare. I wonder if he thinks I'm trying to one-up him.

"Caliban knocked me down the hill." The explanation sounds absurd and I laugh a little.

"That's stupid."

He heads for the kitchen and I take the lift to the basement, stow the vacuum cleaner and dust rags. When I come out, I can hear him climbing the stairs again. I wait until his footsteps fade and I hear the distant click of his door closing. For a second, I feel strangely unsettled, but I shake it off.

The moment I've been waiting for.

I move quickly through the rec room, salute the dusty moose as I pass, and climb the corner stairs up through the now-pristine living room to the second floor. I'm the only one who ever uses the library. Next to it is Kristina's bedroom. The door no one ever opens.

Until now.

1.10: Where Are You?

Mrs. Huntzel never speaks of Kristina, and if Philip does it's only to badmouth her. "She destroys everything she touches." From most people, I'd blow that off as emo bullshit, but Philip is the precise opposite of a drama queen. So I'm not sure what to expect when I enter the forbidden chamber. Black candles and a voodoo altar, maybe. Sculptures made of animal skulls. A closet full of whips and leather. Scientology books. Who the hell knows?

What I find is a small, tidy room with a canopy bed, a child's desk, and an empty chest of drawers. The walls are pale pink, with a border of yellow and blue flowers running near the ceiling. The curtains are lace, and match the doily on the wing chair in the corner. Every surface is clear, barely a layer of dust. I tiptoe around, even though it's the kind of house where you couldn't hear a pitched gun battle in the next room. On the bed, happy little unicorns frolic across the comforter, which is thicker than my entire mattress at the Boobie Hatch. One door opens onto the closet, the other a bathroom. I don't run the water or flush. Maybe no one would notice, but I expect the door to burst open any moment to reveal Philip, Mrs. Huntzel, even the mysterious Kristina herself.

"Intruder alert! Intruder alert!"

I suppress an urge to test the smoke detector, grab a quilt from the closet and plunk down on top of the unicorns instead. The sensation is at once familiar and unsettling. I've had plenty of early nights at the Boobies, confined to quarters. This bed is softer, and the quilt is smooth and cool against my bare arms. I wonder who keeps the room dusted.

My phone vibrates in my backpack. I ignore it. My face hurts. Unless I steal one of Philip's Vicodins, sleep probably won't come. The phone buzzes again. I picture Trisha. I'm hiding out in a room that belongs to a girl I've never met. Dust tickles my swollen nose. The air smells of silence. And what am I thinking about? Not Duncan, or the Bobbitts, or Mrs. Petty and the frown she reserves just for me.

No. I'm thinking about Trisha. Amber eyes and hands clasped below her breasts.

In my mind, she's sitting on her bed, the high wooden headboard behind her with its hidden compartment, its hidden secret. Her Katz laptop is open beside her. She's annoyed at her cell phone because...*buzzzz*...I'm not picking mine up. Doing homework, writing poetry, G-chatting with Denise Grover. Texting me again.

Buzzzz.

I should call her. I *want* to call her.

I don't.

Reid would say it's a trust issue, or that I'm punishing myself. Maybe he's right, but that just pisses me off.

Fosters really only have one thing in common: we're fosters. But everyone acts like we're all supposed to be best friends, as if abuse, neglect, and termination of parental rights are all that matter. Cooper pushed Trisha and me together. "Hey, you two should be friends because, you know, your folks are state-assigned." Not quite, but close enough. With almost anyone else it could have been a disaster, but not with Trisha. She's got her shit together like no one I know. And those eyes don't hurt either.

Maybe I *am* punishing myself. It's not like I don't deserve it.

———

I wake up when a single beam of sunlight falls on my face through a narrow gap in the curtains. It's after seven. Two nights running, I've gotten away with misdemeanor trespassing.

And two days running, I'm wearing the same clothes. No one will notice except Trisha. There's a string of texts from her. Something tickles in my belly and I decide it's safe to text back.

> Sorry. Meant to call but got busy last night, then fell asleep early. See you at school.

I'm such a liar.

I fold the quilt and smooth out the unicorns, then wash up in the bathroom. Everyone is gone, Mrs. Huntzel and Philip to school, Mr. Huntzel wherever he is. Always traveling—I haven't seen him in weeks. I sneak through the basement to the garage, out the side door past the BMW.

I trot down the hill to Hawthorne. I have to skip coffee, but at least I make it through the doors at Katz early enough to grab free breakfast and avoid a Cooper Frowning. In Day Prep, Duncan is all anyone can talk about. I occupy myself by borrowing Sean Ferrell's laptop and logging in to ChalkChat. Nothing too pressing, though I'm behind on Trig homework. Moylan doesn't accept late assignments, but I have to do it anyway, if I want to pass the next quiz.

After Day Prep, there's another assembly. Great.

I hold back, way past done with group hugs and communal weeping. A good time to slip out for a coffee, but when I turn down the hallway toward the side exit, I run into the cop.

"We're gathering in the Commons."

He's as wide as he is tall, with a bullet-shaped head and a frown that seems to start at the back of his neck. Yesterday he was in uniform, but today he hulks over me in a blue suit and a tie printed to look like crime scene tape. Hilarious. The woman with him is smaller and less imposing, but the sharpness in her pale eyes tells me she's a cop too. She offers a smile—bared fangs. "Come along, please." Her voice is bright and high. I can feel it in the back of my mouth.

I have no choice.

At the assembly, they skip the soft soap. No Harley May leading us in a guided visualization of our personal grief process. The cops do all the talking. Detectives Stein and Davisson will be interviewing a number of students today. They emphasize the word *detective*. Per school policy—and probably against cop wishes—parents are being informed and may attend. Wayne and Anita wouldn't have bothered even before The Incident, but I figure Mrs. Petty will make an appearance, should my turn come.

Except not. The cops are using Cooper's office for the interviews.

I'm at the top of their list.

First thing through the door I spot my computer in his glass case, tucked beside a stack of handheld game consoles and other contraband. Inaccessible, but at least I know some fascist district IT tech isn't rooting through the laptop's innards. If I'm lucky, Cooper has already forgotten it—at least until his Outlook alerts him my sentence is up.

Relieved, I slump into the familiar wooden chair. The woman detective sits in Cooper's seat, Man-Mountain on the back edge of the desk. He has to twist around to face me.

The woman starts. Detective Stein, she tells me. Man-Mountain is Davisson.

"I spoke with your caseworker."

I wait for her to continue, but she doesn't. She wants me to fill the silence, but I've been to this dance before. After a moment, the big guy makes a noise in the back of his throat and Detective Stein looks at him before going on. "She's unable to attend, but she said we should go ahead and ask you a few questions."

More silence. I survey the room, see Cooper has added a framed movie poster from *High Noon*. The guy has all the subtlety of an anvil falling off a cliff.

"You've been attending Katz since February. And before that, Central Catholic. Lots of schools, we hear."

In the front office, Mrs. An, the school secretary, is on the phone, but I can't make out her words. Background noise. Always with the background noise. Mrs. Huntzel skipped her volunteer duties again today.

"You've moved around a lot. It must be very hard."

What's hard is not staring at them while they fidget. The room, dense with the desperate weight of Cooper's collection, makes me tired. I lay a hard stare on the glass case. On my laptop.

Detective Davisson takes a turn. "We understand you and Duncan are friends."

His breathing sounds like a lawn mower.

"Joey." The woman again. "If you answer our questions, we can get you out of here. I'm sure you have things to do."

I turn my eyes to her. "You haven't asked any questions."

A look passes between them. Davisson leans forward, his knuckles going white on the desktop. "I get it. You're an old hand at this, am I right?" His voice feigns friendliness, but I know better.

"Is that your question?"

"We're just trying to find out what happened to your friend."

That one isn't a question, either, but a deepening crease forms between his eyebrows. Cops are always looking for a reason to go nuclear. "I was in school."

More breathing, more jabber from the outer office. Finally, Detective Stein laughs uncomfortably. "What happened to your nose?" It's clumsy as misdirection goes, but then I *am* an old hand at this.

"Electric toothbrush mishap."

I want them to think I can do this all day. The sooner they get tired of me, the better. If I'm going to stay on Plan, I need to get to class sooner or later. Moylan's Trig problems aren't solving themselves. I've got Chem too, another class I have to actually show up for.

Davisson's throat rumbles. "You say you were in school."

"All day long."

"And at about one-thirty? Where were you exactly?"

I pretend to think for a moment, and choose my words carefully. "That's when I have Directed Inquiry." I'm still looking at my laptop.

"What's that?" His chuckle sounds like water spilling into an oil drum. "Some kind of study hall?"

Now he's trying to be a dick, but he's closer to the mark than he realizes. "It's an independent study course. We write a big research paper."

"How does that work? Do you meet in a classroom with a teacher?"

In other words, is an adult keeping track of us? "Something like that." Harley May doesn't take attendance, and doesn't expect to see us every day. At the beginning of the term we spent a week or so coming up with our projects and setting milestones. So long as we hit our marks and turn in the final paper, she doesn't care whether we show up or not. As she put it, "I'm available to help you work through research challenges, and to make sure your energies are directed in a constructive fashion." The only time I've only been to class this week was yesterday, a fact that doesn't help me one bit.

"What do you know about why Duncan left school on Tuesday afternoon?"

"I didn't even know he *had* left until I got here yesterday morning." A fudge, but I'm not dragging Trisha into this.

"I understand you and Duncan had a fight last spring."

I've been waiting for them to bring up the fight. Cops always think they're on to something.

"Over—what was it?" Davisson's lip curls into a smirk. "A game of chess?"

"It wasn't over a game of chess."

"I mean, boys fight over girls, or—"

"It wasn't over a game of chess." Irritation sticks in the back of my throat like a wad of snot.

"But it was in Chess Club."

The fight was in the Chess Club *room*. I don't want to get into it. "It was a long time ago."

That earns me the kind of world-weary smile the elderly reserve for those who clearly lack their innate grasp of deep time. "Any lingering hard feelings?"

"Not from me."

"And you two are friends now."

"Yes." My voice snaps. I suppress a wince. They can't have missed my tone.

Davisson turns to Stein. She's studying me. Without dropping her gaze, she nods thoughtfully. "We're done for now, I think. We'll let you know if we have any other questions."

When I open the door to the outer office, Mrs. An's voice breaks against my ears. She's talking to a parent. "—trying to get an idea of the boy's movements on Tuesday afternoon. Very informal. But if you're concerned, please come down—" Some overprotective Katz mommy doesn't want her poor, fragile baby genius subjected to a grueling police interrogation. Shock. Cooper hovers at her shoulder, one hand to his chin.

The surprise is Trisha sitting on the bench next to Cooper's door. I pull up short. "Oh, hey. Did you get my text?"

"Yes. Finally." She rolls her eyes. "Asshole."

"What's going on?"

She looks toward Cooper's doorway. "The cops want to talk to me."

I'm not sure why a band tightens behind my belly button. Trisha and Duncan run in different circles. I don't think they've exchanged a dozen words in all the time I've been at Katz. "Did they say why?"

"I assume they're fans of my poetry."

Ask a stupid question. I manage a sickly smile. Then I do something I've never done before. "Do you want to get a coffee later?"

Her eyes get wide and she smiles. "Jo-o-o-oey Getchie. Are you actually asking me *out?*" Before my face can burst into flames, her grin drops and her eyes shoot past my shoulder. I turn.

Of course. Mr. Vogler has arrived. When he sees me, his cottage cheese cheeks flood red and his lips pull back from his teeth as if he found me stuck to the bottom of his shoe.

You know how it is, Joey.

I head for the door before he has a chance to tell me to get lost.

0.11: Chess Club

In the weeks after I first got to Katz, I learned Duncan was number two in Chess Club in the only way that mattered: he was second board. I'd never heard the term before Katz, but it didn't take long to figure out it was a chess-jargony way of saying he was never better than red ribbon. With the help of his Book, Philip held the first board in an iron grip of obsession. Duncan clawed at him, but from where I was sitting (under the board, apparently), it seemed he never got close to knocking him off. Duncan could be president—an elected position—and run the club. Set rules, issue high-handed edicts. But the only way to be first board was to defeat Philip. And that never happened.

Duncan wanted first board like Wayne wanted creamed chipped beef, like Cooper wanted a pony. I admit I didn't understand—top of the heap in Chess Club? To me, that was like wanting to be in charge of Moylan's Electronic Math Tutor DVDs. When I said so to Reid, he stared me down for about an hour, then said, "Joey. What do *you* want?" Asshole. I didn't answer, but fine—I got it. Still, no one beat Philip.

Until I did.

It was a fluke. Everyone *knew* it was a fluke. I didn't even want to play him. He had two games going and offered to

take on two others. Typical Philip. He's twitchy at school, and
the dead time while his opponents are thinking through their
moves only adds to the twitch. He likes to fill up the empty
space with more chess. You ask me, the dude needs an iPod.

That particular day, no one was interested. I'd just lost
my obligatory game to Colin Botha and was happily eating
beans-'n-franks and reading *A Game of Thrones* when Duncan
went Joffrey on us.

"Getchie, you're against Philip."

"I played my game."

"And you'll play another, or move your dead ass out of here."

Lunches at Katz are long. Not like my other schools, where
they ram you through in twenty minutes, barely enough
time to inhale a gummy slice of pizza and spill your milk.
At Katz, lunch is a full period. I live for the hour of peace.
Lose a game of chess, then relax amid the *tip-tap* of pieces
moving on boards and the occasional murmur. "Good move."
"You really want to do that?" "Check." Even an ejaculation of
chess-thusiasm was no more disruptive than wind scattering
leaves. It was like living inside the Golf Channel.

So I had no interest in Duncan's decrees. But when I hesi-
tated, he added the *coup de grace*. "Your choice, Getchie. Play
Philip, or go eat with the plebs."

Classy.

I put my book down and sat at one of the empty seats
Duncan indicated next to the window. It was an April afternoon, two months after my arrival at Katz. Outside, drizzle fell
with its usual resolve. Inside, Philip paced in the cross-shaped
space between four tables, chewing carrots and spitting veg-
etable matter as he studied the boards before him. I hid a pawn
in each hand, black and white, and held them out for Philip
to choose, but he brushed me off. "Shut up. Just play white."

Everyone was being an asshole that day.

Courtney, Mrs. An's daughter, got drafted as well, but unlike me, she actually gave a damn. I pushed a pawn at random, then another the instant Philip responded. Each time he moved I moved. With four games going, it would take him a minute to get back to me, but I moved again before he could turn away.

I could tell he was getting annoyed, but too bad. Him and me both. Fucking Duncan. I threw pieces around the board, barely aware if the moves were even legal. Philip wasn't used to opponents who cared so little about the outcome. His breath whistled past his teeth every time I moved. Across from me, Colin Botha—club noob but with a strong U.S. Chess Federation rating and my bet for first to knock Philip off his throne—was putting up a serious fight. Courtney and Duncan were holding their own and keeping Philip from giving me his full attention.

Which could explain what happened.

I might not have noticed if I wasn't in particular need of quiet at that moment. Every sound rattled in my ears, from the tap of the felt-footed pieces to the muted chatter trickling in from the Commons. Annoyed, I tossed a knight into Philip's back row, which made no sense even to me. Philip responded with the irritation of a man who'd discovered a pubic hair in his hamburger. He killed the knight with his queen. In the second after he lifted his hand, even as I was reaching for another piece to push, he sucked in a quick breath, barely audible. But I heard it. And I paused.

He'd made a mistake.

Philip didn't make mistakes. Not on the chessboard. I looked up at him but he was already turning away, munching carrots and trying to cover. Maybe he thought it didn't matter, that I would never see what he'd given me. Whatever he thought, I felt something new and different: a tickle behind my eyes, a sudden need. I gazed at Duncan, intent on his own board. Light reflected off the sheen of sweat on his upper lip—so desperate to have what Philip had given me. A *chance.* I sat back and, for the first time since Mad Maddie, tried to win a game of chess.

I studied the board for fifteen minutes to be absolutely sure. Long enough for Philip to knock off the other three, first Duncan, then Botha. When Courtney resigned, Philip turned to me. "Well?" His attitude was impatient, but I sensed concern behind it. He knew I knew—the long delay since my last move was proof of that. What he didn't know was if I would figure out how to exploit his mistake.

Except I already had.

I smiled, casual and a little saucy. Then, when I had his attention, I moved a bishop one space. *Check.* I didn't have to say it out loud. Everyone saw it. Philip's king was trapped, no way to move out of check. My reckless play had left us with a chaotic board, and Philip had no way to block. If he'd ignored my idiot knight in the back row he could have cleared the current problem right up with his queen, but she was out of position now.

"Mate." I *did* have to say that out loud. Duncan needed to hear.

It didn't mean anything. By club rule, you could only jump two boards, and then only after winning four out of seven. One loss by any ranked member to me was no more than a fart in the wind.

Rain whispered against the window. A foot tapped against a table leg. Then Philip shrugged. Losing a meaningless game to me turned out to be a big yawner. He grabbed his Book—in those days, a spiral notebook, not the vinyl behemoth he would soon switch to—in order to log the three games that mattered. I knew he would remember every move, even from my game, but no point in logging that one. Random nitwittery and one unforced error, never to be repeated. But the other three games would give him something to analyze. He'd already forgotten me.

Duncan hadn't. "Such...*bullshit*."

He ranged around the cluster of tables into the empty space where Philip had paced during recent combat operations. Behind him, Philip hunched over and scrawled notation, oblivious to the looming menace at his back. Duncan thrust a trembling finger at me and then Philip in turn.

"*You* can't beat *him*. You're *nobody*."

Blah blah blah. There was only five minutes left in the period. All I wanted was a little quiet before I had to return to the general population.

"You don't know jack*shit* about chess."

No fucking kidding. I reached for *A Game of Thrones*, thinking if I ignored him he'd wind down.

Instead, he spun on Philip. "You're just gonna let this happen? He *beat* you."

Philip looked up from the Book, his face bland, as if he only just noticed the ruckus. "So what?"

The wrong thing to say. The lunchroom—not big to begin with—seemed to contract as Duncan's face went red. My ears popped, and the windows seemed to vibrate. Tendons sprang out on his neck. Maybe that would have been it—an entitled asshat pitching a tantrum—until his bulging eyes fixed on the Book. Philip's talisman, his magic tome, his obsession. Duncan grabbed the notebook and ripped it down the middle, tossed the halves in opposite directions. Then he cocked his arm about a mile over his head as anguish rose in Philip's upturned face. Sheets of chess notation fluttered around us like leaves.

Fosters tend to fall into one of two camps: those who fight everyone and those who fight no one. Up 'til that moment, I would have put myself in the second category. I'd been in some pitched battles over the years, but they were always a matter of self-defense—usually against some sociopath who knocked my dick in the dirt for laughs or to take what little I had. Defending the weak and nerdtrodden was never on my To Do list. But Philip was the one who gave me the chance, however limited, for a measure of quiet each day. I owed him…something.

Not that I took the time to formulate the thought. I was out of my chair before his lips could part.

I have no recollection of balling a fist, even less of the right cross which, according to subsequent reports, connected with Duncan's jaw below his cheekbone. My first awareness was Duncan's hands dropping as my punch snapped his head around. I followed through with my body until our chests collided. He staggered, caught himself against a table. I glared down at him, suddenly aware of how much taller I was. His head rolled back, loose and wobbly.

"Joey, dude…"

"…that was…"

"…didja *see* that…?"

"…fucking master, dude…"

My heart pounded in my chest, and air whistled through my nose. Duncan gazed up at me, eyes wayward. One pupil expanded and contracted. He blinked, tried to smile.

"Heh heh." He actually said the words. *Heh heh.* Then, "Maybe we should kiss and make up before someone gets hurt." There was blood on his teeth.

All I wanted was to lose my game of chess and sit in peace. No student blather, no teachers lecturing, no cable news, no laughing, no crying, no screaming. Just fifty-five minutes of quiet, once a day, five days a week. Too much to ask?

Apparently.

Before I had the chance to tell him to kiss my ass, the door opened. Moylan. I didn't see him, but there was no mistaking his voice. "Joseph. Duncan. What is the meaning of this?"

Duncan and I didn't break eye contact, though in his case I'm not sure it was a matter of choice.

"Joey gave Duncan a beatdown."

To this day, I don't know who spoke. Didn't matter. My days of losing a chess game in exchange for a little peace were over.

1.12: Home Away From Hell

If I'm going to take a chance on entering the Bobbitts' one last time, Thursday afternoon is it. That's when Wayne has his weekly meet-up with his boss. Afterward they continue on to some shenanigan for insurance dorks. He never gets home before nine. The rest of the week, he might go out at any time to meet one of his customers—but mostly he's in his office.

Thursdays are also Anita's physical therapy, an event she never misses since it's when she gets to assign a number to her pain. That number is ten. They won't prescribe any more pills, but at least she can complain and that's important. Plus she gets a massage, paid for by insurance. It's a win even without the Oxy.

What all this means is I can get my tools.

Assuming I can get in. The way the day's gone, I'm not hopeful.

Trisha never made it to coffee. After her time with Detectives Heat Vision and Man-Mountain, Mr. Vogler hustled her away from school. I was in the hallway when they left, math book open in my lap. I heard heels on tile and looked up in time to see him guiding her out the door, hand on the small of her back. She looked my direction, but I don't know if she

71

saw me. Later, I asked Denise if she knew anything, but she hadn't talked to Trisha since Day Prep.

In Trig, Moylan took it upon himself to alert everyone to the fact I was sitting on an M. "Joseph. Your work has fallen off." *My name isn't Joseph.* In terms of grade-point average, a Katz M would be a C at an actual school. My test scores have all been mid-nineties, quizzes high too. No way had two days of missing homework done that much damage. He was just being a dick. I handed in the day's homework, nailed a ten out of ten on the pop quiz, and kept my mouth shut. Moylan could suck balls.

In her screwball way, Harley May was worse. She caught me in the Commons during lunch and suggested a check-in on my DI project. My next milestone, a list of sources on Reconstruction and the Compromise of 1877, wasn't due 'til Monday, so I knew she really wanted to *talk feelings.* I was a clam in response to her interrogation, but I couldn't avoid the OMG<3 hug at the end. Her chest felt mushy against my cheek. I think I picked up a mild contact high which eroded into a brutal headache by the time I arrive at the Boobie Hatch, where I find myself wishing I'd built an outside hide for my tools. In theory, it's a good idea, especially since in an emergency move you may get no chance to crack open your hides. If you cache off-site, you can go back later without having to worry about getting into a house you no longer have access to.

In practice, it's not so straightforward. When I was yanked from the Natrones, it was a month before I could sneak back. By then, my hide in the crawlspace of a neighbor's outbuilding had been found and looted. With indoor hides, at least your stuff is close—ready access can be critical. If you have to pack in a hurry, just fake a few tears and ask for a minute to be alone. That's what I suggested to Trisha, anyway.

Of course, I didn't anticipate present circumstances.

The easiest way in would be to break a window. But that's ammunition for Wayne. Besides, I don't want them to know I've been here—though my empty dresser might provide a clue. Wayne's security bars are going to be a problem, but there is one possibility. If it doesn't work, my only other option may be the Goodwill bins and lice-infested clothes sold by the pound.

The house is quiet, sealed up tight. For the hell of it, I try my key on the front door again. No good. Wayne added a second deadbolt for emphasis. Ferrell claims he knows how to pick locks, but every time I've asked him to teach me he makes some shitweasel excuse.

The backyard is axe-murder private due to the seven-foot cedar fence and a couple of shaggy willows in the corners. The flower beds are bare earth and a few shrubs. Behind an overgrown azalea I find what I'm looking for, a metal hatch inset in the foundation at ground level. An old coal chute, according to Wayne. Anita says that's not possible, because the house isn't old enough. Whatever, Bicker Twins, all I care about is whether I can get it open.

I pull a pry bar out of my backpack. If someone found it on me at school, I'd be on the fast track to expulsion. The padlock is about five hundred years old, rusted solid. Before I can I jam the pry bar through the shackle, I hear a voice.

"Joey. I didn't think it would be you."

I jump back and almost trip over myself. Anita is standing at the top of the back stoop, leaning on her cane, watching me.

"They cancelled my physical therapy. Can you believe it?"

I'm thinking about how there were no cars in the driveway. I straighten up. She had to have seen the pry bar, but I try to hide it behind my thigh anyway. "Where's the van?"

She throws up her free hand, waves in a fluttery way. "Oh, you know. In the shop. Brakes or something. Wayne handles that stuff."

I smell smoke.

"Joey, you upset your father."

She's holding a cigarette.

"He's not my father."

I've never seen Anita smoke. Now in the space of a day I've seen both her and Mrs. Huntzel light up.

"He could have been. You never gave him the chance." She looks at me through bloodshot eyes. If the cigarette didn't smell like Marlboro, I'd wonder what was in it. Still, her voice is slurred enough to tell me she's gotten into something. Painkillers…vodka? Who knows? I still need my clothes and my tools.

"The police asked about you."

Sudden disquiet swells inside me.

"What did they want?"

"They wanted to know if you could drive." She spits out a giggly trill that makes my nose hurt. "Wayne told them you don't have your license."

That's not an answer that helps me. "Is that all?"

"Well, you know how Wayne is. He was emphatic that you had no access to either vehicle. He showed them that cabinet where he locks up all the keys."

I don't know why I'm surprised. I'm the perfect target. Foster kid, violent family background, prior arrest record. Of course I'm a person of interest. Next time they talk to me, they're not going to accept half-answers. The question then is what do I tell them? The truth blows The Plan all to hell. But that's better than having Duncan's hit-and-run pinned on me.

"Don't worry, Joey. They don't think you hurt your friend. They just have to check everything. Routine, they said."

Yeah. Right.

"I need my things."

She inhales cigarette smoke, blows it into the still air. The gray cloud lingers longer than it should.

"I expected Mrs. Petty. Is she with you?"

I stare at the stoop, where she stands in precarious balance. "No." The word comes out slowly.

"He feels terrible about what happened."

I close my eyes. A notion flickers to life in the back of my mind. Not quite a light bulb turning on. A flickering CFL.

"It was an accident...."

They haven't called Mrs. Petty because they figured I would. And now they're hiding behind new locks and silence.

"Surely you understand that, Joey. Just an accident."

"There are no accidents." But I'm not talking to her, not really. My thoughts are churning. The Boobies don't know I'm in the wind. Neither does Mrs. Petty.

I'm...on my own.

She ejects a final long stream of smoke, then throws her cigarette butt into the grass. "I'll get your things." She turns and goes into the house. I notice she fails to grimace, doesn't seem to need her cane. When she returns, she's holding my suitcase.

"I did your laundry." Her voice is apologetic. "It seemed the least we could do." She offers me a sheepish smile, then turns away. Closes and locks the door behind her.

I stow my pry bar, hoist my pack. It's good to have my clothes, such as they are. But my tools—well-hidden in the narrow brown cell upstairs—are probably gone for good.

1.13: Default State

I spend two hours on the animal heads, plus my usual Thursday duties. Philip and Mrs. Huntzel seem to be lurking all over the place. Every time I turn a corner, one of them is standing there. At one point, when I'm at the top of a ladder choking on moose dust, Philip walks into the rec room. He's not wearing his mask, but I wish he was.

"You're stupid. No one cares about those heads."

"Thanks. That's very helpful."

"Just stating the obvious."

Obvious for him, maybe. He never has to worry about where he'll be living tomorrow, or what's for dinner tonight. This is one of those moments when I understand why Trisha talks shit about him. As good as she has it, she knows a foster placement can end at any time. None of us has the certainty Philip takes for granted.

He leaves the way he came before I can bean him with my dustrag. After he's gone, I slip off to scope hiding places. I intend to keep my stuff close by, in Kristina's room. But the debacle of my tools at the Boobies makes me wish I'd already built a few backup hides in Huntzel Manor.

There are storage rooms, the boiler room, a couple of dark cellars, and the laundry room. None offer what I'm looking

76

for. Too much foot traffic or, in the case of the boiler room and cellars, nothing but bare concrete walls. The old, bank-style vault offers more promise. Its door is wedged open—does anyone know the combination anymore?

Inside, the walls are white-painted brick. There's a wine rack on the left, a few dusty bottles here and there. The wide grate in the floor at the back is part of a drain system that runs throughout the basement. Once, when a noxious smell arose in the laundry room, Mr. Huntzel suggested I wriggle in and clean out whatever died down there. Lucky me, Mrs. Huntzel put the kibosh on that idea. Five gallons of bleach water through the grate seemed to clear out the smell.

But what interests me are the floor-to-ceiling shelves on the right, with lots of nooks and crannies—perfect for a false back, hinged and latched. Without my tools, I can't do much, but there are enough loose boards behind the grimy Mason jars that I might be able to fake something up in the short term. I pull out a couple of splintery planks at the back of the bottom shelf to reveal a shadowy recess behind.

Someone got here before me.

I listen for approaching footsteps, but the basement is quiet. Philip has found somewhere else to sulk. From the recess, I retrieve a black nylon duffel bag covered with cobwebs and crud, smelling of foot odor. No telling how long it's been in there. My first thought is to put it right back where I found it. None of my business. But it's a good hiding spot. For all I know the duffel is filled with long-forgotten laundry.

Or, well…money.

Twenties and hundreds bundled into stacks with rubber bands, with a few loose bills mixed in. It's not new money, not fresh bills wrapped at the bank. At a glance, there are several dozen bundles, each about an inch thick. Most of the stacks are hundreds.

A *lot* of money.

For a moment, I imagine what I could do with this kind of cash. The tools I could buy, the distance I could put between myself and the wonderful world of foster care. It's like I'm holding a winning lottery ticket. But almost as quickly, paranoia boils through me.

Normal people don't hide duffels full of cash in the walls.

I look around, unable to shake a sudden feeling I'm being watched. No one is there, but the paranoia lingers. With a tremor in my hands, I jam the bag into the recess and replace the boards. For now, I stick my suitcase on a high shelf in the shadows. I'll deal with it later.

Mrs. Huntzel runs into me as I exit the vault. "Joey! You startled me."

When my heart dislodges itself from my throat, I manage to croak out, "Just grabbing supplies." As evidence, I show her a wad of rags I'm carrying around.

"I see." She peers past me into the vault. I expect her to ask why I was looking for rags in there, of all places. But then she shakes her head. "You boys need to slow down in the house."

I let out a breath. When she turns away, I call after her. "Hey, Mrs. Huntzel. When I'm done, would it be okay if I take a quick shower?" She turns back and I hold out my arms. I look like Cinderella's dodgy brother.

"Of course. I believe there are towels in the guest bathroom at the top of the stairs." Then she's gone.

Philip can say what he wants about the animal heads, but I needed the excuse as much as I needed the hours. Another day without a shower and they wouldn't let me through the door at Katz. When I come out of the bathroom, his bedroom door is closed. I stop in the butler's pantry to note my time—four hours. Forty bucks. Or, about a million less than I found in that bag. I don't want to think about it, so I poke my nose into the fridge. Mrs. Huntzel's sandwich from the night before is still there. I grab it, go open and close the back door in case anyone is listening for the security system tone. I pass back through the basement, stopping to snag my suitcase—moronic to go snooping in the vault in the first place.

When I shut Kristina's door behind me, I wish there was a latch.

Some time afterward, I'm snuggling the unicorns, staring at the dark window and listening to the silence, when my phone buzzes.

only gonna try this once. answer or dont, txt only

I deserve that. I draw a breath and reply with unexpected honesty. Unexpected to me.

I missed you today

She takes her time answering. I get the feeling I said the wrong thing.

bullshit. u just wanna know what they askd

I sigh into the empty silence. Deserve that too. I make a point of not asking what she told the police, even though she's right. I *do* want to know.

how come txt only?

Another long wait. Outside, the darkness deepens from blue-gray to black.

dads in a weird mood. keeps opening my door. checking on me.

Pause.

he doesnt knock

Wayne wouldn't either, but in the days when Anita could still climb the stairs, she always knocked. Before I can figure out the best way to tell Trisha it's seriously creepy for a man to barge uninvited into a girl's room, she texts again.

did he say something 2 u?

He didn't have to. His look of disgust in the Katz office was loud and clear. I wonder if she has any idea of the speech he gave me that day in their driveway.

no.

I almost add, "not today." Decide to stick with the lie of omission. It's an hour before she texts back, a period long enough for my skin cells to recycle a dozen times over.

sorry. cant talk. no school tomorrow. going 2 coast.
c u monday

Is he keeping her out of school so she can't talk to me, or because of something the cops said? The Voglers spend a lot of time at their house in Manzanita. But they also take school seriously. I can't remember Trisha ever skipping to go to the beach. Even weirder is *c u Monday*. Manzanita isn't Turkmenistan.

Text me from Manz?

No response. Alone, in that dark room, stripped to my underwear in a stranger's bed, paranoia is my default setting.

At least the underwear is clean.

1.14: Snoop

Three days squatting. I wonder how long before I'm considered a legal resident.

The detectives haunt the school all morning Friday, but Katz is in an old building with lots of back hallways and odd corners. I avoid any close encounters. They seem to be focusing on staff—fine with me. Still, my stomach stays knotted until I catch sight of them shaking hands with Cooper on their way out the door shortly before lunch.

After school—early Friday—I spend three hours in the computer lab working on sources for DI and writing an AmLit reaction paper—expressions of the American Dream in *Of Mice and Men*. (What dream?) Stuff I should be doing at the coffee shop on my laptop. The lab is run by a misanthropic gargoyle who calls you a cultist if you own something with an Apple logo on it. I bought my phone at 7-11, so he usually leaves me alone. While I work, he noisily slurps a Cup Noodles and lectures no one in particular about open source software. A pair of earbuds may be a necessary investment next time I get paid. Maybe I can pick up a hot iPod on craigslist and really piss him off.

As soon as I click SEND on the reaction paper, I'm gone. On my way out, I peer through the office door. Mrs. An is alone, frowning at her computer as she bangs on the keyboard. Cooper's office door stands open, but there's no sign of him.

Mrs. An lets out a sudden exasperated sigh. "Joey?"

I startle and look at her. "What?"

"Keep an eye on things for me? I need a coffee."

She doesn't wait for me to answer, blows through the door. The phone rings, but since she didn't say anything about receptionist duty, I ignore it. My eyes shift to Cooper's doorway.

My laptop is still on his shelf.

It'll only take a minute.

I check the hall. Empty, but from somewhere in the distance I can hear the murmur of conversation. Far away, Commons distance. It's six long strides into the corral, but when I reach the shelf, I hesitate. I feel like I'm poised at the edge of a trap. Any second, the floor could drop out beneath me. Trapdoor to the Katz Dungeon Annex.

"Were you looking for me, Joey?"

I spin. Cooper stands in the door.

"Um."

As he crosses to his big leather chair he claps me on the shoulder.

"Something I can help you with?" He leans back, eyes glued to mine. The smell of pomade tickles my nose hairs. His gaze flicks to the glass case.

"Duncan!"

The name spills out of me like falling rocks. His eyes turn back to me.

"Did you want to tell me something?"

"I, uh, just wondered what you've heard."

He studies me for a long moment. I feel like an insect pinned to a board. "I just spoke to his mother, as it happens. There's been no change."

I swallow. "Okay."

"Is there anything else?" His eyes flick toward the case. I silently thank my own paranoia and shake my head.

"I gotta get to work." I manage to not knock the returning Mrs. An onto her ass as I make my escape.

When I arrive at Huntzel Manor a little after three, Caliban greets me at the door. I brush the mud off his back, tell him to go terrorize children in the park or something. Friday is my day to clean Mrs. Huntzel's office, the kitchen, and the utility areas. My easiest day.

More important, Friday is the day Mrs. Huntzel takes Philip to the Portland Chess Collective—the only time he faces a real challenge on the board. They won't be home 'til late.

This is my chance to see where things stand, and work out an escape plan, should the need arise.

In Kristina's room, I inspect the broad window frame. There's no evidence of security sensors. Not necessary on the second floor, I guess. Once I'm sure an open window won't bring the alarm company van shrieking up the driveway, I lift the sash. The window has no screens, which helps. Kristina's room looks out over one end of the upper veranda. The outside wall is brick, with stone lintels above each window. Some of the bricks that stick out in a decorative pattern will double as handholds in case of emergency. My first choice isn't to climb out the window—nor my second, third, or tenth—but as the prophet said, you never know when you're gonna need to jam.

Satisfied I can climb down if I have to, I close the window and stash a length of clothesline I'd lifted from the garage into the bottom dresser drawer along with my clothes. The rope isn't for me. If I have to pull a Spider-Man, it's to lower my gear first. I stow the suitcase in the closet. Not much of a hiding place, but one thing at a time.

My next stop is the vault. I can't shake the sensation I'm being watched as I open the hidey-hole. I ignore the loose bills and focus on the bundles. Forty-seven stacks of hundreds, eight of twenties. I keep losing count, but looks like each stack is a hundred bills. Not quite five hundred thousand dollars.

I'm not sure what knowing the amount tells me, besides the fact someone in this house has hidden half a million dollars behind a loose board in an unsecured vault. I can think of more than a few reasons why it isn't in a bank. Money this filthy didn't come from volunteering at Katz or a legit business. I pack up the cash and hide it again, with no temptation to hold back even a single twenty. Back upstairs in Kristina's bathroom, I have to wash my hands twice to kill the stench.

I leave the sink running, turn on the shower. Out in the hall, with the door closed, I can hear the water, but faintly. Same for the library. From the living room, I detect a burble overhead, but I'm not sure I'd notice it if I wasn't listening for it. Trisha says my super hearing would be cute if it wasn't so damn annoying.

I'm not worried about the library and living room. I'm not worried about Philip, either. His thoughts drown out all else when his head is buried in his Book or he's staring at a chessboard. Which is most of the time. The question is what can the Huntzels hear? I don't plan on kicking up a ruckus, but I gotta know if I can take a piss or brush my teeth without having SWAT bust in on me.

I hesitate outside the door to the master suite, as if a bubble of warm air is pressing against me. But then I turn the knob and cross the threshold.

Adult bedrooms aren't something I have a lot of experience with. During the Mad Maddie era, my chores included running the vacuum cleaner throughout the house, but all

I remember of her bedroom is the smell of skin cream. At some placements, the parents locked the doors, and not just bedroom doors. The Tinkels padlocked the fridge. Wayne and Anita never went that far, but their bedroom was verboten. *No problem, freaks.*

Now, as I stare across what feels like a vast expanse, Mr. and Mrs. Huntzel's room is both strange and anticlimactic.

Two wide windows on the far wall let in lots of light, but the air is as heavy as a held breath. I close the door behind me and listen to the silence.

It's perfect.

Twin beds anchor the corners, but there isn't much else in the way of furniture. A couple of wing chairs. A flat-screen TV on a media stand at the foot of the nearer bed. There is a scattering of DVDs and Blu-rays on the floor, commercial releases and home-burned DVDs with handwritten labels. *Bianca on E, Bianca Red Carpet, PM on SdT.* I think about the folder full of pictures in Philip's dresser. Mrs. Huntzel too? I know Philip sometimes watches videos with his mom, but I always figured it was *Haven* or *Star Wars Rebels* marathons.

The layers in the Huntzel weirdness have layers.

A pair of doors lead to the bathroom and a big walk-in closet. The silence holds in both. My professional eye notes the bathroom could use a freshening, but I'm glad I don't have to deal with all the shampoos, conditioners, and beauty implements of strange and vaguely sinister configuration. There's no evidence of Mr. Huntzel, which seems a little strange. Dude has to shave, right? In the closet most of the clothing belongs to Mrs. Huntzel. A wrinkled suit and two grayish dress shirts hang at one end of the rack, along with a lone tie.

I head back out to the main room. One bed is neatly made.

Its nightstand is bare, drawer empty. No books, no slippers on the floor. Could be a bed in a hotel room.

Suddenly I understand why I see so little of Mr. Huntzel. He doesn't actually live here.

Huh.

The other bed is a tangle of sheets and blankets. The brush on the nightstand has reddish-gray hairs twisted among the bristles. There's a nail file, and an empty water glass with a smudge of lipstick on the rim, the television remote. Mrs. Huntzel never struck me as a messy person, but the bathroom and the heap of clothes on the floor kick that idea in the ass.

I pull open the drawer on her nightstand.

Among the kind of clutter I suppose you find in any bedside table—tissue box, pens and pencils, scraps of paper—there's a pistol.

The air drains out of me. As guns go, it isn't much. Wouldn't even make the cut in your average first-person-shooter video game. A small revolver with a stubby barrel and a black plastic grip. I absorb the details in an instant, then rock back on my heels. I feel like I'm standing on the edge of a cliff.

Who does she expect to shoot?

People like me.

I close the drawer and return to Kristina's room, turn off the water. Sit on the bed. Stand. Run my thumb over my phone. I almost text Trisha, but what would I say? *If my bullet-riddled corpse turns up on Mount Tabor, tell the cops to take a hard look at Mrs. Huntzel.*

Instead, I try to distract myself with pine cleaner and a mop. For all the good it does me.

Fuck.

With Mr. Huntzel gone so much, maybe the gun helps

her feel safe. It's not like she waves it around. How long have I worked here? Six months? Never seen it.

Still.

If the money was unsettling, the gun makes me want to swallow my tongue. But at least I know where things stand, right?

That's what I tell myself, anyway.

I finish Friday in an hour. Record time, not the best I've ever done. Restless and edgy, I retreat to Kristina's room, close the door. Find myself thinking about food. My thoughts are clinical. Practical. I gotta eat, even though I'm not hungry. Back in the kitchen, I build a sandwich—with mustard—and grab a bottle of water. I eat standing…pacing…standing in Kristina's room. For a while, I listen at the door but the house is silent. Sometimes, Philip has told me, his mom takes him out for dinner after Chess Collective. I try to remember the last time I saw Mr. Huntzel. Can't.

Finally, as sunlight fades outside, I get undressed and slip under the covers. It's still early but I don't know what else to do.

Leave?

And go where?

Exactly.

This is what you get for snooping, asshole.

1.15: Victoria's Orphan

By the time I fall asleep, I've worked through at least half a dozen ideas.

She's a private detective…

An elite international assassin…

The money's her fee…

It's fake…

Or, the gun's a fake…

A toy…

A cigarette lighter

I picture her in black-and-white on the lower veranda, firing up a cancer stick from the barrel of her snub-nose. At some point I either talked myself into believing she'd never shoot me—I'm Philip's guardian angel, after all—or exhausted myself.

No clue how long I've been asleep when my eyes pop open. There's a presence in the room with me. Not Caliban, unless he's figured out how to turn doorknobs. A person. All I can think of is the pistol and the scent trail of all that cash. Then the light clicks on and confusion roils my fear. It's not Mrs. Huntzel. The girl in the black quilted vest and camouflage pants tucked into shin-high Chucks is holding a leather messenger bag, not a gun.

Which is a good thing. She looks pissed.

"Who the hell are you? And what are you doing in my bed?"

Even if she hadn't mentioned *her bed*, I'd know it was Kristina—I recognize Philip's sour glare. Her hair is dark like his, but with jewel green flashes that match her eyes. Philip's elf features are more effective on her too.

I push myself up, remember I'm only wearing my underwear, and scooch back under the covers again.

"You—"

"Me. Yes." She tosses her vest toward the dresser, doesn't seem to care when it hits the floor. "What happened to your face?"

I thought it was looking better. "It's…I—" The bridge troll crack I'd prepped for just such a moment dies on my lips.

"Wait. You're the stray, aren't you?"

"The what?"

"You're Victoria's stray. The orphan."

"You call your mother Victoria?"

"It's her name. What do you call her?"

"Mrs. Huntzel."

"I guess that makes sense."

She drops her bag and looks around the room as if checking for damage. I know I'm busted, but the fact she hasn't started screaming for blood or dialing 9-1-1 leaves me with this weird, floating anxiety.

"What do you—?" A wad of goo collects at the back of my throat, but somehow I force my voice past it. "It's just, well… Philip said you don't come around anymore."

She studies me for a long moment, and her eyes soften. I wonder if she's thinking I'm not so different from her, another castoff. But then she shakes her head and her gaze darkens again.

"And that's why he's letting you sleep in my bed?"

I don't say anything. Maybe my face gives something away.

Her lips pull back from her teeth into a sneer, another patented Huntzel expression. "He doesn't know you're here, does he?"

"Listen—"

"No one does." Now her sneer turns into an evil grin. "You picked the one room in the house no one will ever enter. The black sheep's bedroom, the prodigal sister. The evil bitch no one talks about."

"I'll leave. Okay? Just don't tell them."

She laughs, too loud. "Why the fuck would I tell them anything?"

I'm confused, but she only laughs again.

"Didn't Philip tell you? We don't speak."

"Why not?"

"None of your fucking business, Oliver."

"Oliver?"

"You never read a book?"

"Oh. Dickens. Sure."

"What's your real name?"

"Joey."

"You'd be more interesting as Oliver." She considers me for a minute. "Are you naked?"

Here's the thing. You imagine this moment, good-looking girl appears in your room in the middle of the night. A blood rush is what you hope for. Just not to the face.

"Not completely, no."

"Good."

"Listen—"

"No, you listen. I know what you did for my brother, and no matter what they say, I appreciate it. But that doesn't give you carte blanche."

"Carte blanche?"

"You don't get to do whatever you want. Get me? This is *my* room. Keep your shorts on. Beat off in the shower. Don't be getting your spunk on my sheets."

"Jesus."

She laughs, but I don't see what's funny. "I just want to be clear about whose bed you're sleeping in. Now move over."

"What?"

"Move over. I'm tired."

"I'll go somewhere else."

"Where? None of the guest rooms have blankets or sheets. Shut up and move over. But keep your hands to yourself. I'm not looking for any action."

She grabs the quilt from the closet and turns off the light. In the moonlight filtering in around the curtains, I can just make out her silhouette wrapping up in the quilt. The bed shifts as she lies down beside me. There's three layers of fabric between us. Not nearly enough. She rolls onto her side, back to me. I hear her shoes hit the floor. It's like an elephant clumping around the room, but I suppose she knows how solid the house is.

No way can I sleep. I wish I was wearing a T-shirt and some sweatpants. My boxers feel like a shadow.

"You have a boner, don't you?"

"Who *are* you?"

She chuckles without turning toward me. "Remember what I said. Shower only."

I don't know which is worse, the gun down the hall or the girl in my bed. My hands twist the covers up to my chin. After a while, my pulse slows in my ears and I realize I can hear her breathing. Slow and regular. Asleep. I have no clue how she can sleep. I can hardly breathe with my heart pressed against the back of my tongue. Moonlight moves across the window, slow as melting glass—

When I awake the next morning, she's gone. Caliban has taken her place, with her permission, I assume. His tail thumps when I stir. On the dresser there's a note and an old, tarnished key.

Oliver—
   The key is for the door next to the fireplace in the rec room. Not wired.
   You're welcome.

                                                        —K

1.16: Tighty-Whities

It's barely eight when I sneak down to the basement, Caliban at my heels. The rec room is quiet and empty, dust-free after my efforts on Thursday. The door next to the fireplace looks like an afterthought, plain and dark, a wooden airlock with an ancient deadbolt and no knob. I'm half-surprised when Kristina's key slides into the keyhole. The door opens with the barest squeak. As promised, there's no bleat from the security system.

Caliban darts out ahead of me into a space shaded by the looming chimney and the laurel hedge. I've worked for the Huntzels for months, but this is the first time I've seen this end of the house from the outside. The slope of Mount Tabor drops sharply here, too steep for landscaping. Last year's leaves crackle under my feet. After throwing me a look, Caliban disappears into the brush. A weedy path spills down to the street, hidden from the house by a wall of arborvitae.

With Kristina's key, I can come and go as I please. I can only guess why she gave it to me—maybe more weird Huntzel gratitude for what I did to Duncan. But who the hell knows? I head to Uncommon Cup for breakfast.

Two hours later, I'm sweeping the upper veranda when Philip appears at the foyer door. He stops to watch for a moment, expression unreadable behind his plastic mask. I don't think he needs it now. Probably thinks it makes him look like some kind of super villain. The Chessinator. He's got his Book in one hand. I assume Mrs. Huntzel chased him outside to "get a little sun." The bruising around his eyes has cycled from wannabe Goth to comical raccoon.

I lean on the broom. "Hey, Philip. What's the deal with Kristina, anyway?"

He jumps when I speak, startled. Stares at me for a long, blank moment.

Why do I even bother? He never answers my questions—a position I approve of most of the time. But Kristina…I don't know where she came from, don't know where she went. Or why she showed up at all. Sleep with a girl within two minutes of meeting her and it makes an impression, even if you never touch each other.

"Why do you care about Kristina? She's an ogress."

Not the word I'd choose. "Just wondering."

He's quiet for a long time. Usually that means he's trying to figure out how to be clever or evasive. Since he sucks at both I'd rather he just told me to fuck off.

"I refuse to discuss Kristina."

Fuck off it is.

He goes looking for somewhere else to obsess, leaving me to my menial labor. Usually I don't mind pushing a broom or scrubbing floors, but this morning the mindless task leaves my brain free to ponder the women in my life.

Kristina. Mrs. Huntzel and her gun. Anita's fearful kindness—*Did your laundry, sorry about the face.*

Mrs. Petty has been dark since Tuesday in the corral. Usually I wouldn't care, but I'm not thrilled she left me to twist with the cops.

When you don't need them, you can't get rid of them. When you do, they're nowhere to be found. Get used to it.

As I work, my mind keeps looping back to Trisha. I wonder how things are going at the beach. Her silence is like a pressure in the center of my chest. While I was at Uncommon Cup, I went so far as to initiate contact. A miracle text.

Hey. Bring me a shell?

Half an hour and one pulverized donut later, I sent another.

That was a joke.

No response. Might be time to rethink my fierce opposition to emojis.

———

At noon, Mrs. Huntzel reviews the clipboard, then takes seven twenties from her purse. None smell like ass. "Thank you, Joey. Good work."

I'm dismissed. One-forty is my best week ever.

As weekends go, this one is meh. I spend Saturday afternoon at Uncommon Cup working on Math and doing my American History reading. The only moment of interest is when I hear two girls rattling off a list of celebs who are "*sooo* grotesquely overexposed.*"* Bianca Santavenere makes the cut. Apparently she's been shopping a "leaked" sex tape. By the time the café closes, I'm a week ahead on History and Trig, and working on my counteroffensive for when Moylan sticks me with an *M*. I steal into the house through Kristina's secret door without incident, lie awake for hours wondering if she's going to make another appearance.

Sunday is dull as dry beans. Me mostly holed up in Kristina's room, Caliban farting at my side. I'm grateful for the company, but, *sheesh, dog*. I probably shouldn't get used to it; last thing I need is him scratching on her door to visit when I'm not around. Still, it's nice to think I'm not the only uninvited guest in the house. When the cops finally bust us, maybe we can share a cell.

Every few minutes I check my phone, resist the urge to text Trisha. I read *The Crucible*. Make progress on my DI project. Sleepwalk through a couple of Chemistry worksheets. At intervals, I sneak into the kitchen to scarf pizza rolls, potato salad, and pretzel sticks. Grazing from the food group P.

During the afternoon, I watch from a second-floor window as Philip pulls the 740i out of the garage and washes it in the driveway. Should be my job, but I *am* burning through a shit-ton of pudding cups so I can't really complain about a missed hour of paying work. It's been a week since I faced a plate of creamed chipped beef.

Sunday night I sneak through the basement to the kitchen—reading alone for hours is hungry work. As I pass through the rec room, I hear the sound of violin music. At first, I think it must be coming from upstairs. I wonder if the Huntzels have guests. But as I near the door to the utility basement, the music grows louder. For a moment I find myself caught up. The sound is strange and resonant, loud, frenetic. And missing something, though it's not clear what until the sound abruptly stops and Philip steps through the vault door. He's carrying a violin in one hand, bow in the other. Wearing nothing but a pair of tighty-whities, his body slick with sweat.

Wriggling bugs crawl through my gut. It's only because he goes the other direction, toward the kitchen stairs, that he doesn't bust me. I slink back to Kristina's room, no longer hungry. Getting late anyway.

As I'm trying to fall asleep, I think back to my dream the first night I was here; the feverish violin music must have been

Philip. I had no idea he could play anything except chess. I don't know classical music, but even I could tell he's good.

What I don't want to know is why he plays alone, in the vault. And definitely not why in his underwear.

1.17: That Was a Joke

Monday morning. I guess it's fall now, since I tramp down to Hawthorne through rain and the smell of wet leaves. But I forget my soggy shoes when I get to Uncommon Cup. Trisha sits with the fish, mug in one hand, *The Crucible* open in the other. I get a regular coffee—cheaper than a double shot—and skip the donuts. Coagulated eggs, soysage, and watery orange juice await me at school—repulsive, but free.

I sit down. Before I can say anything, her eyes spill over me. "Don't worry."

"Don't worry about what?"

"He wouldn't let them ask me any questions."

I can't believe I've forgotten the detectives already. Maybe not forgotten them. Just...other things on my mind. Guns and green-haired girls. Secret money. I meet Trisha's gaze. "Why not?"

"Maybe he doesn't like cops."

One thing Mr. Vogler and I have in common.

"Did you invoke?"

"Is that what it's called?" She grins. "How many times have you been arrested, Joey?"

I look at the fish. "I'm surprised they didn't call your caseworker."

"That guy's useless. Probably doesn't even remember my name."

They can't all be Mrs. Petty I guess. As I sit there wondering what it would be like to have a caseworker who didn't know my name, Trisha tips something into her mug from a silver flask.

"You want some?"

"Uh."

"Good grief. It's just Baileys." She taps the flask with her index finger, but then she tucks it away in her jacket. Her eyes scan the café. "I like it here. Want to come back after lunch?"

I swallow. I can't tell if she's changing the subject on purpose, or actually likes Uncommon Cup. I want to know more about the police, but she's more interested in the café.

"Well?"

"I have to show up for DI today. And then after that I need to spend time in the computer lab before Trig."

"Right." She nods as if she understands, but a shadow of disappointment darkens her gaze. Unless it's my own reflected back at me. "You know, Joey, you could borrow my Katz laptop. I got a MacBook for my birthday." The Comp Lab Troll must love her.

"You don't have to do that. It's only a few weeks."

"Don't be silly. You could come home with me and pick it up instead of going to the lab."

The mental image of Mr. Vogler setting attack dogs on me flares behind my eyes. "Let me see how it goes today." Before she can press, I add, "How was the beach?"

Now I'm the one changing the subject. She hesitates, then lets it go. "Tedious. Mom had some big work project, so it was just me and dad until Saturday night." Her cheeks darken. "He took my phone."

She must see the panic on my face.

99

"Don't worry. I erased all the messages. I always erase my messages."

"I texted you a couple of times."

"I know. He told me." She turns her book over and leans forward, her voice going quiet and conspiratorial. "He got all weird about it, like you were communicating in code. 'What does he mean, *bring me a shell*?' I said it meant you wanted me to bring you a shell."

"It was a joke."

"Obviously, dumbshit." A gleam dances in her eyes, then she leans to her side to root around in her book bag. When she raises up again, she's holding a sand dollar. "I brought you a shell anyway."

Electricity arcs up my spine. She presses the sand dollar into my hand. Part of me wants to run, like I'm caught in a burning building. Instead, I run my thumb over the coarse surface. It's white as milk and fits perfectly in my palm.

"You didn't have to do this."

"I know."

A trace of adhesive on one side tells me she got it at a tourist gift shop. I stare at it for a long time, trying to figure out what to say. *Thank you* would probably do. A random factoid is what trips off my tongue.

"They call these sea cookies in New Zealand."

She snickers. "They do not."

"They do too."

"How do you know that? And don't give me some dippy male-answer-syndrome bullshit either."

It's possible I'm making it up, but it feels like actual information. "I read it somewhere."

"Let me guess. Wikipedia."

"Probably."

"Dumbshit."

At least she's smiling as she leans back in her chair and stretches her arms over her head. My gaze falls on her breasts, rising and falling as she breathes, and the electricity returns. Then I catch movement behind her. From the counter, Marcy leers as my face goes molten. Trisha drops her arms and leans forward. "What?"

"What what?"

"You're blushing."

"No, I'm not."

She cups my hand in hers, hiding the sand dollar inside. "I like it."

I turn to the fish tank and will my flesh to blanch. Fail. "Thanks for the sea cookie, Trisha."

"You're welcome, Joey." With that, she stands up. "I've got to go. Denise and I are getting together before school." Her warm fingers brush the back of my neck. "Think about my offer." After she's gone, I catch Marcy gazing at me, a half-smile on her lips.

For the first time in days, the overheated pressure in my chest is gone. The lack of sensation throws me, as if I've lost something important. Tension gives me an edge. Worry reminds me of the danger lurking behind every encounter. Anxiety keeps me from making mistakes. Trisha feels like a mistake. A beautiful mistake. I'll see her again before the day is out, but already I miss the feeling of her hand on mine.

I grip the sand dollar in my pocket, walk to school in a daze. Not wanting what I want.

At Katz, the corridors are jammed with people, moving in clots, talking, opening and closing lockers. I lose my way in the hallways, hear nothing, forget to eat free breakfast before Day Prep.

The noise comes crashing back in the form of the two cops who cut me off on the way into Harley May's classroom. Detective Man-Mountain puts a hand on my shoulder, heavy as a sandbag. Detective Heat Vision does the talking, her squirrelly voice sharp in my ears.

"Joey, we need you to come with us."

At first, the command makes no sense, but slowly the meaning penetrates my fog. *Where?* But I'm unable to speak aloud, or to twist out of Man-Mountain's grip. He smiles grimly, and guesses my question.

"Not to Directed Inquiry, that's for sure. It's time for you to explain to us where you *really* were when your buddy Duncan got run down in the street."

0.18: The Book

It's fair to say my idea to escape school, the Boobies, and even Mrs. Petty and state custody grew out of the punch I threw at Duncan Fox. Not that The Plan came to me in the moment.

In that moment, last April, all I knew was my fingers were tingling and Moylan was demanding an explanation.

"Joey gave Duncan a beatdown."

Moylan stormed across the room to separate us, eyes like boiled eggs, but the words seemed to dampen the fire in me. Philip was already on the floor collecting pages of the Book. Trying not to cry. I exhaled, turned my head toward the rain-swept windows. Saw nothing but gray light and uncertainty. I imagined my next school. Somewhere with yellow lines painted on the floors.

"Boys. With me. Now."

I only knew Moylan as the Chess Club advisor—I didn't yet have him for Math. The tournament season was over, so he worked with the ranked players after school. Since there was no danger I'd ever be one of those, I sat at the back of the room during club meetings and did homework while I lost my game.

I had a feeling I was about to get to know him better.

He didn't push us. Didn't touch. Smart teacher. But I could

feel his eyes guiding us through the door, up the hallway, and across the Commons. We passed near Trisha, who sat with Denise and Beth Black and a senior I knew only as Jen the Amazing. Their table was covered with printed manuscript pages, marked up in red and purple ink. "What happened?" Trisha mouthed, concern darkening her eyes.

Moylan didn't give me a chance to answer. He marched us to the office, barked at Mrs. An as we came through the door. "Is Mr. Cooper available?"

"I'll page him." Mrs. Huntzel was there, too, but rushed out when Moylan told her to "see to Philip in the chess room."

He turned on us. "You two. There."

There was a bench against the wall outside Cooper's office. We sat as far from each other as possible, a four-foot expanse of oak between us. Not far enough. Moylan vanished and the office hum settled in around us. I exhaled adrenalin vapor and stared at an ink-jetted sign taped to the counter. NO TALK-ING. From the other side, Mrs. An chatted with a student aide who came in after Moylan left us to stew. Maybe they couldn't see the sign.

Duncan put his elbows on his knees, grabbed his head. I'd never really looked at him, but now his hands drew my gaze. Tufts of his hair stuck out between long, meaty fingers. His forearms were as thick as my calves, his shoulder muscles piled up around his ears.

If I hurt him, it was only because I landed a sucker punch. "Duncan."

"Don't talk to me." He sounded like he had marbles in his mouth. I didn't want to talk to him. Or maybe I did. I remembered the look on Philip's face as he gathered up his scattered pages of notation. Thought about Duncan's big hands and his desperate need to be first board. It was all so stupid. Not just the fight, but everything leading up to the fight. Hell, wind it all the way back to the moment Cooper first led me into the lunchroom and the original act of stupidity was mine, thinking I might have a place there.

All wanting something ever gets you is trouble.

"Listen—"

"Read the sign."

"You want me to tell you how to beat Philip or not?"

When he answered, "Shut up," I could tell his heart wasn't in it. He sat clutching his head for a minute like he was trying to hold his skull in place. "Fine. What?"

"I didn't beat him."

"What do you call it?"

"He made a mistake and I jumped on it." The aide laughed at something Mrs. An said, then greeted a newcomer with way too much enthusiasm. Lunch must have ended—I recognized Beth's voice.

"So all I have to do is wait for the next time Philip Huntzel screws up? Great tip there, Einstein."

"Just listen for a minute."

He slouched away from me, radiating nervy heat. I closed my eyes, inhaled a scent like warm metal. Tried to ignore the noise and chatter on the other side of the counter. A pencil tapping, phone ringing. Lockers slamming out in the hall. Finally Duncan let out a long breath.

"Okay. Tell me."

"You don't lose to Philip because of the Book."

"What do you know about it? You're not a student of the game."

Which is why I won. I thought about Philip's mistake, my unexpected victory, and wondered if what I was about to tell Duncan was an apology—or an act of revenge. Maybe a little of both. "I know Philip can only see things his way. The Book is all about trends and analysis. What did you do before? What are you likely to do next?"

"So?"

"So you play against the Book, you lose. No way can you analyze better than Philip. His brain works like a spreadsheet."

He lifted his head. One side of his face was twice the size of the other, but what got my attention was the sudden intensity in his gaze. The Book was Philip's greatest asset, a looming presence in every game. Philip's muscle-bound thug menacing every opponent.

"What are you suggesting?" Duncan's voice was urgent now.

"Do what I did. Make screwy moves. Surprise him. If you go off-Book, he can't fit you into his analysis. He gets frustrated."

He was quiet for a long moment, then nodded thoughtfully. "Like Fischer-Byrne."

"Who?"

"Fischer against Byrne, 1956." He stared at me. "The Game of the Century?"

"If you say so."

He shook his head at my tragic ignorance. "In 1956, Bobby Fischer beat Donald Byrne. Fischer was thirteen, Byrne an adult champion who didn't expect a challenge, even from a prodigy. Fischer won by exploiting a Byrne error in the development phase and then luring him with an unexpected queen sacrifice which netted him a material advantage. Byrne never recovered."

I had no idea what he said. "So there you go."

I leaned my head against the wall. Felt a slight vibration, like a motor. Behind the desk, the aide answered the phone. I couldn't see her, but it sounded like Courtney. Fresh from her loss to Philip, witness to Chess Club Fight of the Century. When she got off the phone, Mrs. An asked her and Beth to stuff envelopes in the supplies nook. Based on the giggles, a hilarious chore.

"You're not a student of the game."

Duncan was back to holding his head in his hands.

"So you said."

"You open with your rook pawns, then bring your rooks out. You think you're being aggressive, but you concede the center."

I regarded him for a moment, realized this was his *quid pro quo*.

"Aren't the rooks my strongest pieces, aside from the queen?" Mad Maddie taught me that.

"Not if you concede the center."

I didn't have an answer to that. Maybe he was right.

He lifted his head to look at me, guessing my thought. "I *am* right. Think about it."

At that moment, I realized Cooper and Moylan were standing there eavesdropping. Cooper had a faint smile which dropped when Moylan cleared his throat. He directed us into the office, told us to have a seat. Moylan stood at one end of the desk, arms folded. Cooper sat on his throne and made church fingers. The stench of pomade just about brought my lunch up.

"You boys have been very disruptive today. I think I speak for both Mr. Moylan and myself when I say we're very disappointed."

I remember thinking the *verys* were a bit much. He waited, but I didn't know if he expected us to say something, or if he wanted his words to settle in. I wouldn't have spoken up either way. Duncan glanced at me, then looked down at his hands, palms up in his lap. He probably figured I had more experience getting reamed in the principal's office. If I wasn't going to talk, neither was he.

Cooper proceeded to outline our offenses as Moylan nodded in stern agreement. They'd done a whirlwind investigation; neither Duncan nor I disputed the facts as presented. Aggravated assault against the Book seemed to bug Moylan more than the fight itself. Duncan never raised his head.

"Fighting will not be tolerated. You're both on three-day in-school suspension, effective tomorrow." He looked at me and added, "The only reason it isn't more severe is because this is your first strike." *At Katz*, he seemed to be saying. "As for Chess Club itself…?"

Cue Moylan. He opened his arms like a spider uncurling. "Joseph. You are dismissed from the club. It's clear you're not interested in the game."

Back to the general population, but at least I wasn't facing another school. Three days ISS was easy time.

"Duncan, you've been an important part of the team since your freshman year. However, our club officers can't be brawling. You'll have to step down as president. Your rank is unchanged, of course. Should this kind of thing not happen again, you'll be eligible to run for club office for your senior year."

I didn't think Duncan was surprised either. He seemed even less troubled than I was by my sentence. He could power-trip with the best of them, but I don't think he wanted president nearly as much as he wanted first board.

"We've also decided the club meeting behind closed doors creates too much opportunity for mischief. From now on, the club can use my classroom during lunch so I can supervise."

I didn't care that Moylan could see me shake my head in disgust. Typical adult overreaction. Duncan's the one who lost his shit; I'm the one who threw the punch. Nobody else did anything wrong, but everyone had to pay. I looked into Moylan's eyes. Something smoldered back there, a flame that flared when he turned my way. *This is all your fault.* I could have said something, but when someone like me tries to defend people like Colin Botha and Courtney An, we only make things worse for them.

Cooper cleared his throat. "Duncan, you can go. Mr. Moylan, thanks for your help."

What that told me was Mrs. Petty was on her way. Duncan shuffled out. I wondered how hard Moylan would land on him for ripping up the Book. Philip was the golden child of the chessboard, after all. I was more worried I'd be stuck alone with Cooper for hours. But a minute or two after Moylan closed the door, Mrs. Petty burst through.

It was like hearing the chorus of some Cranky Adult song. *Fighting will not be tolerated...running out of options...had I forgotten why I was here?* I thought I was being empowered by critical thinking. I guess I'd never be allowed to forget the nun. I faded, but somewhere in there among the lassoes and six-shooters, it hit me. My problem was too much school. Each day of internment was another opportunity to fuck up. Escape was my only hope, the sooner the better.

Eventually the ass-chewing ended and I found myself in the outer office. Mrs. Petty stayed with Cooper to plot behind my back. My adrenalin rush was gone. Mrs. An was gone, too, but the cabinet next to her computer monitor hung partway open—a gleam of metal inside caught my eye.

I scanned the office, the windows looking out into the corridor. All clear. Courtney and Beth were in the supplies nook, too busy getting stoned on envelope glue to notice as I slipped behind the counter and reached into the cabinet. A couple dozen keys hung on hooks, each tagged. I grabbed one labeled "Lounge/Public Conference" and hoped I'd guessed right. The aides were still giggling as I slipped the key into my pocket and headed for the door. Mrs. An passed me on her way back from the Commons with a fresh cup of coffee.

I bumped into Mrs. Huntzel in the corridor. I sorta knew her, of course. She was practically an employee.

"You looked out for Philip." Her first words ever to me.

The way I saw it, I punched an asshole in the mouth. Philip may have been the trigger, but I wasn't thinking about him so much as Duncan. Then I turned around and told Duncan how to beat Philip. The way she smiled at me, honesty would get me nothing. "His notebook is pretty important to him," I offered.

"It's *very* important to him."

"Yeah." I figured that was enough. And I wanted out of there anyway. Any second Mrs. An could notice the missing key and call in an air strike. But when I turned away, Mrs. Huntzel put a hand on my arm.

"I have some work I need done up at the house. Odd jobs. Is that something you'd be interested in?"

No.

That was my first thought. If she knew my story—working in the office, she'd have to—she probably saw me as a charity case. But then I thought about how hard it was to come by cash. Carpentry supplies weren't cheap. My treatment plan required that I earn spending money in exchange for chores, but Wayne had a Scrooge-like approach to that idea.

And anyway, I *was* a charity case.

"What do you have in mind?"

"There are rooms in the basement which need cleaning out. After that, we could see."

Rooms? What kind of basement was she talking about?

"I can pay you ten dollars an hour."

Better than McDonald's. I was sure Mrs. Petty would be cool with it. Wayne wouldn't care. Hell, he'd be glad to be rid of me for a few hours.

"Sounds great. After school?"

"You can ride with Philip and me."

That day was my first ride in the BMW, my first look at Huntzel Manor. A month later, after I built a new set of shelves for the butler's pantry and proved I could use a power buffer, she made me houseboy. Turns out Mad Maddie's cleaning lessons were of some use after all.

1.19: Boys Have Their Secrets

I don't think the detectives like me. That's okay. I don't like them either.

They drag me into the corral past a grim-faced Mrs. An, this time with Cooper in tow. I sit in my straight-backed chair. The cowboy display is more than I can take this morning, so I focus on the shelf of contraband. The answer to their question is right there in my laptop. Dumbshits.

Except I'm the dumbshit if I forget juvenile detention is full of kids who thought they could outsmart the police. There's only one way to beat a cop: STFU. Name and prisoner number only.

"Joey..."

Since I won't, they do all the talking. Occasionally they drop a question in there, but mostly it's thinly disguised accusation delivered with a sneer. Trying to piss me off.

We know you weren't in Directed Inquiry.

We're not assuming you were anywhere near the accident...

It was an accident, wasn't it?

Just tell us what you saw.

What I saw was nothing.

They never read me my rights: another trick. Present the

illusion this is all informal. Just a chat. If I invoke my right to an attorney, they know I have something to hide. If I try to talk my way clear, they twist my words to trip me up. The second I say something of significance, the cuffs come out. "He surprised us by confessing, Your Honor. At that point, we Mirandized him—" This is why you keep your mouth shut.

The big guy is the patient one today, friendly-*lite*. The woman barks the questions that imply I know things I don't. Cooper sits behind them, ass on the credenza, chin down around his knees. I steal glances at him, only to find him staring from beneath his eyebrows every time. At last he clears his throat.

Detective Stein sighs. "What?"

"Perhaps we could send Joey out for a moment."

From the looks on their faces, they think I'll bolt the second I'm out of sight. No chance of that; they'd look for me at the Boobie Hatch. Detective Davisson runs his hand over his buzzed head. Detective Stein frowns and turns to Cooper.

"I think Joey understands the next step will be a drive downtown."

Cooper exhales sharply. "I'm sure that won't be necessary. Come on, Joey. Duncan is your friend." There's an edge to his voice I don't like. He sounds flustered.

Stein waves Cooper off and stands up. "Forget it. We're taking this—"

Davisson puts a hand on her arm. "I'm sure we can sort things out." He smiles at me. The Good Cop/Bad Cop act is so obvious I have to bite the inside of my cheek to keep from laughing in his face. He settles himself on the edge of the desk and hunches over, no doubt trying to reduce his intimidating bulk.

"Joey, I understand where you're coming from." His voice is soft, coaxing. When he leans close, I can smell the Barbasol. "You've been through a lot in your life." In other words, he's read up on me. My DHS file is supposed to be confidential, but it's probably not that hard to get. "And hell, we all know boys have their secrets. I respect that." There are police records too, stuff he can pull up on his computer. From ten years ago, from five. "I also know you have your reasons for mistrusting us." He shows me his teeth—

—and an alarm goes off in my head.

"I'm guessing you don't remember me, but I was friends with Zach Yearling—"

The room goes dim. My fists clench and heat boils through me, like a flashback to that day in chess club. Stein jumps to her feet—Cooper moves too. Their mouths fly open; their eyes spark. They look like stick puppets dancing on a stage. The atmosphere bleeds from the room with a crackling roar. In a split second of clear thought, I realize they think I'm going to throw a punch, or try something more drastic.

Idiots.

What I do is puke on Man-Mountain's shoes.

It's not much. A little coffee and stomach acid. The smell burns in my nostrils, floods my eyes with tears. In a heartbeat, heat drains out of me and I slump back against the chair. Someone shouts for towels. The cops are making noise, so much noise. Cooper tries to calm them down, but he might as well be a mouse against a couple of alley cats. Doesn't matter.

—because nothing ever changes.

They almost got me last time. Zachariah Yearling almost got me. He missed, but cops are like hornets. Hive memory runs long and deep.

Sixth grade—almost five years ago to the day—I was an ass hair away from Screwed for Life. My beige foster mother, the Missus, died in a fire at the bar Sergeant Yearling owned with a couple of other cops. I'd never been within a mile of the place, but that was beside the point.

The way Mrs. Petty put it, "They circled the wagons." Cared more about protecting one of their own than finding out what really happened. I was convenient. Cops looked at me and thought, "He survived the fire that killed his family. He *must* have set this one." With Zachariah dropping blunt-force hints—"The boy has all the signs: withdrawn, hostile, prone to violent outbursts."—I was hours from being charged. Arson. Murder. Some were even calling for me to be tried as an adult. Just, you know, *because*.

I was eleven.

A lucky break saved me. One detective broke ranks to pull at the threads of the investigation. By then, I was in the pediatric psych ward at Good Sam—suicide watch. You want to know about noise, visit a psych ward. Crying, shouting, screaming—all day, all night. I may not have been crazy when they locked me up, but the noise just about drove me there. Three days in, I was curled in a ball with my fingers in my ears.

Then, out of nowhere, Mrs. Petty unlocked the door and drove me to my new home, the Tinkels. Yearling had been arrested. The rogue detective had unearthed surveillance video proving I was forty miles away when the fire started. Then, traces of the accelerant used to start the fire were found on Yearling's cop shoes and he cracked. In his confession, he still tried to blame me. The convenient orphan with a fiery past.

On the news, they showed cops camped out at the court-house for a chance to serve as character witness at Zach's trial. I'm betting Detective Davisson was one of them.

"Joey!"

They're all staring at me. I blink. Sometimes my thoughts are so loud I miss what's going on around me.

Cooper is on the phone. "Mrs. An, would you get hold of Mrs. Petty? It's urgent. I need the district legal counsel too." When he puts the phone down, he stares at Stein.

Davisson and Stein exchange a look. Someone has wiped at the vomit on the floor, but Man-Mountain's shoes are still wet. The room is strangely hushed until Cooper's phone rings. When he picks up, it's obviously Mrs. Petty.

"Yes, the police are here. The situation is…exactly." His eyes fall on me. "I've called the district lawyer too." He listens for a moment, then offers the phone to Detective Stein.

It's awfully quiet for Jaeger versus Kaiju. Detective Stein doesn't say much. No one does when Mrs. Petty is talking. Finally Stein hangs up the phone. She lets out a long sigh. "All we want to know is where he was."

Even if I tell them, I can't prove it. I was alone. If I open my mouth, I blow up The Plan without escaping their crosshairs. I've got a rhythm here at Katz, but I've been bounced from too many schools. One more move, especially after an expulsion, and I may never recover.

As for the cops, they're out to screw me, no matter what I say. I can't count on a rogue detective twice in one lifetime.

Cooper leans forward. "Joey?"

Never admit to anything.

But Cooper's need is a ball of pressure squeezing my skull. I rub my face and sigh.

"I don't remember where I was." That's a lie. "But I never… left…*school*." That isn't.

Stein's fingers grip the edge of the desk so tight they turn white. "You're going to have to do better than that."

I put my head in my hands, like Duncan did after the Chess Club Fight of the Century. "There's too much noise."

Davisson finally cracks. "What in holy hell is that supposed to mean?"

But Cooper jumps like a man at sea who just found a life raft. "Joey needs a quiet place to work."

"Like where?"

"The gym." I never go in the gym. Cooper must know it. But they don't.

Davisson doesn't understand. "Since when is a gym quiet?"

Cooper smiles sheepishly. I know he's thinking about how we don't have a basketball team. I say, "This is Katz." If they can't figure it out, they're lousy cops.

At that moment, Mrs. An opens the door. Her expression is grim, steel in her gaze. "The attorney is on the phone." That doesn't matter, unless I invoke my right to counsel—which I won't unless there's no other choice. But it's enough to suck the heat out of the air.

The county has lawyers, too, an entire prosecutor's office. Stein and Davisson grant Cooper this round. Next time, I won't be so lucky. They shuffle out, sputtering bullshit apologies no one believes. In a dozen thudding heartbeats, it's just me, Cooper, and Mrs. An. She puts a hand on my shoulder, then leaves us alone as an almost alien realization settles through me.

Cooper had my back the whole time.

I meet his eyes and nod a fraction of an inch. He acknowledges me with a nod of his own, but there's a strain there, a sharp vertical line on his forehead. He turns his head. I can tell he's looking at the picture of himself on the horse.

As Mrs. Petty would put it, "Joey, you don't make it easy for any of us."

1.20: Watch Your Back

I can't imagine what brought me to the Commons. It's too early for lunch and long past breakfast. The space is only half-full and quieter than usual. Despite what Man-Mountain would like to believe, Katz has no scheduled study halls. If you have a free period or an open-attendance class, you make your own study hall. The Commons or the library is favored by those who want a work surface. Otherwise, any wall or corner will do.

As a rule, I spend as little time as possible in the Commons, but today I drop into a chair at an unused table. In my lap, my hands shake. A sensation like ants creeps down my neck. My eyes steal around the room, unable to find what I'm looking for.

Who.

Damn it.

If she's not in class, I suspect she'll be at Uncommon Cup. I don't know her exact schedule—the only class we have together is AmLit. Right now, I should be in Chemistry. I think. I've lost track of time. Part of me wants to go look for her, but I have no energy. Or maybe my legs are smarter than I am. I don't know what I'm doing with Trisha. My Plan is on the verge of coming unraveled and here I am, wiggy over a girl.

A shadow falls across the table. For a moment, my stomach flip-flops at the sight of dark hair. But it's too short, too straight. The eyes are all wrong—gold-flecked brown, distant. I blink the fog from my gaze and find Courtney An standing there.

"Hey, Joey."

"Hey."

"My mom said you were upset."

I drop my chin, bite back a smart-assed comment. A chair scrapes across tile. I hear her fingers drum the table. Before I can engage my mouth to say I want to be alone, she heads me off.

"Fucking cops."

I shake my head. What would Courtney An know about cops? Chess maven, school secretary's kid, insider favorite for valedictorian this year. But when I look up, I glimpse the curl of a tattoo on Courtney's wrist, a thorny vine illustrated to look like it's piercing her golden skin. Inked blood drips from a jagged slash. The rest of the tattoo is hidden by her sleeve, but it serves as a reminder I don't actually know anything about her. Her sweatshirt reads, "Ask Me About My Grandkids."

"Don't they know you're his friend?"

A grim smile steals across my lips. Isn't delusion grand?

"It's just all so sad. I don't understand why they're here." She gestures vaguely with both hands, like she's shooing away flies. "He didn't get hit in *here*."

I shrug. "If there's one thing cops are good at, it's looking the wrong way."

"Tell me about it."

We sit there for a while, neither speaking. Around the wide space, others are talking, or tapping laptop keyboards. The rush of blood in my ears is too loud. Courtney's fingernails tick silently against the table. She's somewhere else, lost in her own thoughts. Only her eyes show any sign of life, but I can't read them. Angry. Or calculating. I wonder what her story is, but I won't ask. I don't want to invite questions.

After a while, she lets out a long breath and for a split second her eyes mist over. "He didn't even get a chance to enjoy being first board."

Her words are like a punch to the gut. "First board? Duncan?"

"Philip didn't tell you? I thought you practically lived with him."

Paranoia washes over me, but I push it down. My job with the Huntzels isn't a secret. She must think we're closer than we are. "Philip and I don't really talk." I've been completely out of the loop on the chess team.

"Well, you should have been there." Like Moylan would allow that…he barely tolerates me in Math class. "He spent the summer refining his game, then finally made his push against Philip. It was pretty dicey for a while. Duncan won three in a row last week, then Philip responded with three wins and it looked like he would hang on. But at lunch that day Duncan took game seven. Got inside Philip's head, broke his legendary concentration. It was awesome."

"He went off-Book."

"*Way* off. Just like you told him."

"He told you about that?"

"Yeah." Courtney grins, a sad smile, yet proud. I find myself wondering about her relationship with Duncan. Last I heard, she'd made third board, the only ranked girl in the club—I know she takes shit for that. She and Duncan must spend a lot of time together. "Remember him in the hall that day? He was so excited."

That must have been what the slap-fight was all about. *Yo, Getchie, you missed the show.* "He'd been trying for first board for a long time."

"Then an hour later he's in a pool of his own blood."

My heart jumps in my chest. I watch people moving through the Commons. For a moment my gaze falls on the hallway leading to the private lunchroom. I could use some time in there right now. But it's locked and my key is gone.

"Mrs. Huntzel was so pissed."

"Well, Duncan did break Philip's nose."

"I mean before the nose thing."

"Seriously?"

"Yeah. I saw her in the office after the game, all up in Mr. Moylan's face about how Duncan *must* have cheated. Steam was coming out of her ears." She grabs a sheet of paper someone left on the table, a flyer for an open mic night at a coffeehouse nearby. Not Uncommon Cup. She starts scribbling on the back with a stubby pencil. Her gestures are angry, her lips a hard line. I smell sweat. At first I think she's scrawling a note, but a series of interlocking boxes begins to fill the page. I watch, hypnotized. After a moment I realize she's talking.

"We're sitting here. You're…moping, pouting. I'm drawing squares. Your girlfriend's off writing a poem or a novel or whatever she does." Breath. "People around us are studying, or blowing off studying. Making out in some corner. Out there—" another gesture "—people are drinking coffee, working, fighting with their boyfriends or girlfriends, riding bikes. Having sex, eating bacon, slamming shots. You name it. Meanwhile Duncan has to eat, pee, and crap through tubes. All because one of those people out doing other things right now—*living life* things—is a coward." She crumples the page, tosses it across the table. "Makes you wonder why Mrs. Huntzel hasn't shown up for her volunteer thing the last few days."

A hollow forms in my chest. I try to swallow, but my tongue sticks to the roof of my mouth. "What's that supposed to mean?"

"Hey, I'm just talking." Courtney raises her hands. "You're the one who knows them."

I think about Philip in his underwear, violin in hand. The folder of Bianca Santavenere clippings, the DVDs at the foot of Mrs. Huntzel's bed. Then the gun, and the money—Mrs. Huntzel's strange moods. Finally, Philip washing the BMW Sunday afternoon. I've never seen him lift a finger around the house.

Jesus.

She stands, hits me one last time with a glare. "Watch your back, Joey." Then she strides off, straight-armed and brisk. All I can do is stare.

2.0

Events are like a frayed cloth.

2.1: Here's the Thing

Cooper heads me off at the pass before I can sneak out to Uncommon Cup to look for Trisha. "Joey, not even *you* are allowed off campus during the school day. You heard what we said at the assembly." I didn't, but I suppose it was something about locking us down because of what happened to Duncan. I don't have it in me to argue. Not after the way he cockblocked the cops.

For the rest of the morning, I wander the bowels of Katz Learning Annex, listless and edgy all at once. Unlike me, Trisha evades Cooper's lasso. She fails to appear even at lunch, which is when her crit group meets. Denise says she's working on something new. "She needs to be alone when she has a new project, Joey." Apparently Mr. Vogler still has her cell, so no point in texting.

The afternoon continues the suck. In Directed Inquiry, Harley May says my source list "shows a disappointing lack of range and depth." After that, I get four out of ten on a trig quiz. Moylan's sad smile might be more convincing if not for the twinkle in his eyes. By the time the final bell rings, I'm ready to chew glass.

There's no sign of Trisha at Uncommon Cup, so I trudge through rain to the Huntzels. First stop, the garage. I examine the front end of the BMW, but I don't know what I'm looking for. There's no damage, but maybe there wouldn't be. People are soft; cars are hard. Philip would have washed off any blood. CSI, I'm not.

Short of asking a direct question, I have no way of finding out if Philip or Mrs. Huntzel had anything to do with the accident. All I know for sure is Courtney belongs to Team Duncan. Beyond that, her dramatic speech, a little innuendo, and a Sunday afternoon car wash don't add up to much. And even if it did, what can I do about it? Call the cops? I can picture *that* scene. "Hey, Detective Heat Vision, why are you hassling me when you could be looking at the notorious Huntzel crime syndicate?" That'll work. Besides, Philip and Mrs. Huntzel would have been at the hospital getting his fright mask about the time Duncan's head was cracking pavement.

I can't let Courtney knock me off The Plan. So far, I've managed seven days on the lam. A mere two-hundred-fifty to go 'til early graduation.

Sure.

I work through my Monday set—foyer, conservatory, and dining room, wax and buff—on autopilot. Philip and Mrs. Huntzel hover on the fringes; I ignore them. But later, as I'm rolling the floor buffer off the lift in the basement, Philip shambles down the stairs. Courtney's punch line—*You're the one who knows them*—pops into my head.

What I know about them is precisely jack.

"Hey, Philip." When he stops, I realize I have nothing to say. Obviously, I can't ask him if he or his mother committed hit-and-run assault. His eyebrows drop and I spit out the first thing which pops into my head. "I haven't seen your dad in forever."

Without his mask, his reliable glower is on full display. "What do you care?"

Good question. I feel like a cretin. "I noticed you guys have been driving his car. Something wrong with the BMW?" Subtle.

His bruises have turned yellow, which makes him look sicklier than usual. "What's it to you?"

In anyone else, his testiness might be suspicious.

"Never mind."

I put the buffer away, then head down to Division and 50th for food cart tacos. I don't like spending the cash, but I'm sick of waiting around for Philip and Mrs. Huntzel to clear out of the kitchen. Or maybe I'm sick of pudding cups. If such a thing is even possible.

An hour later, back in Kristina's room, the evening dies under the weight of Harley May's demands on my source list. The job is made more difficult by my lack of internet access, which means I spend hours shuffling pages printed in a computer lab frenzy. After I take it as far as I can—I'll be keyboarding handwritten revisions at school tomorrow—I pound through trig homework, then open *A Clash of Kings*. Reading comprehension eludes me until my book light dies. I set the book aside and peer into the darkness. I couldn't sleep if you hit me in the head with a hammer.

Near midnight, the door opens and closes. I'm looking at her when she turns on the overhead light. Tonight, her green hair is pulled back in a clip. She's wearing her vest over a short pink skirt and black turtleneck.

"Oliver! You're dressed! I'd actually expected you to go the other way."

"What would that have got me?"

"Dick cut off." A blade longer than my hand *snikts* from a black metal handle in her hand. She grins fiercely when I flinch.

I'm not in the mood for crazy girl antics tonight. "I'll sleep in the rec room. Or under a bridge."

"Stop whining." She clicks the knife shut and stows it in her messenger bag. "I promise I won't hurt you."

"Why doesn't that reassure me?"

"Is there some reason I *should* hurt you?"

"You tell me."

"I gave you the key, didn't I? That should tell you all you need to know."

All I need to know? I know precisely jackshit. If there's a good time to break my rule against asking questions, this would be it.

Why the key?

Why do you have to sneak in to your own house?

Why does Philip hate you?

Given how well my interrogation of Philip went, I keep my yap shut. She kicks her Chucks into the corner, then disappears into the bathroom—leaves the door partway open. I can hear her pee. After a moment the toilet flushes and water runs in the sink.

When she comes out again, she mistakes the look on my face.

"Don't sweat it, Oliver. No one can hear anything from this room unless they got their ear pressed to the—" She stops, glares at me. "What?"

Spit collects in the back of my throat, but I manage to spit out, "You're naked."

"Don't be absurd." Hands on hips, she looks down at herself. "You've never seen a girl in a bikini?"

I don't see a bikini. I see underwear, thin and edged with lace. The green fabric matches her eyes.

"Is this going to be a problem?"

Her nipples cast crescent moon shadows through her bra. A few hairs curl over the waistband of the panties in sharp relief to her cream-colored belly. I focus on the long, smooth expanse of her stomach, her belly button the least dangerous target.

Her fierce smile returns and she regards me for a long, agonizing moment. Then she strides across the room. Heat pours from my head through my chest, crashes against a matching wave rising from my groin. I lean back, hands on the arms of the chair, as she straddles me and rests her ass on my thighs. She grips my shoulders and leans forward. The pressure of her breasts against my chest bleeds the air from my lungs. Her breath is moist in my ear. "*Oliver,* is *this* going to be a problem?"

I want to answer, but a dizzying scent of flowers and earth throws my brain into a kernel panic.

She takes my earlobe between her lips, giggles softly as a shudder runs through me. When she reaches down between her legs and grabs the inside of my thigh, her touch is so electric I almost buck her off. She kneads my leg for a moment, then runs her hand up my chest. My gaze follows her own as she leans back. Her eyes seem to have their own gravity. "You've never been laid, have you?"

"Jesus."

Her laughter is like stones falling into a well. She caresses my arms, shoulders to wrists. Without breaking her gaze, she guides my hands up to her chest, centers my palms on her breasts. When she releases my wrists, I start to pull away but she shakes her head. "Leave them."

A shiver runs through me. I nod a little as if I have a choice. "You like that?"

I don't respond.

"You're allowed to like it. I'd be surprised if you didn't like it, unless you're gay—in which case you'd like something else." She giggles, licks her lips. "But you're not gay, are you?"

The smallest shake of the head.

"You're holding my tits, Oliver."

"Okay." A whisper.

"You're allowed to like it. I like it too. Not right now, but as a general rule, I mean." A throaty chuckle. "Would you like to know what else I'd like?"

I do, even though part of me is afraid of the answer.

"I'd like you to get used to this, Oliver."

I try to swallow, fail. "Used to this?"

"Used to *me*." She does a little hip shimmy in case I'm not clear about who she's talking about. "I may not be here that much, but when I am, you have to deal."

Deal?

"This is my room. I want to feel comfortable here."

"Okay."

"I need to be able to change clothes and take a shower and walk around in my underwear, because that's what I do here. In *my* room."

"Okay."

"Stop saying okay."

"Okay."

More laughter, less gentle. Her eyes flash emerald. "You're not hideous or disfigured." Her eyes are nothing like Trisha's. They're hard as gems, cold as ice. I want to look away, can't. "Someday, *Joey*, I'm sure some girl will want you to fuck her."

I feel like I'm going to choke.

"I am not that girl."

She stands. I gaze at her breasts, no longer in my hands. Perfect and upright. But receding…receding. She drifts across the room, just a few paces. Might as well be miles away.

I close my eyes and shudder one last time. Philip was wrong. She's not an ogress. She's far more dangerous.

2.2: And: Scene

Trisha doesn't show up for school Tuesday or Wednesday. If Denise knows why, she's not telling. I only ask once—I don't want to look like some kind of stalker, an effort at which I apparently fail. At lunch, Beth Black puts a hand on my shoulder and says, "She's writing a poem, Joey. She'll be back."

"Okay."

"She told me about the sand dollar, an interesting token. You should use it."

"For what?" Beth wanders off without offering an explanation. In rapid succession, Cooper, Mrs. An, and Harley May stop me from stealing off to Uncommon Cup. Just as well, I guess. I have work to do. I finger the sand dollar, then grit my teeth and tell myself to stop being such a Bella. The Plan leaves no room for romantic entanglements.

The good news is no cops. At a short assembly after Day Prep, Cooper tells us they have finished at the school, but may have follow-up questions with some of us individually. I hope that doesn't mean they could show up at the Boobie Hatch unannounced. Cooper also tells us there's been no change with Duncan, though doctors remain hopeful. Harley May leads us in a creative visualization meditation. I visualize escaping through one of the Commons skylights with rocket boots.

More good news is no Kristina Tuesday night. The night before she had mercy on me and didn't sleep nude, but in the morning she walked out of the bathroom naked and dripping from the shower. Laughed at the abrupt flow of blood to my cheeks. I hope it was just the blood in my cheeks. I make a point of sleeping in sweatpants and a long-sleeved tee-shirt I stole from Philip, just in case.

Wednesday is more of the same. I ace a quiz in Trig, manage to turn in a source list which passes muster. When I'm not in class, I'm in the computer lab, hammering out a paper on *The Crucible* or catching up on ChalkChat messages. My laptop remains on Cooper's shelf, out of reach. But still no cops. If only I could skip my Reid appointment.

He's not himself. No cryptic smile, no scrutiny drenched in hidden meaning. His office smells like microwave popcorn, but when I make a joke about him not bringing enough to share, he doesn't pretend to be amused.

"The police spoke to me, Joey."

And: scene.

Not really, but might as well be. 4:01 p.m. and I'm thinking about those rocket boots.

"They wanted to know about your background. What kinds of trouble you've been in."

4:01…4:01. The clock on the wall over his shoulder is old-fashioned. The sweep hand clicks silently around the face, second by agonizing second, but I feel like I can hear it anyway. *Tick…tick…tick?*

"As you know, there are limits to what I can tell them. Your confidentiality is guaranteed."

Thanks, Reid. 4:01. How fucking long does it take for a minute to pass? I blink. It's as if the second hand has bounced backward on me.

"They asked if you had told me where you were when Duncan was injured."

4:02. Finally.

"I didn't tell them what you told me—that you were in Harley May's class. Because I can't. I wouldn't. Do you understand that, Joey?"

There. It actually did jump backward a tick. I'm sure of it. Bastard clock. 4:02.

"Joey?"

One of the foster kids I lived with in middle school had a collection of comic books, *X-Men* mostly. He acted like they were made of gold, even though they were beat to hell and torn. Hard to keep things nice when you live the life of a foster.

"The nature of our relationship is such that nearly anything you say is between you and me only."

The kid let me read them sometimes, but only *he* could touch them. The little control freak sat across from me at the dining room table, then reached over and turned the page when I said okay.

"There are only certain things I can reveal without your permission."

I remember a character—I think it was a girl—who could move things with her mind. 4:02. *Tick...tick tick.*

"If you make what I believe to be a credible threat against another person..."

Right now, I'd give anything to be able to turn the clock ahead with my mind.

"...or against yourself."

But I couldn't even get permission from a whack-job to turn the pages of a ratty old comic book.

"Or if you reveal a sexual encounter with a child."

I wonder how old Kristina is. Eighteen? Twenty-five? A well-kept forty, like Bianca Santavenere? Do I count as a child? If she was here instead of me and confessed to sitting in my lap and pressing her tits into my hands, would Reid have to call the cops?

"But pretty much anything else, it's private. Between you and me. You understand that."

Sweat cracks across my palms as I remember the feel of her breasts.

"It's about trust. You can trust me, Joey. You understand that, don't you?"

I let out a breath. Feels like I've been holding it an hour. *Tick...tick...tick?*

"You can trust me."

I've heard this speech before. A hundred times. *I get it, Reid.*

"But trust goes both ways."

Here it comes.

"I need to be able to trust you too."

Reid will never give up.

"Joey, please understand what I'm saying here. It is in your best interests to answer the police's questions fully and honestly. You need to tell them where you were that day. It's important...for you. For your future."

4:03. Twenty-five minutes to go.

"Joey, please."

I look at him now. "Et tu, Brute?"

"Joey—"

"*Julius Caesar.* Act Three, Scene One. I had to read it twice my freshman year. October at Forest Grove, then again at Parkrose in January. Same curriculum, totally different page."

That's the last thing I say. Not even goodbye when—days later—4:28 arrives and I flee.

2.3: I Never Use It

All evening, faces swirl in my head. Courtney and Duncan. Reid. The detectives. Even freaking Bianca. Mrs. Petty makes an appearance, though she's been so quiet the last week it's only a cameo. I try to concentrate on covalent bonds at Kristina's desk. Failing that, I scratch at a sheet of paper with my pencil, notes for my *Crucible* paper. Reading back over them, they make less sense than my feelings about Trisha.

It's after ten when the solution hits me. I need food. I haven't eaten since lunch. After Reid, my stomach was too knotted. When I arrived at the Huntzels, I watched through the kitchen window as Philip and his mom slurped soup before I crept to the other end of the house to Kristina's door. I haven't risked coming out all evening, but they have to be in bed by now. Mrs. Huntzel is such a grandma about crap like school nights.

Silence follows me down the north stairs through the living room and into the rec room, the only sound the faint *tap-pad* of my feet on the slate floor as I pass under the glass eyes of the animal heads. But halfway across the landing between the rec room and the utility basement, I hear a voice.

"Philip?"

Mrs. Huntzel stands at the head of the spiral stairway. Acid surges into my throat. The basement landing is dark. My first instinct is to dart back into the rec room. But she moves before I do, descending and calling out again. I hesitate, then slink into the darkness under the curving stairway. Halfway down, she pauses, one foot a step lower than the other. Her slipper is inches from my nose, visible in the gap between the stair treads. She's close enough to hear my heartbeat. The scent of Gold Bond sucks fluid from my eyes.

The scuff of a footstep draws my attention to the utility basement door.

"What are you doing, honey?"

"Nothing."

Philip materializes in the dark doorway. He's in his underwear, feet bare. His violin hangs loose in one hand, bow in the other. I press back against the wall, crouch into a tight ball. If either of them hits a light switch, I'm looking at jail time.

"Philip, you need to be more careful with your violin. It's too valuable to sling around like that."

"It's fine."

"Think about your future. If you take care of it—"

"Who cares?"

She draws a sharp breath. For a second, no one moves.

"Honey...why do you do this to yourself?"

"Leave me alone." He reaches around and scratches his back with the end of the bow.

"You're only making it worse."

"It's the only thing I'm good at."

"That's not true. You're good at lots of things—"

"I *hate* chess." The venom in his voice is chilling.

"Philip, please."

"She—"

"We all agreed."

"I didn't."

"You were so young." Her long sigh seems to fill the space around me. "You'll understand someday."

I can hear him breathing, but the shadows are too deep for me to make out more than his form. Pallid skin, the dark hollows of his eyes. Most of the time, Philip comes off as little more than a high-strung crank stuck on the *fuck you* setting. But right now, I'm wondering why he doesn't have a Reid of his own.

"Come on, honey. I'll make you some cocoa."

"I don't want any cocoa." But he shuffles across the landing and climbs the stairs. His mother makes soothing sounds. He grumbles in response.

I don't move until silence falls, then I return the way I came. Caliban nearly gives me a heart attack when he shoulder-bumps me in the library. I'm too flustered to stop him when he follows me into Kristina's room and joins me on her bed. Sleep eludes me—if not him—for hours, but now only one face swirls in my mind.

I hate chess.

"You're the one who knows them," Courtney claimed.

Yeah. Sure.

In the cold morning light, I see Caliban has filled Kristina's bed with dried mud and leaves. I'm going to have to do laundry soon, a practical need I find weirdly comforting. Laundry: sheets and my own clothes—an achievable goal. But first I have to eat, and free breakfast won't come soon enough. Fortunately, Marcy has day-old donuts at Uncommon Cup. I can get twice my usual quota without breaking my budget.

A couple of olds have corpse-camped the fish tank table,

frowning at dead tree news over bran muffins and coffee. They probably don't like the Pandora station Marcy plays in the mornings—music from my own lifetime. I sit near the door and stare out at the rain. The donuts are stale and taste like sand, but they fill the void in my middle. I try not to think about Philip, but that just means I think about Duncan instead.

And someone else.

Then, as if in answer to a wish I'm not willing to make, she's there. I look up and in the space of a breath, I fall into her amber eyes.

"Jo-o-o-oey."

I've missed you. I don't know why I can't say it out loud. Maybe she'll pick it up telepathically. That works. Right?

"You've done a number on those donuts."

The tabletop is a field of crumbs. My coffee cup is empty. Butterflies flutter through me and I jump to my feet. "Sit down. I need a refill. I'll get you something."

She smiles and slides into the chair across from me. "You're sweet."

My nerves crackle inside me. Marcy smirks when she takes my order—double shot for me, salted caramel latte for Trisha—then refuses my money. "On the house, lover boy."

I've no doubt my face is the color of a baboon's ass when I return with our drinks, but Trisha doesn't say anything. It's her turn to peer out at the rain. She glances my way and smiles gratefully when I pass her the latte.

"It's been a while."

"I needed some time."

"Beth said you were writing a poem."

She nods. Sips her latte. I notice she doesn't pull out her flask. Maybe Baileys doesn't go with salted caramel. "You didn't text."

"Your dad—"

"He gave it back this morning. My bitching finally wore him down." She looks at me. "If you'd texted, he probably would have had held out longer."

"He doesn't like me." I'm sure it's obvious to her, but it feels like a confession when I say it.

"That's okay. I do." We sit quietly for a while. I catch myself enjoying the warmth of my cup. Her presence is calming. My mind clears as a patch of blue breaks through the clouds. I want to ask her what she's been working on, but the silence feels nice. I'm sure she'll tell me when she's ready.

At some point, without thinking, I pull the sand dollar from my pocket.

She breaks out into a grin. "You still have your sea cookie."

I run my fingers over the rough surface. "Of course I still have it."

"I'm glad." She reaches out to stroke the sand dollar's edge. Her fingers brush my own. The touch is like a jolt of electricity. She pulls away quickly. Her gaze returns to the window. As her eyes follow rivulets of rain down the glass, a confusion of emotions seems to war across her face: surprise, uncertainty, sadness. After a moment she shakes her head and blinks. "I almost forgot." A sheepish smile turns her lips up as she reaches for the backpack at her side. "I brought you my laptop."

My face goes hot. I'm sick of my face going hot.

"I can't use it at school. Cooper will freak."

"Tell him to kiss your ass."

"That should work."

She laughs. "So use it at home. Or here. It's got Jeff's script on it, so they won't even know you have it."

"Thanks."

She knocks off her latte, then shoulders her bag. It's only 7:05. We have plenty of time before Day Prep.

"Denise?"

"Yeah. But I wanted to see you first."

She turns toward the door, then looks back over her shoulder. "By the way, the battery is all charged." There's something in her voice, a playful lilt, which makes me wonder if she suspects what's in the battery compartment in my own laptop. I open my mouth, but I can't think of how to ask without giving the secret away. She waves goodbye, then heads through the door with a jangle of bells and a gust of rain-scented air.

When she's gone, I lift the lid. No need to power up. The display awakes, a document open. A poem. *Untitled*, but with her byline at the top. At first I'm confused. *I got a MacBook for my birthday,* I remember her saying.

I've never written a poem, except for some poorly rhymed nitwittery in English class during middle school. I have no idea what's involved when you give a damn and have something to say.

Trisha gives a damn.

I read it twice, then slip the laptop into my pack as a chill settles into my bones. I don't think my coffee will help.

by Trisha Lee

Mother distracts herself with poetry: Haikus about wind
Whispering and scurrying
Through autumn's last leaves.
I wait, but all she's got for me
Are quoted lines about the contradictions of ice
And murmurs: "A girl can always use new clothes."
I ask her to stop—

I ask him to stop—
But my voice flies like leaves on the wind.
He channels Mother's breezy promises of new clothes.
Voiceless, I'm the girl in every brown leaf—
His waxy hands creep like spiders, their need as sharp as ice.
Eyes closed, I compose poems to myself.

A haiku wind blows, a litter of leaves lifts me
I ask it to stop—
My body slaps against a windowpane of ice
Raw, naked, and unwound.
"After," he breathes, as I tremble like a leaf
"I'll let you pick out some new clothes."

My heart ticks, a broken clock wrapped in his clothes
A sound too loud to come from inside me
"Just think of after—" he breathes, and I quiver like a leaf.
—as if it will ever stop—
A trick, a trap, his voice is a pleading wind
Falling through caverns of jaundice-coated ice.

He announces himself with clinking ice,
Consoles himself with a gift: for once it's not clothes.
I compose a failed haiku about wax and wind
And how, if only for a moment, I want to own myself.
I cannot breathe until everything stops
I cannot leave—

I fall like autumn's last leaves
My voice shatters like ice
"He'll never stop—"
I gather the coins, the needless clothes
Like shards of glass littered around me,
The abomination caught in the wind...

In life, at least for me,
Events are like a frayed cloth.
They continue to unwind.

2.4: Lifeline

Trisha will be with Denise in the Commons. I want to see her, but I need time to make sense of things, in a place where no one will bother me. The library, maybe, enforced quiet at a time of day when almost no one else will be there. I'm barely through the school doors when Courtney cuts me off. She puts a hand on the center of my chest.

"The cops are here."

My stomach, already in knots, lurches. "What else is new?"

"They want you." Her lips sink into a frown. "Your caseworker is in with Mr. Cooper too."

I close my eyes, at a loss for where to go. Mrs. Petty knows about Uncommon Cup. If they don't find me there, they'll head to the Boobies looking for me. Once Wayne and Mrs. Petty get their wires uncrossed, my sojourn at the Huntzels is over. It was stupid to think I could make it work all school year, but the thought of going back into custody depresses me. I suppose I could throw myself on the mercy of the court. "Look...my Katz Meow!"

Like that ever works.

I give Courtney a sad smile and shrug, turn back to the door. She pulls at my arm. "One more thing."

"What?"

"Duncan opened his eyes."

"He's awake?"

"Not exactly. He's not talking, but he's responding to people." She squeezes my arm. "The doctors won't let the cops see him yet. But they are encouraging friends and family to visit. People he trusts."

I'm not his friend. But I don't say that. I don't mention Reid's opinion of my trust issues either. "Have you seen him?"

"Before school. I told his mom I'll come after too." *But you can go right now,* her eyes seem to say. She gives me a shove.

I have a thought and dig my heels in. "Listen. Can you do something?"

"What?"

"My laptop is on Cooper's shelf." It's probably stupid, too-little, too-late. "Any chance you could snag it for me?"

Her eyes narrow. "You think I owe you something?" Her glare radiates challenge.

I shake my head. "Forget it. I'll figure something else out." As problems go at this point, the potential discovery of my laptop's hidden treasure ranks about the same as finding creamed chipped beef in my shorts.

But then Courtney's gaze softens. "Sorry." She licks her lips. "I'll try. No promises." Then she pushes me through the door. Cold rain hits the back of my neck. I hesitate. Down the hall, Mrs. Petty steps out of the office, Man-Mountain hulking in her wake. That makes the decision for me.

The number 14 bus is coming down Hawthorne as I run from Katz, so I jump aboard. No one appears to be following from the school. I let out a breath and drop into an empty seat behind the driver. The bus smells like someone took a dump on it.

My hands bounce in my lap. Every face drips with suspicion. Just across the Hawthorne Bridge into downtown, I escape the bus. Rain chases me through Waterfront Park and across the Steel Bridge, but I hardly notice. Nerves push one foot ahead of the other. The hospital is farther than I expect, yet I spot the sign directing me to Emanuel Emergency sooner than I'm ready. The main entrance is even closer.

Inside, I'm at a loss. There's an information desk, but I don't think I can handle talking to an actual person. A woman behind the counter sees my hesitation and takes matters into her own hands. "Are you here to see someone, young man?"

My voice finds its way up from a hole in my belly. "Um. Duncan Fox?"

She taps the keyboard in front of her, peers at her monitor through the bottom of her glasses. "Are you a friend or a relative?"

"I'm his brother." Where did that lie come from?

"Damon?"

That computer knows more than I do—I had no idea Duncan had a brother. "Yeah. That's me. Damon." It feels like I've thrown away an opportunity.

"He's in ICU, honey. Do you need directions?"

Without giving me a chance to say yes, she points me toward an elevator bank, tells me which button to press, which turns to take. I must pay attention on some level, but I can't remember what she said. My hand acts of its own accord, my feet follow. Men and women in scrubs and lab coats brush past me, impatient or indifferent. The plants are all made of plastic. I hate the smell of the place, Betadine and body odor, shit, and bleach. The PA system murmurs, too quiet to make out, too loud to ignore. My shoes squeak on tile, swoosh across carpet. The layout makes no sense. Steel-edged corners seem

145

to appear in all the wrong places. Doors big enough to drive a truck through bar my way, then open the wrong direction at the touch of a button. At some point I stop. A man is looking at me. A nurse. His eyebrows seem knitted to his forehead.

"I said, may I help you?"

Dry saliva has glued my lips together. They open with a pop. "Duncan Fox?"

He turns and gestures. "Through there."

Beyond the nurses station, a broad, open door leads to a tiny room full of tubes, wires, and machines. A smoke detector blinks on the ceiling. Duncan lies back on a narrow bed, a smooth white blanket tucked up under his armpits, hands on his belly. His face is oddly flat, misshapen, like a mud cast left out in the rain. An IV runs into the back of one hand. Another clear tube is looped under his nose and around the back of his ears—a nasal cannula, I inexplicably remember. I also remember how mine tickled my nose during my own hospital stay, ten years before.

"Are you one of Duncan's friends?"

His mother, I presume—she has Duncan's chin and sandy hair. She's sitting in the corner next to the bed. When I meet her eyes, she jumps to her feet and crosses to me.

"Uh. Joey."

"Of course, Joey. It's good to see you again."

We've never met.

"I don't want to bother you, Mrs. Fox." I start to edge out of the room, but before I can make my escape Duncan's mother gloms onto me like a lifeline.

"Actually it's Mrs. Blount." Her fingers are cold and as dry as old paper. "I remarried after Duncan and Damon's father left us."

"Oh."

"You can call me Patty."

It's been nine days since the accident; she doesn't look like she's slept nine hours in that time. Sunken holes for eyes, blotchy cheeks. Her face is a map of tragedy. I look away.

"They said he—"

"Yesterday, yes. He looked right at me. This morning he spoke."

"What did he say?"

A crazy trill comes out of her. Laughter, I think. "He said he was thirsty." She releases my hand. Sensation is slow in returning.

I'd expected to see his head wrapped in bandages, a mummy turban. His head has been shaved, but aside from a single white gauze rectangle behind his ear, there's no evidence of injury.

"Maybe I should go."

"No, please. You can talk to him. Familiar voices are important, they say. You can help him find his way back to us."

"I wouldn't know what to say."

"Just the sound of your voice is enough." Her own voice pleads. "I'll leave you two alone."

"You don't have to do that."

"I don't want you to feel self-conscious. I need a coffee anyway. Would you like me to bring you some chocolate?"

Duncan must have never explained me to her, the pleb foster kid who knocked him haywire in an accident of physics. Before I can say anything else, she clasps her hands and backs out of the room. "Talk to him." As she disappears around the corner, I hear her final plea: "Please."

I sit on the edge of the chair she vacated.

I don't know why I'm here. In a day or two, he'll tell the cops who hit him. When it isn't me, they'll leave me alone. Right?

Right.

If not this, it'll be something else. Most likely Wayne will convince them I assaulted him. *Joey's brutal facial bleeding caused my urinary PTSD. I'm pressing charges!* As if simply running away isn't enough reason for them to fuck my life.

"Getchie."

Duncan's voice is so weak I'm not sure he spoke at first. His eyes are half-open, milky and unfocused. I lean forward in the chair, try to think of something profound to say. All I come up with is, "Hey."

"Your face."

I reach up, touch the memory of the scab next to my nose. The bruises are fading, the swelling long gone. "It's nothing. A disagreement over a game of chess." I smile, but I can't tell if he gets the joke. His face still has that muddiness. But when I stand up to move to the side of the bed, his eyes follow.

"Off—" He closes his eyes for a moment and his tongue runs over his lip. When he opens them again, his gaze is clearer. "You said."

"What did I say?"

"You said...off-Book."

"Yeah, go off-Book. I heard it worked."

"Yes." He draws a breath. "No."

"No? Courtney said—"

"Where...Court?"

"She's at school. It's school time now."

"Where...Courtney?"

I don't know how else to answer his question. Maybe he doesn't understand me anyway.

"Tell me about the game. You beat Philip. You're first board."

"First."

"That's right. Four out of seven." According to club rules, Philip can't challenge Duncan to recapture the rank until he wins three games each against the two board ranks below him. Courtney and Colin Botha, I guess. Will he bother? *I hate chess,* he told his mother. Losing first board might be what he really wants.

"Court…helped."

"She's smart. Sure. Said you got inside his head."

"Where is she?"

"She's at school."

He half nods, but I can't tell if he understands me. "I won… at school."

"I know. Good job."

"He didn't like…the violins."

At first I think he says something else. *Violence.*

"What's that?"

"The violins…the violins."

His lips twist into something which might be a smile.

"He didn't like…I saw Italy…the violin."

He's not exactly making sense, but it's clear Duncan found out about Philip's hidden talent. Such a weird thing to hide, especially at a school like Katz. Chess genius *and* violin virtuoso? Philip would be a rock star.

He must have his reasons, but still.

I wonder if that's how Courtney helped Duncan. I bet she's good at unearthing skeletons. If Duncan sprung the big secret at a key moment during the deciding seventh game, it might have been enough to rattle Philip.

Maybe that's what Mrs. Huntzel was angry about.

Angry enough to…?

Duncan's gaze drifts. I let out a long, slow breath. It's come down to it. The question. For a moment I'm afraid to open my mouth, but then I picture Courtney's face and it spills out of me. "Do you know who ran you over on Forty-ninth?"

His eyes go wide and level on a spot past my shoulder, but I can't tell if he hears me. Or if he could understand the question if he did.

Either way, it doesn't matter. One of the machines beside his bed starts to beep. A second later I'm at the center of chaos.

2.5: Détente

A nurse drags me out of the room. "What? What's happening?" No one answers. Grim-faced figures in scrubs rush past me. I recognize Mrs. Blount as she blows by. Someone guides me past the nurse's station. "You'll need to wait out here."

"Is Duncan okay?"

A firm hand pushes me into a small waiting area. Vomit-green carpet, one of those ubiquitous plastic plants. A TV hangs from the wall, tuned to some bottom-feeder reality show. Shouting women in a restaurant, all looking like a cosmetics counter exploded in their faces. One of them throws wine. The sound, mercifully, is off.

I sit down in a chair that feels like it was made from modeling clay. Duncan's beeping invades from beyond the nurses station, beeping and voices. So many voices, I can't make out the words. I can't see into his room. I'm far from home. I don't know where else to go. I have no home. I tilt my head back against the wall, close my eyes and see Duncan's muddy face. But when I open them, it's worse. The words of Trisha's poem bounce at the edge of sight, beyond the angry women and shaking fists. A tampon commercial offers the only relief.

I lean forward and rest my forehead on my hands. Think of Duncan on the bench outside Cooper's corral.

"Who are you?"

I open my eyes. Across the waiting area there's a flash of copper hair and surprised eyes. Too quick, the figure disappears past the nurses station.

"I asked you a question."

With a start, I realize someone is sitting near me, back in the corner. Long-legged and lean, sandy blond hair and a heavy face, a few years older than me. Leaning back with arms folded and legs crossed at the ankle.

He looks like Duncan, taller and older. And angrier.

"You're Getchie, aren't you?"

I swallow and nod. He wasn't here when the nurse pulled me out of Duncan's room. He must be Damon, but my mind is on the figure with the copper hair, a woman. Did I imagine her? Was it Mrs. Huntzel?

"What are you doing here?"

I shake my head, a bag of nerves. "Uh—" I turn to Damon, flustered. His glare is like an interrogation lamp in an old movie. "Courtney told me he woke up."

He regards me for a long moment, longer than I can hold his gaze. I find the television, still silent but now showing a news broadcast.

"Yeah. He woke up. For all the good it did him."

"What do you mean?" I don't know how long I've been here. Too long. I feel disconnected from time. Somewhere, a high-pitched tone squeals. Mrs. Huntzel is nowhere to be seen.

He unfolds and gets to his feet, looms over me. "What I *mean* is my brother is dead." He pauses for a beat, not long enough for me to react. "Does he have you to thank for that?"

Does he?

I asked the question after all, and then all hell broke loose. I shake my head, horrified.

"No." Damon takes it as a denial. "Of course not." The fury in his voice makes clear what he thinks.

"I just wanted to see him." I peer across the room, still searching for Mrs. Huntzel.

"You saw him. Satisfied?"

I'm not sure what I am. Numb. Confused. I stand. A helicopter shot of a wreck on I-5 fills the TV screen, three cars a tangle of twisted metal. A hollow disorientation fills me. I never should have come.

I duck my head and try to move past him, but he grabs my forearm.

"What I don't get is why he liked you."

"What?" I speak into his shoulder, try to pull away.

"Duncan. He liked you." He doesn't let go. "You didn't even know."

Détente. According to Merriam-Webster, it's "the easing of hostility or strained relations." It never occurred to me Duncan liked me. How could he? He didn't even know me.

"He liked that I told him how to beat Philip at chess."

"You're an idiot."

Tell me about it. I pull away again. This time he lets me go.

2.6: Springtime of Death

For a while, I wander the hospital corridors looking for Mrs. Huntzel. I don't find her, can't be sure she was even here. At some point, I'm outside, one foot in front of the other pulling me along. A long time. I don't remember how I get to Uncommon Cup. I find myself standing at the counter staring at a barista I've never met, an old guy with a red birthmark on his neck, visible above his V-neck tee and gray cardigan. One gray eyebrow crawls up his forehead like a caterpillar, a shaggy question mark.

"What?" If Marcy was working, I wouldn't have to speak.

"Anyone home?"

"I'm sorry?"

"I said, what'll it be, bud?"

"Oh." I can't remember what I usually get. I look up at the menu board as if it can tell me. The letters might as well be Chinese. After a moment of indecision, I order a coffee with room. He pours me a mug without asking if I want to stick around. It doesn't matter. I don't have to be at work for at least an hour. Assuming I still have a job to go to after I bailed on the cops and Mrs. Petty this morning. My next foster home will probably be in Idaho.

When I turn around, I see Trisha sitting with the fish. Pages are spread out over the table in front of her, along with a half dozen pens—all different colors. She's not writing. Her nose is aimed at a book in one hand while the other strokes one of her long braids. I can't tell if she's even noticed me. My body is a shadow cast through ice.

The half-and-half pitcher is empty, but I don't want to face the old guy again, so I continue to the fish table and sit down. I wrap my hands around my cup, trying to wring warmth from it. The coffee has no more flavor than the color brown. Maybe it's just me.

Trisha looks up from her book. "'It was autumn, the spring-time of death.'"

"What?" I search for her eyes, but I can't quite find them.

"Tom Robbins?" She waves the book at me. "*Still Life With Woodpecker?*"

"Oh."

"Don't you read?"

The question makes me think of Kristina, but then I wonder if Trisha is referring to her poem. I shake my head, attempt a laugh to cover my confusion. "Sure, I read." I just read *The Crucible*, I think. Or was that last week? I can't remember.

"Not enough, apparently."

"Okay."

"Joey."

I'm still cold.

"What's wrong?" Her voice changes.

"I'm still cold."

Now she's staring at me, but her eyes are like dark, orbiting stars. A little coffee splashes out of the mug onto my hands. Distantly, I imagine heat.

"What happened?"

"Duncan is dead." I can't believe I come right out and say it. *Duncan is dead.* I don't say things like that. Maybe I do.

Do you know who ran you over?

She sets the book down. I close my eyes, but I don't like what I see on the backs of my eyelids. When I open them again, her face is a sheet of glass.

"How did you find out?"

I caused it. I suck in a breath and watch the coffee splash out again.

"From his brother."

A long, heavy silence hangs between us. Then, "Why did it have to happen?"

The question makes no sense. Trisha understands as well as anyone there is no why. *Shit happens* isn't just some hipster tee-shirt philosophy. Fosters know this better than anyone. Our lives are one long string of shit happening. Life's a bite and then you die. Along the way, you leave bits of flesh on every snag. *What's up?* Oh, you know, bleeding out. Same as every other day.

Trisha knows this. Her hands press against the tabletop as if she's trying to keep it from flying away. I look at the manuscript pages and their riot of multicolored lines, tiny, carefully scripted words. I've never seen how she does it. How the words happen, how they become something from nothing. Is it like a puzzle, pieces moved with colored pens? I've only ever seen the poem on her laptop.

"I never—" *got to talk to you about your poem.* She cuts me off. "When...?"

She's still thinking about Duncan. I want to think about anything else.

"A little while ago."

A long time ago, I woke up strapped to a gurney as a sagging house burned. I coughed blood across the white sheet wrapped across my legs and chest. Someone tried to put an oxygen mask over my face, but I shook it off. Through the open doorway beneath the blazing roof, I could see my sister's crib—a bonfire, the flames so hot they screamed. "Brave kid," a voice said. "The fire was too much for him," someone else added. They didn't know what the fuck they were talking about. I wasn't brave. I was responsible. Then I was rolling away, rolling away, wheels of the gurney rattling across hard dirt, as Trisha's face pushes through the smoke. A hand squeezes my shoulder, the grip hot and iron tight. I flinch and twist in my chair. Drop the mug.

It shatters at Mrs. Petty's feet. With it, the real world crashes down around me.

2.7: Back in the Boobie Hatch

Where are we going?

I'm afraid to ask out loud. My new home, I assume. We're in the Impala, awash in the stink of rust and burning oil, like we're riding inside the muffler. The stench of exhaust and the terror of being in her passenger seat cuts through the fog in my head. A little.

"It's not your fault, Joey."

"Says who?"

She shuts up. Fine with me. I don't want to fight with her. She wouldn't call it fighting. She'd call it trying to have a conversation. Conversing with Mrs. Petty can be a contact sport, especially when I don't know what's on her mind. As we tear along, bouncing over curbs and dodging oncoming cars on one-way streets, I think about Reid. Next appointment, he'll want to talk about Duncan again. Some days, twenty-eight minutes is a lifetime.

How do you feel about Duncan's death?

I don't know.

Do you miss him?

Why would I miss him?

You weren't friends?

You know we weren't.

Do you wish you could have been friends?

He was an asshole.

But do you wish you could have been friends?

I get it—I'm an asshole too.

Do you feel responsible for his death?

Fuck you, Reid—

Well, do you?

"Yes."

We've stopped. Mrs. Petty shuts the engine down and looks at me, her eyes sharp. "What was that, Joey?"

"What was what?"

She shakes her head and gets out of the car. I sit there for a minute, relishing the stillness. Already Trisha and Uncommon Cup feel like ages ago. Somehow that thought fills me with an unaccountable sadness, but I tell myself I've survived a trip in the Pettymobile. One problem down, another staring me in the face.

We're at the Boobie Hatch.

I don't talk. Can't. Mrs. Petty doesn't seem to notice. Wayne is talking enough for all of us.

"So good to see you again, Hedda. Anita was just asking about you the other day. She's doing fine, by the way."

There's pink in Wayne's cheeks, sweat in his crew cut. The day is anything but hot. When he meets my gaze, his eyes narrow and I detect the slightest shake of his head.

Is he covering for me?

We follow him inside. The old TV has been replaced. Forty inches of flat-screen gazes at me, the high def so crisp I can make out cracks in the news anchor's foundation makeup. Is this what a week's worth of foster stipend buys? The sound is off, a development I find even more unnerving than Wayne's speed-jabber. The place is tidy, too, despite the fact I haven't been around to act as Cinderella. Even the mildew base note has been Febreezed into submission.

But the next surprise is my cell.

It's not empty. And by not empty, I mean there are shirts hanging in the closet, socks and boxers neatly rolled in the dresser. It's not great stuff. Goodwill pickups, but it's clean and not so different from the stuff I've been wearing all my life.

I catch myself staring at Wayne. He's still running at the mouth, but I can barely hear him, or Mrs. Petty's clipped attempts to get a word in. She's mostly focused on her search, ignoring the hides she already knows about but tapping the bottoms of drawers and looking on the underside of the bed springs.

"How's he been?" I hear her say.

"Oh, you know Joey!"

I feel myself backing into the doorway. The temptation to run is almost irresistible. A voice in the back of my head tells me I have to sit tight. It makes a kind of lunatic sense. Wayne Bobbitt—ex-Marine—may be a coward, but he's a *clever* coward. For nine days he's been sitting in this house, distracting himself with his new TV, waiting for the hammer to drop. With a single phone call from Mrs. Petty to set up this visit, he realized I haven't ratted him out. I've been somewhere else, hiding just like him. And now, if the truth comes out, we're both busted.

If he wants to play pretend, the only way to make it work is play along.

Clever, indeed.

I pop out of my daze at the sound of a crack, gunshot loud. Mrs. Petty snaps her head around at me from inside the closet. She has one hand on the back wall. With her eyes glued on me, she pushes and the crack sounds again, quieter now. Maybe it wasn't all that loud to begin with. Nothing happens, but she can feel the give on the top latch. The deranged smile on Wayne's face loses some of its gusto as she leans into the back wall. She moves her hands up and down, pressing at different points. *Click...click...click.* Finally she happens on the combo, hand pressing upper left, foot lower left. The latch releases. She steps back and lets the back wall swing open to reveal the compartment behind.

Wayne shuts up. That's something. Mrs. Petty inspects the space behind, running her fingers along the latch release and the countersunk screws of the frame. After a moment she steps back and lets out a low whistle.

"I gotta hand it to you, Joey. You do good work." Up in cabinetmaker heaven, Mr. Rieske must be so proud.

Wayne can't seem to decide how to react. He wants to be pissed, that much is obvious. But his desire to maintain the status quo wars with default outrage across his brow. Finally he figures out how to use his words. "What's in it?"

She's looking at me when she answers. "Tools. Screwdrivers, a hammer, a couple of saws. An auger." The same auger I used to make Trisha's hidey-hole. I bought a one-and-a-quarter-inch bit, a foot long, just for her project.

She turns to him. "We've always known he was a builder, Wayne. It's a quality job."

He sputters a bit, then manages a weak grin. "Yeah. And not full of bomb-making supplies, right?" His attempt at a joke falls flat.

Mrs. Petty turns a hand over. "What do you say, Joey? Is this it?"

I surprise everyone in the room, myself included, by answering. "Yeah. That's it." I can hear the truth in my own voice.

I'm not sure if it's Duncan's death or Wayne's fear that has knocked me more off balance.

"Well, I think we're done here."

"Of course, Hedda. Of course." Wayne follows her down the stairs. I find myself swept along in the wake of his jabber. At the front door, he shakes her hand and thanks her for looking out for me—a chilling fiction. She turns to me and says, "Joey? A moment?"

I follow her down the steps, stop next to the Impala. I pray she doesn't suggest another ride. "I can only protect you from the police so far."

A shiver runs through me. She either doesn't notice, or ignores it. "I don't know what to tell them."

"Try the truth. It won't kill you."

After Mrs. Petty drives away, Wayne steps out of the open front door. The oily smile is gone. His eyes are hard and empty. Same old Wayne, back again. "Well?"

"Can I get my tools?"

"Tools?"

I feel like a tire with a slow leak. This can't last. Even Wayne has to recognize that. But his expression remains dead.

I have no idea what the story is with the Huntzels, but the uncertainty there feels safer than the reality here. I turn and walk away. He doesn't try to stop me.

2.8: Huntzel and Huntzel

Thursday—upstairs public areas and finished parts of the basement—is blown. I return to the Huntzels after dark, sneak
into Kristina's room without bothering to pretend to show up
for work. I don't even know if Philip and his mom are home.

The night passes in a wash of sweat and dark dreams. Trisha
ignores my texts. I awake exhausted, shower as a substitute for
rest, and escape the house before anyone else is up.

The old barista is working with Marcy. He fills a cup without asking what I want, offers me two chocolate donuts and
a stack of napkins. I pay without argument. Trisha isn't there,
so I pull out my phone.

Are you coming to UC?

A crushed donut later, she responds.

dad is driving me to katz

She usually buses.

Anything wrong?

I destroy another donut without hearing from her, then
gulp coffee and rush to school. It's early, but breakfast starts
at seven. I can't remember the last time I ate something other

than room temperature pudding and donut crumbs. The food tastes like ass, but it fills the hole in my center. While I eat, Trisha walks in with Denise and Beth. They sit in a huddle, talking in hushed tones. At one point, I make eye contact with Trisha, but her expression is a shadow. The Commons fills around us, the chatter achieves full-tilt cacophony just as the warning bell for Day Prep rings. Duncan's name is on everyone's lips as we pass through the halls to our classrooms. I lose sight of Trisha without ever speaking to her.

After a shortened Day Prep they drag us to assembly, begun by Cooper but turned quickly over to Harley May. She talks us through the five stages of grief, a clinical lecture easy enough to tune out. But, when she suggests we find a sharing partner, I slip out the back of the room and make for the exit. Sean Ferrell chases after me and thrusts a sheet of paper into my hand.

"What's this?"

"Krokos is throwing a wake for Duncan tonight."

"You are fucking kidding me."

"Dude, you *gotta* show. Deets on the flyer."

I don't know whether to be horrified, or burst into tears. I pick door number three and sprint to the coffee shop under sunlight filtered through high clouds. My phone is already in my hands as I drop into a seat at the fish table.

Join me at UC?

Marcy gives me a look from the counter. I realize I haven't ordered anything.

"Is it okay if I just sit here a minute?"

"Stay as long as you want."

I smile gratefully, then feel my face fall when the phone vibrates.

Can't. sorry

I'm staring at the empty chair across from me when Marcy slides a steaming mug in front of me, then sits down in Trisha's chair. It feels like an invasion.

"What's this?"

"Vanilla steamer. Drink up. You'll feel better."

"I'm fine."

"You are definitely *not* fine. I don't know if it's something with your girlfriend, or your buddy who got hit by the car, or what. You look like someone bit your dog. So, do what Doctor Marcy says and drink your goddamn steamer. Don't make me cut you." She's smiling, but I take her at her word. The steamed milk is warm, sweet, soft in my mouth. It pisses me off that it also soothes my turbulent gut. I sip slowly and watch bubbles rise in the fish tank.

"You wanna talk about it?"

If Reid asked the same question, I'd clam up, or toss some him some bullshit. Marcy doesn't sound like she's probing my secrets for her own—or the State of Oregon's—ends. I realize I do want to talk about it—the only question is what *it* is. Trisha's poem? Yes, but not here, not now. She didn't write the poem for Marcy.

"Duncan died yesterday."

The words come out surprisingly easy. Probably because they're not a betrayal of trust, or a confession. It's all over the news.

She nods in sympathy. "That sucks." My lips compress and she raises an eyebrow. "Or does it?"

I shake my head, then nod. Shake my head again.

"You're confused."

No kidding. I feel like the punch line in an *xkcd* comic. "Everyone says he's my friend. Was my friend."

"Everyone but you."

"His brother claims he liked me."

What Reid would say, or Cooper—maybe even Mrs. Petty—is, "Well, you're a likable boy, Joey."

I'm the handsomest and the smartest boy ever too. Vomit.

Marcy is quiet for a long time, then turns a hand over. "The way I see it, you have two choices. You can let it go. Or you can earn it."

"I don't know how to do either of those things."

"So? Figure it out."

Why can't Reid ever talk like that?

After a while, Marcy leaves me. I finish my steamer and, belly soothed if not my spirit, slink out into watery sunshine.

And walk. I'm hungry, which makes my bust out of school idiotic. No way am I going back, so I make for the Fred Meyer at Cesar Chavez and get a couple plates of conveyor belt sushi. When I come out of the store, the 14 is just pulling up. Without thinking, I climb aboard. Based on the smell, it's the same bus I rode yesterday. Eyes watering, I pull out my phone. I can't think of what to say.

Hey.

Lame. Her reply comes almost immediately.

u left in a hurry

I can't tell if it's an accusation or an observation.

Couldn't deal. You want to get together?

Early release Friday, she wouldn't even have to stage a breakout. The poem looms between us. She showed it to me for a reason, but I'm starting to wonder if she regrets the decision.

sorry. got a drs. appt downtown.

I imagine us running into each other, which makes me think I'm starting to get a little creepy. Once across the Hawthorne Bridge I jump off the bus at a random corner. My brain feels like mush as I crisscross downtown streets. After a while I find myself at Pioneer Courthouse Square. A dude in silver body paint and spray-painted cardboard armor stands dead still on the corner, but when a passerby drops a buck in a can at his feet, he bows like a robot. HAVE A HEART 4 THE TIN MAN, his hand-lettered sign reads. As I stare at him, my phone vibrates.

gonna hit duncan's wake. c u there?

The last thing I said to him looms in my mind.

Sure.

Somehow I manage to transmit my reluctance via text.

promise?

I want to go anywhere else.

Promise.

The Square is a city block of brick, with a raised section on the west and south sides, creating a kind of amphitheater with a fountain under the Starbucks at the northwest corner. It's the kind of place where they put on art festivals, non-threatening musical acts, and light a giant Christmas tree every year. Most everywhere I look are homeless teens of the sort everyone's afraid I'll become. Begging spare change and cigarettes by day, taking it in the rear for a fin at night.

Portland's Living Room, they call it. Whatever.

I grab a seat at a table beside "Umbrella Man," a bronze

statue supposedly emblematic of the city. Good a place as any to try to make sense of my life.

But there are no answers, and too many questions. What was Mrs. Huntzel doing at the hospital, if that was even her? Is that where she's been spending her days the last week? She wouldn't be there out of concern for Duncan—she's hated him as long as I've known her. Unless it's guilt, not worry, that took her there.

Unless I imagined the whole thing. Jesus.

As I search for a coherent thought, Kristina appears at the far corner of the Square. Her face is unreadable, but she seems in a hurry as she crosses the bricks and climbs to the upper level, barely a dozen feet away. She stops at the Honkin' Huge Burrito cart, then—burrito in hand—turns toward the cluster of tables.

Her eyes lock on mine.

For a moment, she looks like she wants to run the other way. *Race you.* A breeze blows her green hair across her eyes. "What are you doing here?"

Something in her tone pisses me off. "It's a public place." It's not like I'm in her bedroom.

She closes her eyes for a second. When she opens them again, her gaze has softened. "You're right." She sets her plate on the table and sits down. "Sorry."

"Do you live near here?"

She scans the crowd. "Sometimes." An approaching MAX train toots and she flinches. I'm about to ask what she means when she reaches across the table and grabs my hand.

"Listen, I'm meeting someone."

Your boyfriend? I don't know where the thought comes from. At least I have the sense to keep it to myself. "Don't let me keep you."

Her eyes jump to the Umbrella Man. "Here."

"Here what?" I try to pull my hand back, but she hangs on. Heat pulses between us. For a moment I picture her green bra. I blink the image away.

"I'm meeting them here."

"At this table?"

"Joey. *Please.*"

I'm being a dick. I survey the Square, trying to guess who her meeting might be with. No clue, but a weird thought boils through my head. *Trisha, she's here to meet Trisha.* My jaw clenches. Obviously I'm insane. Even so, my nerves seem to buzz.

Trisha has a doctor's appointment downtown.

And? So what?

Kristina is what. Everything about her, from the emerald highlights in her hair to the red Chucks on her feet, knocks me off-kilter. Sitting here next to her, the world feels upside down.

"Okay. Whatever." I jump to my feet, free my hand. Kristina looks startled, but I mumble something about seeing her around and dart down the steps. Some gray-hair swears at me when I clonk into him and spill his coffee, but I don't stop until I'm across the Square. When I turn around, Kristina is looking the other way. I'm forgotten, just like that.

Fine.

But as I turn away, I spy a figure who stops me in my tracks. He approaches Kristina's table from Broadway and gestures at the chair across from her. She nods, and he sits. Mr. Huntzel.

I can't remember when I last saw him, but it's been at least a month. Now he appears out of nowhere for a secret confab with my mystery host. He's the father of a family he doesn't live with—a fact no one seems to acknowledge. She's the daughter who lurks in the shadows, doesn't talk to her parents, and sleeps in the same bed as a stranger after sneaking into her own house in the middle of the night. That she's eating a Honkin' Huge burrito with her old man *shouldn't* be weird.

Right.

They talk for a few minutes, the conversation clearly heated. At one point, he points a finger in her face and seems to be almost shaking with anger. I wish I was close enough to hear, but then Mr. Huntzel looks my way. I can't tell if he recognizes me, but paranoia floods through me as Kristina turns to look too. I take a step back, stop at the sound of bells and a horn. The MAX arrives at the stop behind me. It's going nowhere I want to be, but I jump aboard before the doors close.

I sit down across from a girl engrossed in a copy of *Us Weekly*. Brangelina is either dying or pregnant—not sure which, but that's not what interests me. A familiar face looks out from the lower right hand corner of the cover. Bianca Santavenere apparently up to shenanigans again. Idly, I wonder if the story will make it into Philip's folder.

But, now that I think about it, the real question is why Philip has that damn folder in the first place.

2.9: Stravaganza del Talento

Huntzel Manor is empty when I arrive. I *should* work—Thursday on Friday: upstairs public areas and the finished parts of the basement—since yesterday got blown. Friday on Friday too. The way I'm burning cash on street tacos and conveyor belt sushi, I need the hours. Instead, I scout the house from basement to second floor. Philip is supposed to be with his mom, off playing chess, but I'm starting to wonder if anything is what it's supposed to be. Once I'm satisfied no one's home, I head for Philip's room.

You're the one who knows them.

I don't know if such a thing is even possible.

But I do know a place to start. In the dresser, under the socks. The folder of clippings is still there. I sit down on Philip's bed and go through each page, one by one.

It makes no sense.

Bianca Santavenere is a has-been, once an actor now turned into a reality TV spaz-twit. Near as I can tell, the only thing she does is show up places where cameras are likely to be. The stories in the folder cover appearances at Hollywood parties, run-ins with cops, her efforts to stay in the public eye. For a while she had a perfume, a line of shoes, a workout program, but all that seems to have died. Her TV show was so long ago it might as well have been in black-and-white.

I've seen stories over the years—you can't miss them if you're ever near a TV or grocery store checkout lane—but nothing that would explain Philip's interest. The folder doesn't help. I tuck it back under the socks and make my way to the master suite.

Mr. Huntzel's bed remains crisp and unused, Mrs. Huntzel's still a mess. This time, I skip the bathroom and closet, as well as the armory in the nightstand. I'm interested in the DVDs.

Bianca on E, Bianca Red Carpet, others. A shared interest, mother and son.

The DVDs are right where I remember. Mrs. Huntzel must not have been watching TV the last few days. Too busy lurking at the hospital?

I take a moment to figure out the remote, then power up the TV and DVD player. The first DVD auto-plays on insertion, a spot from *E! News*. Bianca mugs for the camera at the opening of a club in Miami Beach, makes kissy faces. Her hair is oily black, her flesh orange, her lips fat as slugs. I can't make much sense of the story. Something about her husband opening the club for A-List celebrities, though we never see him. There's a shot of LeBron James, but it looks like he's somewhere else. After a minute or so, the video cuts off.

O-kay.

The next DVD is a bit slicker, since there's an actual menu and a PLAY icon on screen. Some iDVD theme. Only one selection. *Bianca on the Red Carpet at the Grammys*. More kissy face, this time with a lot of attention on a gown that looks like it's made from banana peels. The show host pretends she loves the dress, but I'm not convinced. Bianca's date is a slickster in a shiny suit. Her husband, I gather. A nobody—but a *rich* nobody.

The rest of the videos seem like they'll be more of the same. *Bianca TMZ, Bianca Press Conference.* Press actually show up to listen to this woman talk? I stick the DVD in, curious in spite of myself. The quality is shitastic. If it's a press conference, it's happening on the run. She's crying as she trots along a palm-lined walkway next to the man in the shiny suit, tossing out lots of "I'm sorrys." Questions pepper her, but the sound is too choppy for me to make them out. Then, she stops and faces the camera, and for a moment I can hear. "My addiction kept me from being there for my family when they needed me most. For them, I promise to get clean. For them, I promise to do whatever is necessary to help the police in their investigation. For *them*," dramatic pause "I *will* be whole again."

Something about the video rings a bell, but I can't pull the memory up. I make a mental note to Google it later. Eject.

The only disc label that differs from the rest is the one which reads *PM on SdT.* At a loss, I stick it in the DVD player. Another auto-play.

The show is called *Stravaganza del Talento.* High-speed gibberish spills from the TV, Spanish maybe. I don't know. Three people who must be judges, *American Idol*-esque, sit bantering in front of an audience. A foreign version of Ryan Seacrest is on stage. He talks for a minute or two, grinning and waving his arms. I pick up one word which I think sounds familiar, but I don't realize what it is until the music starts.

Philip.

He's a lot younger, maybe nine or ten. But there's no doubt. He's scraping his violin, as good then as he is now—to my ear, at least.

I watch, transfixed. The camera views bounce all over the place, from the judges to Not Ryan to the crowd and back to Philip. The audience is vocal and appreciative. Then it hits me. They're speaking Italian.

"I saw Italy," Duncan said. He must have been talking about this video.

The camera flashes on two women in the front row and it all makes sense. Sort of.

Okay. Not really.

Bianca Santavenere and Mrs. Huntzel—smiling, excited, hands clasped before them. Bianca's face is less warped and orange. There's no gray in Mrs. Huntzel's hair. When Philip finishes, to nutbag applause, the camera shows the two again, this time hugging each other.

A moment later, the video ends. I turn off the television and sit, silent, on Mrs. Huntzel's bed.

I have no fucking idea what's going on. But I gotta wonder if this video is why Duncan is dead.

2.10: Suck For a Buck

I spend an hour or three pacing Kristina's floor, talking myself in and out of going to Duncan's wake. There may be a few people who actually give a shit what happened to him, but for most it's just an excuse for a party. Like anyone needs an excuse.

But as daylight fails, morbid curiosity and/or my text promise to Trisha overcomes good sense and I pull out Ferrell's flyer. Because Katz Learning Annex is a magnet school, the students live all over town. In the Learn Something New Everyday category, the flyer tells me Yancy Krokos shares a backyard with the Huntzels. Sure, the backyard is Mount Tabor—all two hundred acres—but still.

It's full dark as I climb down from the park into the steep backyard of Chez Krokos, an uninviting hive seemingly constructed from stacked shipping containers. The exterior is half glass, half rust-streaked steel—the landscaping faux-*naturel* to the point even a dandelion seems planned. Signs inform me all wastewater is recycled; the house is heated by passive solar and compost. *Sunset* magazine did a feature.

In other words, an ideal location for a Katz Karouse.

The house is one box after another, each space sparsely furnished with objects of no apparent use. The floors look like cork, the walls are colored panels pop-riveted onto metal studs. I don't see any smoke detectors.

Katzoids swarm through every room. The chatter sets me on edge, both the noise and topic: Duncan. In what might be the dining room, Somers and Ferrell pass around growlers of beer home-brewed from Honey Nut Cheerios. My nose wrinkles at the scent of clove cigarettes. Beth Black offers me a drink from a flask with Hello Kitty printed on the front. Vanilla schnapps.

"You're late, Joey."

"The flyer said six till whenever." I hand her the flask and grab a cup of Somers/Ferrell ale to kill the taste of schnapps. "It's nowhere near whenever."

"Trisha didn't think you were going to come."

A hitch in her voice fills me with sudden anxiety. A burst of laughter and the pulse of house music sounds from deeper in the hive.

"Where is she?"

Beth's eyes flick toward the opening leading to the next container. "Joey..." I leave her and head into a dim, crowded room with a view of the Tabor hillside. A pounding drum track assaults my ears and I blink at the sight of Trisha on a low table in front of a gas firepit. She's wearing a black skirt and a white tee-shirt dotted with buttons, which glow beneath an overhead UV light. Blue flames silhouette her dark figure as she performs a slow, rhythmic dance, arms twisting over her head. Onlookers—mostly guys—cheer and hoot, or maybe they're egging each other on. When I draw near, the buttons resolve into Lifesavers, most sewn over her breasts. A hand-written sign on the table reads:

SUCK FOR A BUCK
No Hands!!!

She spots me and reaches out, fingers beckoning. "Jo-o-o-oey!" Her eyes flare in the black light. "You want a Lifesaver? Only a buck. Lips only, no teeth!" A few damp threads indicate she's already made some sales.

If the world felt upside down with Kristina at the Square, I don't know what it is now.

"Me first!" Sketch Echols pushes through the crowd and throws a wadded up bill onto the table at her feet. As Trisha bends over for it, he grabs her ass. Hoots and shouts greet the move as he jumps onto the table. She spins around, the dollar bill forgotten, and smacks at Sketch's grabby mitts.

"I said no hands."

"What'll a hundred buy?" He's a foot taller than Trisha, looming and wraith white next to her.

A shadow passes over her face. "Read the sign..." Her voice drops; I can barely hear her over the music. "...asshole." Bodies press closer to the table. I look around and spot Denise and Courtney in a far corner, engrossed in conversation. Courtney's face is a mask of grief. Neither seems aware of what's going on.

"Lighten up, girl."

Sketch is typical Katz glitterati, right down to the fedora and lensless horn-rimmed glasses. Last year, after his parents bought him an eighteen-hundred-dollar digital SLR for an elective photography class, he traded it for a baggie of Adderall and turned in a portfolio shot with a one-dollar app on his iPhone. Word is his folks didn't blink since he came home with all E's that term. He's six-six and wire thin, too noisy during his quiet moments. Right now, his bullshit is deafening.

"Two hundred!" As Sketch lunges at her, I push through the crowd, snag his arm.

"Keep your hands to yourself." I spit the words through clenched teeth.

He spins, wrenching his arm free. "Is a bitch trying to talk to me?" At my back, his bros laugh. He grins their way, head tilted back so he can see out from under the rim of his idiot hat.

Heat boils up my spine. "You heard me, fucklips."

Someone jams me from behind. I hold my ground and throw an elbow from my hip. The whuff at my back is satisfying, but then fingers grab my arms, pull me away from Echols. I twist and fight back.

A voice in my ear shouts, "Watch out, Sketch. He hit Duncan last year and now he's *dead*." People seem to think that's hilarious. I whip my head back, crack a chin. As the hands slide off my arms, I jerk forward. Sketch grabs me around the middle before my shoulder drives through his gut, but the momentum is all mine. He staggers, realizes too late his feet have found the table's edge. He topples over and pulls me after him. We land on the cork floor with a whump, most of my weight slamming into his chest. I'm on my feet again in a heartbeat. From his back, Sketch kicks out at me. I catch the ball of his foot with my hip, twist away from the follow-through. As I raise my arm, some part of me thinks about how this is supposed to be a party in honor of the last guy I pummeled. Sketch Echols is far more deserving of a beatdown than Duncan ever was.

"*Stop—!*"

Trisha's shout is so loud and piercing everyone in the room goes quiet. Only the throbbing music continues. On the table, Trisha stands rigid, arms tight at her side.

Sketch untangles himself from below me, scrambles to his feet. He throws a shoulder into my back, but when I don't react, he turns his attention to Trisha. "Yo, bitch, I bought me some coconut—"

A sudden storm rises in her eyes. "You didn't *buy* me." I can't tell if she's yelling at Sketch, or me. Both of us, maybe. "I'm not for fucking sale!"

Or neither of us.

The desolation in her voice smothers the fight in me. My hands drop, my fists uncurl. It's like she's gazing at me from a deep, dark place. Trisha, I remind myself, is why I'm here. Sketch Echols is nothing more than an empty bag of wind.

I suck in a deep breath. "You're right, Trisha. I'm sorry."

From behind me, Sketch's rage charges the air like static. "You know what, orphan? Fuck your sorry."

Something in Trisha's face changes. Sketch's words seem to drain the spirit out of her. She sags, all but falls off the table. I catch her in my arms.

"I want to go."

"Let me help you—"

"I don't need any help."

But she leans into me. Where her cool hands grip my neck and arms, my skin feels alive. As I guide her through the crowd, I spot Sketch stalking through the doorway into the next shipping container. He glares over his shoulder at us. I meet his stare with cold resolve. It probably didn't occur to him I'm not the only orphan in this room. Or maybe it did. Either way, he's lucky I have someone more important to worry about right now.

2.11: The Department of Things Best Left Unsaid

In an act of mercy, someone switches the music to acoustic guitar. Most everyone finds somewhere else to be. Trisha and I are left with blue flames in the firepit and a few people at the margins, oblivious to the scene that just unfolded. "I was being an entrepreneur." The trill in Trisha's voice tells me she's been drinking. "My dad is an entrepreneur."

Her Baileys-scented breath warms my neck. Hard as pebbles, Lifesavers press through my shirt. A few pop off, bounce across the cork. No one bothers to give chase.

I make eye contact with Denise, still talking to Courtney in the corner. Her cheeks are taut, but her gaze loose. "Can you find her a shirt?"

Denise hesitates for a moment, as if she wants to say something, but then hands Courtney her cup and disappears through a shadowed doorway. Courtney meets my gaze, but misinterprets my anxiety. "I didn't have a chance to get your goddamn computer, okay?"

At the moment, my laptop is the last thing on my mind. Before I can say so, a shout from the next room—"Is it too late for a suck?"—causes Trisha to cringe.

"Can we go, please?"

"Denise is getting you another shirt."

"I have one in my bag. Where's my bag?"

"I have it, honey." Denise reappears and pushes an oversized leather purse into my hand. I guide Trisha from the room. A nervy titter trails us through the house. Trisha doesn't seem to notice. I pick a path through shipping box after shipping box until I reach the sliding steel door leading to the front porch. A frosty clutter of stars hangs overhead.

We're alone at last. Trisha leans against the wall next to the door. "I'm okay. Give me a second." The only light is the glow of east Portland stretching away below us. Somewhere down there is the Boobie Hatch. I turn back to Trisha.

She holds her head in her hands for the space of a dozen breaths. The tension seems to bleed out of her. Finally she pulls off the tee-shirt and drops it, oblivious to the cold.

She catches my stare. Not all of her is oblivious.

"Don't pretend you've never seen a bra outside a Victoria's Secret catalog."

This isn't the moment to mention Kristina. Trisha takes a wobbly step. "I have an idea." She starts to slip sideways. I reach out to catch her, snag a finger in her bra strap.

"I'm sorry."

She rights herself. "Oh, shut up." Her eyes scan the dark porch. "Where's my bag?"

I hand it to her. She finds a sweater and pulls it over her head. "I didn't ask to be rescued, you know. Sketch Echols is the least of my worries."

Before I can respond, she charges down the steps to the street.

"You coming?"

I catch up with her at the sidewalk. She grabs my hand and pulls me up the steep street, her breath billowing in the night air.

"Trisha, slow down."

"I have an idea."

"What idea?"

"We're going to Philip's."

I pull up short and shake my head. "Bad idea."

"Shut up. You have a key, right? You have a key to everything. I want to see how normals live."

The Huntzels are anything but normal. "They won't like—"

"So don't tell them. It's a castle, right? I can't believe you don't know how to sneak in after all these months working there."

She turns and trots up the hill, her heels clacking on the sidewalk. I give chase, begging her to come up with another idea. She doesn't listen. By the time we curl through the dark neighborhood on the north end of the park and come up on Philip's house, my lungs are burning. But Trisha just laughs.

The house is mostly dark, the only lights above the exterior doors, plus a silver glow from the kitchen nook.

"No one's home," she says.

Chess Collective Friday. Philip might hate chess, but routine is routine.

"How do we get in?"

I sigh. "We can't stay."

"I just want to see. It'll be fun."

At least I don't have to reveal Kristina's entrance. I use my key on the kitchen door. The security system beep tells me no one is home. Small relief. All I can hope is Trisha gets bored quickly. As the warmth of the butler's pantry envelops us, Caliban trots up from the basement and rubs mud off on Trisha's calf. She bends down to scritch his scraggly head.

"Awww, what a cute dog."

She's clearly insane.

"Okay." She straightens up. "Show me."

Evidently, I'm the insane one. I give her the tour.

She's most fascinated by stuff I never think about: Oriental rugs in the conservatory, carved woodwork over the broad doorways on the first floor. To me, those are things to fit into my schedule. Dust, sweep, polish. To her, they're alluring evidence of wealth and security. We linger in the formal dining room. "They never actually eat in here?"

"Not that I've seen."

"But you still have to clean."

"It gets dusty."

"Oh, forfend!"

The lift enthralls her, down to the basement, up to the second floor. I follow on the stairs, then along the upper hallway as she runs ahead of me. I try to stop her from opening the door the Philip's room, too late. "He's a slob. I'm surprised you haven't tidied up for him."

"I'm not responsible for personal spaces."

"Shocking."

She slams the door and heads toward the library. A breath catches in my throat as she passes Kristina's door, but she doesn't slow. We spend twenty minutes inspecting the books. She fixates on titles I never noticed: poetry by Rilke and Angelou, a biography of the pirate Jean Lafitte. Finally she passes down the north stairway to the living room. The ceramic figurines seem to confuse her.

"Isn't this crap all granny stuff? How old *is* Mrs. Huntzel, anyway?"

"I don't know."

"Weird. Do they actually live here? Maybe they're squatting." Before I can answer, she spots the liquor cabinet. "Is that what I think it is?"

"Trisha, you shouldn't—"

"Baileys!" She opens the bottle and tosses back a slug, then thrusts it at me.

"That's not—"

"Just drink it."

Her laughter rings in my ears as I lift the bottle to my lips. The creamy liqueur is better than I expect. I take a second gulp. Almost immediately my head starts to swim.

She smirks. "Drink some more, lightweight."

"Trisha—"

"I want to see you fall down." I try a third sip, then swallow a mouthful, coughing as she tilts the bottle in my hand. She laughs again, snagging the bottle and darting through the wide doorway into the foyer. I follow, stumbling, up the corridor to the kitchen. A trail of laughter leads me to the south stairs and down into the basement. I finally catch up with her at the vault door.

"My dad has a safe behind a picture in his den. Nothing like this, though."

Everyone needs a hidey-hole, I guess.

She continues to the basement landing. For a moment, the lift tempts her again, but instead she heads into the rec room. The animal heads and grand piano are worth only a glance. She swigs Baileys and crosses to the couch, then turns and beckons. The only light shines from a small lamp on the mantle.

When I join her, she leans against me and I inhale a faint musk. Her hand finds my neck and she falls backward onto the couch, pulling me after her. Our lips meet and our teeth click, drawing a husky laugh from her. I feel her tongue on mine, taste Baileys and a lingering hint of cherry Lifesaver.

"Joey." In her way, she draws my name out. "Why haven't you ever tried to kiss me?"

A moment before, I'd have said because of The Plan, because I didn't want to introduce another layer complexity into my life.

Now? I have no clue.

"You're such a dumb fuck. You know that?"

Her eyes carry a disconcerting longing that makes my chest ache.

"Yes."

A cocoon of warm air seems to surround us. I feel light-headed and loose, not just from the Baileys. A quiver runs through her, a soft sigh slides from her throat. But when I cup her breast, she goes rigid.

"Joey. I can't."

I pull my hand back.

"It's okay."

"I'm sorry."

"Don't be."

She slides away from me, sits back on the couch. I close my eyes. The Baileys bottle sloshes. I want a drink too, or something stronger. I try to breathe instead.

"I'm sorry anyway."

I know why—I think I do. *I read your poem.* I want to say it aloud. For two days I've been chasing this moment, Trisha and I alone in a place where I could finally draw back the curtain and see what she's hiding inside. But now we're here and all I can think about is how secrets are meant to be kept. Drill a hole in a headboard, affix a latch no one else can see, and box up the darkness.

She stirs beside me. I open my eyes, sure she's getting up to leave. But she only takes something from her bag.

"Have you ever seen one of these?"

She hands a coin to me. A nickel is my first thought, but the weight is all wrong. In the dim light, I can make out the image of an antelope on one side. "What is it?"

"It's called a Krugerrand."

"It's gold."

"A quarter ounce. They come in different sizes, but all mine are a quarter ounce."

"All yours? How many do you have?"

"A few." She's quiet for a while. Then, she sighs and lies down against me. "A lot."

"This is what you hide in your headboard, isn't it?"

"Were you curious?"

"It was your secret to keep."

"And now it's yours." Her words are like a band across my chest. I draw a long breath as I return the coin.

"Trisha…"

"What?"

"What's this worth? Hundreds?"

She's a foster, like me. In a good home, maybe, but no matter the placement, fosters don't have stacks of gold coins.

"I didn't steal it, if that's what you're thinking."

"Of course not." I'm thinking about the poem. And what she said at Yancy's.

I was being an entrepreneur.

"It was a gift."

My dad is an entrepreneur.

"From who, Trisha?"

"From *whom?*"

Ever the writer. "Fine. From whom?"

"It doesn't matter." She kisses me again, her lips sticky with Baileys and evasion.

"Did Mr. Vogler give you the Krugerrands?"

Her hand presses hard against my chest. "So what if he did?"

"Trisha…"

She's quiet for a long time, but it's not until I feel her shaking beside me that I realize she's crying. For a moment, I'm not sure what to do, or what to say. So I worm my arm underneath her and pull her close. She turns and presses her face into my chest. I can feel her tears.

"What does he make you do?"

"Who says he makes me? I'm well-compensated." Her voice seems to tear the air between us. "This one paid for my trip to the gynecologist this afternoon." I don't say anything. I don't know what *to* say. She's shaking in my arms, choking back deep, wet sobs. I hold on to her and let her cry. After a while, she draws a breath and coughs. My shirt is wet beneath her cheek.

"Trisha, you need to tell someone."

"I told *you*, didn't I?"

"Someone else. Someone—" *who can do something about it.*

"And then what happens?"

I know what she means. She reports the situation to her caseworker. The one who doesn't remember her name. An investigation opens. Most likely they pull her from the house right away while they sort everything out, which means a new placement. Mr. Vogler denies everything. His wife backs him up; she's never seen *anything* improper. Trisha's the transient, no matter how long she's lived with them. There will be interviews, therapists, but the way the world works, the worst thing likely to happen to the old fucker is he gets dropped from the foster rolls. Meanwhile, Trisha is shuffled off to strangers. The new situation could be no better, and you can be damn sure there won't be any Krugerrands the next time.

Sometimes it's better to screw one old man for some gold coins than to roll the dice on another placement.

After a while, she pushes herself up onto her elbows. I can feel her warm breath stir my eyelashes.

"You look as sad as I feel."

I open my eyes, find her gazing at me. "It's been one of those weeks."

"Aren't they all?" She runs her fingertip across my face, pauses at the fading scar beside my nose. "What's been going on with you lately, Joey?" I can feel her breath on my cheeks. "Seriously."

And there it is. She showed me hers, now I show her mine. Only fair, right? But I swallow thickly and hesitate a moment too long, betrayed by a lifetime of keeping secrets.

She pulls back.

"I see how it is." Her lips compress.

"Trisha—"

"No, I get it." She starts looking around like she's misplaced something. "You've got your thing—whatever that is—and I've got mine."

"It's not like that."

"How is it, then?"

I gaze at her in the dim light, mouth agape, but no words will come. All I want to do is sink through the couch and disappear.

"How about this, then? Tell me one thing." She pins me with her amber eyes. "Who was that girl?"

"I—" The temperature suddenly drops ten degrees. "What girl?"

"The one with the green hair at the Square today."

"That was just—"

"Just? You were holding her hand."

"She's…" *a naked girl I have to get used to.* "…Philip's sister."

She pulls at one of her braids, and her gaze shifts to the empty air between us. "Philip's sister. Of course."

I try to understand why she held on to this all day, all evening. The answer seems obvious enough. She believed one thing about us right up to the moment I wouldn't answer a simple question. Then she started believing something else.

"I guess you got yourself a—" Her voice cracks and she shakes her head. "You got yourself a *rich* girlfriend now."

I'd give anything for an undo.

"At least I have my Krugerrands." She jumps to her feet and storms across the rec room. I should follow, but something holds me back. From the landing, I hear the bathroom door slam.

I grab the Baileys, suck down a long gulp. Then another. The creamy booze curdles in my belly and I feel like I'm going to be sick. *She'll come back,* I think, or hope. *Then I'll fix this—somehow.* I lie back as the room spins around me. But I drink again, and again—until the bottle is empty. After a bit, I doze off. Or pass out.

Then wake—abruptly. For a moment panic surges through me, but the room is dark and still. I push myself up and shuffle out to the landing to check on Trisha. The bathroom is dark. I suppose she could be roaming the house, but after what happened, I can't imagine why she'd stick around. She must have slipped out the kitchen door before Philip and his mom got home, or if she left after, maybe they didn't notice the security system alert.

I return to the couch. A bit later, when I hear Philip playing his violin, I flee to Kristina's room. The atmosphere is thick with dread. I crack open the window, desperate for fresh air, and fall back on the bed.

My shirt is still damp from Trisha's tears, but I don't bother to change. It's not much, but it seems the least I can do. In the end, maybe the only thing we have in common is our status with the State of Oregon. Rejected, neglected, abandoned, molested. But aside from that, she's a girl desperate for someone to share her secrets and I'm a boy who will never tell.

2.12: Are You Awake?

At some point during the night, I awake to find her in bed, curled around me. My head is mush from the Baileys, my tongue glued to the roof of my mouth. I didn't hear her come in. Now she has one leg thrown across my thighs, an arm draped over my chest. Her breast makes a hot spot on my chest. She breathes into my ear. In my sleep, I must have snaked an arm around her back; my hand rests on her hip. She shifts slightly and coos in her sleep. Then she's still again.

I don't know what to make of her presence, nor how she found me. Rather than ponder questions I can't answer, I leave my hand on her hip and breathe in her scent. Her exhalations are steady and soft. Half lost in a dream of her amber eyes, my thoughts clarify. Together in the darkness, I match her stillness.

And then her breathing changes.

"Are you awake?"

It's Kristina.

For a second I feel like the bed has vanished beneath me. My body goes stiff and seems to shrink in on itself. Then a laugh presses upward through my throat, something wild and out-of-control. I'm afraid to let it go, because if I do, I'll sound like a mad man.

"Jesus."

"I was cold."

We're under a sheet, a comforter, a quilt. We're in a house heated by a steam boiler the size of an SUV. She's not cold—she's on fire.

"Are you familiar with the concept of pajamas?"

"You're too tense."

"I can't imagine why that would be."

"I told you to get used to this."

"No, you told me to get used to a naked girl traipsing around the room, changing clothes and stuff. Not a naked girl wrapping herself around me in bed in the middle of the night."

"I'm wearing underwear."

"A distinction without a difference."

She's quiet for a long time. "Maybe you have a point there."

I sigh. Sleep is impossible. The fog returns, centered on my forehead and chased by pain the shape of an axe blade. Inside, a tiny voice tells me to pull my arm from around her if I want to calm the flutter in my chest and the awkward stirring below my waist. Instead, I wriggle uncomfortably, unable to remove my hand from her thigh. A sound leaks from my throat, half-moan, half-whimper. After several minutes, she expels an exasperated sigh.

"You are *such* a baby."

"What?" I hate the whine in my voice.

"You heard me." She slides her hand down my belly and snaps the waistband of my sweat pants. I squirm to escape, but she throws the blankets off and draws away. In that instant, my mind fixes on the memory of her breast pressed against my chest.

She goes into the bathroom and clunks around for a while. When the door opens, I catch a glimpse of a tee-shirt and yoga pants before she flicks the bathroom light off. She climbs back under the covers, but keeps to her side of the bed. My body tingles like there's a buffer of ionized air between us.

"Better?"

What the hell am I supposed to say to that? As she exhales agitation and drums her fingers on the comforter, I lie there, staring at the blinking smoke detector on the ceiling and wondering where they'll stick me when all this comes crashing down. Mars, I hope.

But after a while, her breathing slows and she turns onto her side toward me.

"You *are* a baby, you know."

Sigh.

She chuckles for a moment, then goes quiet. "Listen, I know it was weird today at the Square. It would have been weirder if you'd stuck around though."

You're telling me. I wonder what she'd say if I admitted to spotting her with Mr. Huntzel.

"It's fine."

"If it's fine, why are you lying there huffing and puffing like I'm the third little pig?"

I sit up. "*I'm* huffing and puffing? You're the one who—"

She laughs and smacks me on the arm. "Got ya!"

"Jesus." I drop back on my pillow. "You are a total mystery. Hell, you're miles past a mystery. I mean, you act like...*this*... is nothing." Why my mouth is running is the real mystery. "You don't even *know* me."

"I know more about you than you think."

"What's that supposed to mean?"

"You think you can keep your secrets from me, Oliver?"

"I don't have any secrets."

"Everyone has secrets." She leans toward me. "Tell me one. See if you can surprise me."

"I'm an orphan."

"That's not a secret."

"It's the only thing you need to know about me."

"We're all orphans."

I don't feel like arguing. Her mother is asleep a hundred feet away. Talk about secrets—that woman has secrets. Bianca and Italy, the sack of money, the hospital? But before I tumble down that rabbit hole, Kristina asks a question that makes me wonder if her secret is the ability to read minds.

"What do you remember of your mom?"

Ice water runs through me. It's been a long time since Reid asked me the same question. "Nothing."

"You were still with her until you were almost six."

"How do you know that?"

In the darkness, I can sense her smile. "Maybe I've been checking up on you."

Her mother must have told her father what she knew, and he shared my life over a Honkin' Huge burrito. "Why are you asking me this shit?"

"My house, my rules." Her tone is suddenly combative. "Answer or find somewhere else to squat, orphan."

"I don't remember anything!"

"Bullshit."

Her heartbeat thumps in the darkness. The scent of my own sweat stings my nose, draws tears from my eyes. "What the hell is with you?"

"I was raised by wolves. Now spit it out."

I sigh. "Well, I was born under a tree—"

"You remember being *born*?"

"Obviously not." I rub my eyes, swallow a thick wad of phlegm. "Do you want to hear this?"

"Sorry. Born under a tree."

"It was in the forest on a hillside above Sandy."

"Sounds nice."

"This is how nice it was." I lick my lips. "Eva Getchie, my alleged mother, went into labor while out hunting mushrooms. She sat under a tree for ten hours until my head appeared. Then she grabbed me by the neck and yanked me out and threw me down in the dirt. Got up, walked home. Some other mushroom hunters found me the next morning, barely alive. So even if I did live with her off and on for a few years until her rights were finally terminated, don't you think it's just as well I don't remember any of it?"

For a long time she doesn't say anything. I'm glad she doesn't ask questions, because I don't want to explain how Eva spent time in jail, how my first caseworker tried to reshape her into a proper mother after her release. Parenting classes, counseling. A spectacular failure, but the worst of it, I'm told, was before my memories begin. An emptiness balloons inside me. I feel stupid and guilty, find myself aching for the oblivion of sleep. Based on past history, I won't wake up till after she's gone—though I may suffer dark dreams.

Of course, she's not finished. "Bloody Christ, you're a walking tragedy."

This is why I never tell Reid anything, though I suppose there are rules to keep him from openly mocking me. Still, why Kristina? Why not Trisha, for fuck's sake? A few hours before, if I'd had the courage to answer a single question, I might still be downstairs. Trisha and I could listen to Philip play his violin, unburden ourselves in the dark.

Would it have been so bad to tell her about Wayne, or about Eva? To explain the strange doings of the inhabitants of Huntzel Manor, including the girl with the green hair? To give her more than silence? Surely that would be preferable to feeling so raw and exposed. From that scene in Yancy Krokos' shipping container to the revelation of the Krugerrand, it's clear all she wanted was someone to understand, someone like herself. A foster, an orphan. And if anyone might understand me back, wouldn't it be Trisha Lee?

Yet, somehow, Kristina Huntzel is the one who peeled me open and laid bare every raw nerve.

Jesus.

2.13: YouTube

Trisha doesn't respond to my texts. I spend most of Saturday away from the house, unable to face hours upon hours in Kristina's pink room. My phone is effectively dead in my hands.

I'm at Uncommon Cup. Come hang out?

Silence.

We could talk. Or just do homework.

Nothing.

Too bad I can't concentrate on Chemistry worksheets or Trig problems. My thoughts rattle around inside my skull like ball bearings in a tin can. In a fit of childish mortification, I left Trisha's laptop in Kristina's dresser when I escaped the house. Seemed like a good idea in the moment, but now I'm stuck with no way to work on half my assignments, or scour Google. My crap 7-11 cell phone doesn't do Internet. True, at Uncommon Cup, I'm surrounded by laptops, but instead of asking a stranger to do a search, I wait till I go to the counter for my fourth double-shot of the day to ask Marcy what she knows about Bianca Santavenere.

She thinks for just a second. "Well, she's no Lindsay or Charlie, but on the Famewhore Catastrophe Continuum, Bianca is at least a C-list calamity. Why?"

"I dunno. Her name came up."

"You never struck me as an aficionado of three-digit cable channel pseudo-celebs."

I feel stupid. "I saw a video, this Italian show where she was cheering for a kid playing a violin. But I don't speak Italian."

"You don't say." She gives me a look. Another customer appears, so I return to my seat with my espresso. It's still hard to concentrate, but I tell myself the math won't do itself. Based on my pathetic progress, it won't get done by me either.

After a while, my legs start to bounce in my chair—too much caffeine, I tell myself. The café feels claustrophobic, so I gather my unfinished assignments. My first thought is to walk off the twitches, circle the block once or twice and return to my station to await the girl who will never come. But hours of forced marching end with me standing across the street from Trisha's house. It's become the kind of glorious fall day Portlanders rave about during fits of denial about the winter bearing down on us. Dappled sunlight through leaves just starting to turn, a warm breeze smells of grass.

Oppressive.

The Voglers live in Alameda, northeast Portland—five miles one way as the boy hikes. I've come so far it seems stupid not to take the last dozen steps to the front door. I can't do it. After a minute or an hour, I hunch my shoulders and turn away.

They're probably at the coast anyway. I hope Mr. Vogler didn't bring any Krugerrands.

When I return to the house, I dig out the laptop, only to discover the Huntzels don't have WiFi. A few spotty networks from the neighborhood come up, all password-protected. I don't want to slog back to Uncommon Cup, find myself reading Trisha's poem instead. It feels like a punishment, so I read it again. A few lines stand out.

I gather the coins, the needless clothes
Like shards of glass littered around me,
The abomination caught in the wind...

One day last summer, a few weeks before Mr. Vogler in the driveway, Trisha and I were sitting in the grass on the Mount Tabor summit watching a pair of crows dive-bomb a hovering hawk. It circled lower and lower, dodging its assailants, until at last we lost sight of it in the trees. After it was gone, the crows perched atop a couple of Doug firs and bragged to anyone listening.

"Guess they wanted rid of him," I said.

"I know how he feels."

I looked at her, wondering if she was referring to the Voglers. She scratched one eye under her sunglasses.

"Did I ever tell you about my grandmother—my biological grandmother?" I shook my head. "She used to call me the Abomination." I could hear the capital letter in Trisha's voice. In a moment of weakness, I asked her why.

She put her out her hand next to mine and seemed to compare them, hers warm brown and mine the color of spackle. I waited, but she only shrugged. "Doesn't matter."

A lot of fosters—the ones who come into the system when they're old enough to remember—have little stories like that. At the time, I thought about Eva Getchie driving off in the pickup, but I kept that to myself. I never learned what Trisha's grandmother meant.

I wish I could ask her again.

Feeling foolish and alone, I hide the laptop in the bottom dresser drawer under my clothes. That night, I sleep fully clothed.

Sunday morning, I catch up on Thursday and Friday work. I'm afraid to face Mrs. Huntzel when it comes time to get paid, sure she'll say something about the hospital. But she doesn't blink when I finish and pays me with a terse thank you. After a loop around Mount Tabor through lingering fog, I slip back to the pink room to brood the day away. I should be working, or down the hill trolling the Internet using Trisha's computer. I can barely bring myself to sneak out to snork pudding cups. At least Kristina doesn't make an appearance.

Small favors.

Monday morning, the rain is back. Even so, the first person I come across through the doors at Katz—Denise Grover—is wearing sunglasses.

"Good weekend, Dee?"

"Fuck off."

"How long did the party last?"

"Don't make me repeat myself, asshole."

She must have talked to Trisha.

In Day Prep, even Ferrell and Somers are subdued. Honey Nut Cheerios must a killer ale make. I find a chair, wave a hand when Harley May calls roll—something she never did before Duncan. I half-wish I'd brought Trisha's laptop to do a little Googling, but it's just as well. The moment I pulled it out, Cooper would probably materialize in front of me.

After a minute, the PA system burps and the announcements start. I rarely listen anyway, but Krokos emits a long, low whistle from his desk, then starts laughing.

"Dudes. You have *got* to see this." He's got his Katz laptop open. Ferrell and Somers scoot around in their chairs. Neither seems much interested at first, then Jeff's eyes pop. Harley May frowns at me when I join them, but doesn't say anything.

Krokos has a video up on the screen. YouTube is supposed to be blocked on the school network, but these guys always figure out a way. At first I can't make out what's on the screen. The video is obviously shot with a cell phone. It looks like a view through fog, dark at the edges with an object, pale and shapeless in the middle. The camera shakes and for a second there's a clear shot of a white brick ceiling, cobwebby and half-familiar. A bare yellow light bulb. Then the camera moves again, focuses and music starts up.

It's Philip.

My breath catches in my throat.

Philip in the vault.

Philip playing his violin.

"This is not happening."

The voice sounds shrill. With a start, I realize it's my own. The video was posted by someone whose username is a random string of characters, with a very unrandom "clmz_zebretta_" at the beginning. A new user account, no other videos.

I have no doubt who it is.

Other people pull out their phones. The hangover energy transforms into something else, something feral.

"Look at the views count."

It's at nearly fifteen thousand for a video posted Friday at midnight. Three hundred Katz students can't possibly be responsible for so many hits.

Sometimes you don't know what makes a video go viral. But this one is easy. Guy playing the violin—whatever. Sure, he's good—clearly Philip is a virtuoso. But that's not it. Not the venue either. Not even the fact he's in his underwear. That kind of detail might generate a little buzz, but we're still talking mostly local interest.

The boner has a certain explanatory power. Even in the grainy video, Philip's response to his own performance is unmistakable.

But the money shot is, I'd say, the money shot. At 01:48, Philip's face twists into a grimace and the front of his tented briefs darkens.

Or, as Krokos puts it, "Dude made squirt for Mozart."

2.14: Worst Person Ever

A long time ago, when I complained to Reid about the kid who beat off to his family photo album, he said, "The range of sexual need and expression is vast, Joey. Even among neurotypicals there is no normal. Who can say what this kid has been through, or what his personal challenges may be? Try to show a little understanding."

He may as well have been talking about Philip.

Harley May tries to stop me, but I blow past her. My search runs from the library to Moylan's room, but Philip's not in the building. I find him out on the sidewalk, backpack at his feet, Book tucked under his arm. The rain has soaked his hair and jacket. He doesn't seem to notice.

"Hey, Philip. What's going on?"

He flinches at the sound of my voice. His mouth works for a moment, as if he's trying to decide what to say. At last he settles on, "My mother is coming to pick me up."

His voice is calm, but his jaw is clenched and I can almost hear his teeth grinding. As I stand there trying to figure out how to explain without revealing my fortnight of trespass, he turns to face me. I don't know if the fluid on his face is from the rain or something else.

"I know what it looks like—"

"You let her in my *house.*" He all but spits as he adds, "You're the worst person I've ever met." Considering his feelings about Kristina, that's saying something.

"Philip—"

"Stop talking to me."

"Please. I didn't…" He put his hands over his ears, squeezes his eyes shut. On anyone else it would look childish. On Philip it looks a little childish too, but mostly it looks angry. And justifiable.

I didn't know.

I can't tell if I spoke aloud or not. Doesn't matter. Even if I shouted, first in one ear and then the other, he wouldn't hear me. I leave him there, eyes still closed, ears still clamped. I can't be around when Mrs. Huntzel arrives.

Back inside, the nightmare compounds. I find Trisha sitting outside the door to the library, her MacBook in her lap. She's not wearing braids—her hair hangs loose and frizzy on her shoulders, half-hiding her face. I stop beside her, but she doesn't look up. I'm not used to being the first one to speak. Her name sounds garbled coming out of my mouth. "Trisha." I repeat myself, louder. Clearer. "Trisha."

The hallway chatter—all about Philip—is loud enough to bleed eardrums. How it happened, I can only guess. Maybe she heard him from the bathroom off the basement landing, then slipped out to find him in the vault. And saw her chance for a little revenge for all his little digs and derision—*zebretta, graham cracker.* Less certain is whether she realized Philip would realize I was the one who gave her access in the first place. Maybe that was a bonus—for Kristina, for holding back. If so, I'm not sure I blame her.

"Trisha?"

She closes her laptop with a snap and stands.

"Listen," I say. I'm thinking about Philip. And I'm thinking about myself too. A little bit. Feeling sorry for both of us. But mostly I'm thinking about her. "Trisha, please. Listen."

She's already moving down the corridor.

"I'm sorry." I don't know if she hears me. "I fucked up."

Of course she hears me. She doesn't turn around, though. If being a foster kid teaches you anything, it's how to walk away without looking back.

3.0

They continue to unwind.

3.1: Trespass

Monday—dining room, conservatory, and foyer. Not that I'll be waxing and buffing today. Or ever again. With the YouTube hitting the fan, it's time for new digs.

On the Joey Getchie Catastrophe Continuum, today falls somewhere between Mr. Tinkel on the toilet and the Rieskes slamming concrete on I-84. It's two weeks ago all over again and my options are still crap. Maybe I could pitch a tent on Mount Tabor. If I owned a tent. I foresee a knife fight with a hobo in the near future.

Unless I make one more trip into stately Huntzel Manor.

I've circled through the park so I can observe the house from above without being seen. For most of the day, I've only watched. The windows are dark, no sign anyone is inside. Of course, it's still daylight. I'm being paranoid maybe, but I gotta be sure. The rain has passed. Blue sky is visible through the branches of the Doug firs on the slope. I sit at the top of the hill, back to a tree on which someone has graffitied a huge heart with a peace symbol in its center. Knotted bark digs into my back, but I don't care.

For the hundredth time, I pull the magazine out of my backpack. Buying a dead tree tabloid to read about a fake celeb feels like something Anita would do, but it was four bucks well spent. *Us Weekly* stared at me from the checkout line at Fred Meyer when I stopped for conveyor belt sushi. The issue the girl on the MAX was reading, the one with the story about Bianca in the lower right-hand corner. The tagline below her picture reads *Reality Bites For Bianca*.

Inside, there's not much. Two photos, a big one of grim-faced Bianca clutching a shopping bag, and a smaller one, inset, of her oily husband. The story is one 'graph.

"Reality television personality Bianca Santavenere finds herself getting the wrong kind of attention—if there is such a thing for the fame-starved ex-child star. For the second time in four years, her sugar daddy husband, Florida businessman Nick Malvado, finds himself in the federal crosshairs. This time, it's a joint FBI/DEA task force probing Malvado's alleged ties to the Mexican Los Zetas drug cartel. Seen here leaving Luca Luca at Bal Harbour, a dour Bianca actually seems upset by the attention of the paps for the first time in history. She probably wishes her first husband, celebrated lawyer Pip McEntire, were still alive. Word was, he ate federal investigations for brunch."

At least now I have a pretty good idea where the money came from. And why it smells so bad. It's Nick Malvado's drug money. How it got into the Huntzels' vault, I don't *even* want to know, but I do know I won't feel bad about snatching some now. Even a single bundle of dirty twenties will buy me a lot of nights in one of those no-tell motels down on Powell.

As I tuck the magazine away, Caliban charges out of the undergrowth and clonks into me. He wrassles me onto my side and scrubs me down with his sandpaper tongue before taking up a post at my side. Apparently he hasn't seen YouTube. "Anyone home, dog?" I scratch his mane between the ears. He responds with a tail thump on the fir needles and a string of drool. After a while, he gets bored and hops up. "Where you going?" I watch him trot down the hill toward the laurel hedge, then jump into a hole. I'm abandoned, again.

I take out my phone, try to compose a message. Nothing sounds right. Finally I settle on the one thing I know is true.

> Used to be all I wanted was to be invisible. Now
> I wish I'd let you see me.

She doesn't respond. I wonder if she ever will.

The sun is just touching the West Hills when I climb to my feet and brush fir needles off my ass. Part of me thinks I should hold out until full dark, but the longer I wait the less chance I'll have to find a secure spot to spend the night. If there is such a thing.

I don't have much of a plan. Get my stuff from Kristina's room, stop by the vault, then jam before anyone knows I was there. If I get caught, I'll pretend I've come to clean. Worst case is they kick me out for being a trespassing dickhead.

But when I open the bedroom door, I realize I should have gone to the vault first. Mr. Huntzel is sitting on Kristina's unicorns. As I turn to flee he freezes me with his voice.

"No need to rush off, is there, Joey?"

Yes.

In the last six months, I've fought for Philip, eaten with Mrs. Huntzel, but exchanged fewer than a dozen words with this man. There's a smell to him, a strange cologne. Something exotic—from Italy maybe.

"I have known for some time, in case you were wondering."

"I needed a place to stay."

"So Kristina insisted. She felt we owed you something. But circumstances have changed, have they not?"

I wish there was some way to make everyone understand I didn't know about the video. "Not in the way you think."

"Does that really matter?"

My fight-or-flight response is pinned at *RUN*, but somehow his gaze locks me in place. No spit will form in my mouth. When I speak again I feel like my tongue is ripping open. "Now what?"

He shrugs, his eyes at once regretful and unfriendly.

"You're going to turn me in."

Now he smiles. It's like looking into the face of a reptile. "I have *already* turned you in."

I practically fall down the staircase. He doesn't follow, but then I guess he doesn't have to. The animal heads gaze in judgment as I fumble with the key to Kristina's door—I'm a dumbass for locking up after myself. Finally the deadbolt clicks and I yank the door open, stumble out to the dead leaves.

And into the arms of a waiting cop.

3.2: In the Boobie Hatch

They bind my wrists with a zip tie and shove me in the back of a patrol car parked on Yamhill. I can see the house, can see when Mrs. Huntzel and Philip pull into the driveway in the Toyota. The cops are on the front porch with Mr. Huntzel. From time to time, they glance my way, making sure I haven't slipped the zip, broken through the steel mesh barrier between me and the front seat and started hot-wiring the car. I'm too busy trying to figure out how to sit on the hard vinyl without cutting off circulation to my hands.

When Philip gets out of the Toyota, he stares down at me. Bug in a jar. At this distance, his expression is unreadable, but I can guess. Mrs. Huntzel doesn't even look. She stalks into the house past her husband and the cops. Philip continues watching me until Mrs. Petty pulls up behind the cop car and parks. Then he turns and follows his mother. The cops move out of his way. Mr. Huntzel ignores him.

Mrs. Petty raps on the window as she walks past the cop car. The vinyl almost melts under the heat of her glare. She then marches straight up to the cops. Mr. Huntzel offers her his hand, which she shakes without enthusiasm. They talk for a while, turning to stare at me every now and then. At one point, Mrs. Petty gets out her cell phone and makes a call. Then more talking.

Finally Mr. Huntzel goes back inside. Mrs. Petty marches back down the driveway toward me, the two cops hot-stepping it to keep up. Their legs come up to her shoulders, but no one out-trots Mrs. Petty. She heads straight up to the car and yanks the door open.

"Out."

I have no feeling in my hands, but somehow I manage to twist around and push my way out of the backseat.

What's going on? is the question on my mind, but the fury in her eyes keeps my lips zipped.

"I'm releasing his hands."

The cops had plenty to say when they grabbed me outside Kristina's door, but now they're fumble-tongued as she whips out her Leatherman and walks around behind me. I hear a pop, then my hands are free.

"Thank you, gentlemen." Mrs. Petty puts a hand on my shoulder and guides me to her car. She waits at the passenger side door until I'm belted in—no shoulder strap in the old Impala, then goes around and gets behind the wheel. Tosses my backpack onto the seat behind her. The cops look at us, bug-eyed, as she peels out from the curb and tears down the hill. I assume the reason they aren't in hot pursuit is they got their fill on the Huntzel driveway. All I can do is embed my fingertips into the door handle and hope for the best.

She drives in circles. Belmont to Thirty-ninth to Burnside to Sixtieth and back down to Belmont again. I can tell she's thinking because of the way her jaw moves as she takes the turns. Eventually she finds an on-ramp to I-84 and my lips compress under the rising G-force. I figure we're heading to the middle of nowhere to abandon me. Good riddance to bad rubbish, as Mad Maddie used to say.

Turns out she wants to talk instead.

"Stealing, Joey? That's where we're at now?"

"What am I supposed to have stolen?"

"You deny it?"

"Would it make a difference if I did?" My mind flashes to Sergeant Zach. It sure as shit didn't make a difference with him.

For a minute she actually concentrates on driving, which lowers the overall terror quotient by an order of magnitude.

"He said he caught you walking out with Philip's Xbox—"

"Philip doesn't even *have* an Xbox."

"That's not what Mr. Huntzel told the police."

"Philip wouldn't even know what to do with one."

"Are you suggesting Mr. Huntzel is lying?"

"Like I said, would it make a difference if I did?" It *is* true I ate a lot of pudding cups.

She takes the exit onto I-205 and we head south, approaching Mach One. I wonder why Mr. Huntzel didn't tell the cops I was sleeping in the house. Maybe that didn't sound criminal enough. I am the hired hand, after all. I could claim I thought it would be okay, just a misunderstanding. But thievery of imaginary game consoles would be harder to explain away— ample revenge for YouTube.

"Here's where things stand. You are grounded to the house and school for the foreseeable future. Mr. Huntzel hasn't decided whether or not to file charges."

"You're taking me back to the Boobies?"

"We have an appointment with Reid tomorrow afternoon."

Tuesday: living room and library, dust and vacuum. Except now it's a Reid day.

"I take it I'm fired."

"Joey, are you even listening?"

Everything I own of significance, little as it is, is still at Huntzel Manor. Trisha's laptop is the most important item. I don't give a damn about whether charges will be filed. I only care about where I'm going next. The Boobie Hatch, for all its failings, is better than juvenile detention. I might be able to escape from the Boobie Hatch. Or sit tight and maybe even keep The Plan alive, even if it feels like a long shot at the moment.

Despite nearly killing us both on the way, Mrs. Petty manages to navigate to the Hatch. She marches me through the door and turns me over to Boobie custody. Two weeks ago, if I'd only known, I could have gone to Mrs. Petty, and Wayne would be history. Now the balance of power has reversed. After a brief confab about my failings as a human being, Wayne pushes me up the stairs. That's when I learn he intends to lock me in.

"I'll let you out in the morning. And I'll be driving you to and from school, so don't get any ideas about striking out on your own. We'll all be watching you with eagle eyes."

I look around the small room. "What if I have to pee? Should I wet my pants?"

He ignores the jab, or is too caught up in the moment to notice. With his fat hand, he indicates a Folgers can on the desk. "That should do you till morning."

"When I tell Mrs. Petty—"

"Tell her what? You stole from people who trusted you. I fought in the first Gulf War and have an honorable discharge."

Anita once let slip that Wayne spent the war at the naval base in San Diego. His honorable discharge was really medical. Abdominal hernia, congenital. I don't mention this. He's right about Mrs. Petty anyway.

Advantage: Boobie.

3.3: Carte Blanche

After Wayne's footsteps die at the foot of the stairs, I go to my closet. He's looted my hide. The door is gone, ripped out of the frame by the hinges. The counterbalanced latches hang in ruins. I look away. The only difference between Wayne and the Vandals is I'm pretty sure the Vandals could read.

There's a pry bar in my pack—wherever that ended up—along with my phone and my school crap. Downstairs, maybe, unless Mrs. Petty kept it. The pry bar was a cheapie, but the rest of the tools are a real loss.

Note to self: next placement, rent a safe deposit box.

I turn off the light and sit on the bed. I'm not tired, but I can't stand the sight of my brown cell. Outside, the last sunlight ignites clouds heaped on the horizon. As the first satellite winks into view overhead, I hear a tap on glass. A silhouetted head appears at the window and a hand reaches between the security bars to tap again.

I lift the sash and the silhouette resolves into Kristina Huntzel, perched on the peak of the porch roof. I might wonder how she knew where to find me, but nothing about Kristina surprises me anymore. She's exchanged her red Chucks for black sneaks. Black pants and a turtleneck complete the ensemble. Ninja girl.

"I should've thrown you out on your ass that first night."

I can't really argue the point. "I didn't know anything about it until I saw it at school with everyone else."

"Bullshit."

"Listen, I get it. I'm responsible. I brought someone over and I shouldn't have—"

"A girl?"

"Does it matter?"

"Yes, it fucking matters. I did you a favor and you shit all over it."

I let out a sigh. "I'm sorry. It never should have happened. I know that, okay?" I can't look her in the eye. "I tried to apologize to Philip, but he didn't want to hear it."

"Do you blame him?"

Her breath whistles in her nose, a siren of anger. I know it's a waste of time, but I try to point out the one true fact of high school. "This'll blow over. A new Katz drama always comes along."

"I don't care about school drama. I care about protecting Philip."

The only one who was ever a threat to Philip was Duncan, and only on the chessboard. So much for that. Once the laughter dies down, everyone else will go back to worrying about their own narrow interests and how they rate on the Katz Meow.

"Kristina, seriously. Just give it a couple of days."

"You're not listening to me." She pushes the words through her teeth. Her hands grip the security bars like she's about to pull them apart and drag me out. The only question is whether she'll beat me to death on the roof or heave me off to die on the lawn.

"I'm sorry. What else do you want me to say?" There's

nothing else I *can* say, but it's clear from the look on her face an apology isn't good enough.

"That video has been seen twenty thousand times already, maybe more."

"Kristina—"

"They're going to *find* us. They're going to find *him*."

She doesn't say anything more for a long time. I try waiting her out, but it's not like dealing with cops. The silence forms a void in my brain, an emptiness that fills with shame and worry. And unwelcome thoughts of Huntzel weirdness—guns and secret money, violin music and reality stars.

"This isn't about Bianca Santavenere, is it?"

Her face goes blank. "What do you know about Bianca?"

The sudden chill throws me. "Besides Philip's creeptastic obsession with her?" I guess I'm trying to be funny. But her eyes flare with a bitter fire in the cold light of dusk. "Sorry. It's just—"

"Just *what?*"

Clamped on the bars, her hands tremble.

"Nothing."

"Who have you been talking to?" Her intensity pushes me back from the window. "Where did you hear about Bianca?"

Us Weekly?

I hesitate, as always. But the heat in her stare erodes my resolve. The truth is…what? That I lurked in stately Huntzel Manor, snorking up pudding cups and snooping? She knows all that.

When it comes to Kristina Huntzel, I'm running out of secrets.

"I saw the DVD of Philip performing on the Italian TV show with your mom and Bianca. And I know he—" *has a porny folder of gossip mag pictures.* I shake my head and shut the hell up. Her gaze remains hard but after a bit her tension bleeds away.

She turns her head and seems to study the sky. "He was so happy that night. You could hear it in the way he played." There's pride in her voice. Whatever Philip thinks of her, she obviously cares about him. I wonder if he has the first clue.

"Were you there?"

"No. I had to stay with—" She turns back to me. "It doesn't matter."

"What was the deal anyway? Bianca got him on the show? Like some kind of celebrity talent scout—Simon Cowell in drag?"

She shakes her head, but then says, "Something like that." Despite the darkness, I can see her expression cycle from anger to uncertainty and back again. "She wasn't doing it for him. Everything is always about her."

"So you know her...knew her." They must have been fairly close at some point, even if the thing with Philip had more to do with her than him. Whatever her scheme, things obviously didn't work out. But then what? On their way out the door the Huntzels found themselves in a position to make off with the sack of Mr. Bianca's dirty money?

"The situation is a lot more complicated than you realize."

No fucking kidding. I wait for her to tell me about Nick Malvado and the joint task force. But she doesn't. It's possible she doesn't know about the cash. If I was going to pin that on any of them, it would be Mr. Huntzel—the dude is a total creeper. But she must know *something*.

It can't be Simon-Cowell-In-Drag who's got her scared.

As she sits there on the porch roof, the cold invades my little brown cell. I don't move. Overhead, the clouds push in, low and heavy, blotting out the faint stars.

When Kristina speaks again, the words sound like they're being torn off her tongue in strips. "You've have to understand, Bianca is *dangerous*. When she sees that YouTube…" Her fingers tie themselves in knots against her belly. "Ludolph and Victoria think they can hide in the house, ride this out. They won't…" The air seems to drain out of her. "I can't explain it."

She doesn't have to. My whole life is a big fat *they won't*.

"I tried to go talk to Philip myself, to convince him to come away with me. But Ludolph jammed something in the rec room lock." She locks eyes with me. "I was hoping you would help me find another way in."

Now I have to fight back a crazed laugh. "You've been sneaking around that place a lot longer than I ever did."

"I always had a key."

"So did *I*." She doesn't need to remind me why Mr. Huntzel fucked up the lock. "Why don't you call?"

"He won't answer. He's my *brother*, but he won't answer the phone when I call him."

The hurt in her voice is sharp enough to strip paint. I'm afraid to ask what happened to the badass girl who threatened me with a knife. As if to reinforce the unsettling transformation, she reaches between the bars and strokes my cheek. At her touch, guilt stirs below my belt buckle. For a flash, I'm back in her bed that night after the party and Trisha. "I'm not saying you wanted it to happen. But that video is out there, and now I've got to do something about it."

The Plan hangs by a thread. I still don't know if Courtney can get my laptop. Even if she can, leaving this room—now—would be the last straw. Assuming that straw hasn't already broken.

This isn't my problem. My problem is downstairs on the couch in front of cable snooze. My problem is on a shelf in

Cooper's corral. It drives a muscle car like zombies are hanging off the bumper. It hides...

"I'm not looking for a white knight—"

...hides gold coins in her headboard.

"—just a little help. An idea, a suggestion. Anything. You don't even have to come with me."

We all have secrets, and our own reasons for keeping them. All Trisha wanted was a little understanding, a friend to share her burden. Not so much to ask.

Stupidly, I rub fluid out of my eyes, then look through the bars at the Ninja Girl. I don't know what's going on with Kristina, what's *really* going on. Why Philip hates her, why her father is more gone than home, why she has to sneak in and out of her own house. I can't imagine what mistakes brought her to this moment, perched atop the Boobie Hatch porch, asking a fuck-up like me for help.

I run my hand through my hair. "There might be a way—"

A car turns into the driveway. Kristina drops onto her hands. I pull back from the window, but keep the car in view. As Kristina lifts her head to peer over the edge of the porch, two people get out of the car.

"Who is it?"

Stein and Davisson. "Cops."

"What do they want?"

Me, obviously. "They're investigating Duncan's death."

I can hear Davisson's voice rumbling on the porch. "—aware Joey has been using Mrs. Huntzel's car to run errands? She thought he had his license—"

She's pinning Duncan on me. Of course. If I had any lingering doubt about who was driving the car that day, it's gone. I not only don't have my driver's license—no way would Mrs. Petty stand for that—I've never been behind the wheel of any car—not the Toyota and certainly not the almighty 740i. Anything Mrs. Huntzel says to the contrary is a lie.

I press my forehead against the cold, steel bars. A single padlock between me and freedom. If Ferrell had ever taught me to pick locks, or hell, if Wayne had left even one tool in my hide—

Then it hits me. *Maybe he did.*

I hiss through the window. "Get out of here."

"What about—?"

"I'll meet you at the house." My voice carries a confidence I don't feel.

"But—"

"*Go.*"

She slides out of sight. Now it's my turn—I hope.

Without turning the light on, I use the edge of a dime to unscrew the fake power outlet.

The key for the security bars is right where I left it.

3.4: What Haven't You Told Me?

I don't know if Wayne couldn't find the key, or never looked for it. Probably too busy pissing himself.

I climb out onto the porch roof and shut the window gate behind me. As I snap the padlock, the doorknob rattles and Wayne calls from the other side of my bedroom door.

"Joey, the police want—"

I don't stick around to find out what. I scoot down the shingles, catch myself on the gutter before I slide off. An old rhododendron knots its way up beside the porch. The branches are gnarled and dense enough to hold my weight. From above, Wayne shouts as I crash through the leaves.

I'm running before my feet hit the ground, skid past the end of the detectives' car. Halfway up the block, I cut through an apartment complex, then weave my way through neighborhood streets. I listen for sirens, but all I hear is the smack of my shoes on pavement and the blare of horns as I dart across Eighty-second on my way to Mount Tabor.

About the time I reach the park's edge, the sky unloads. I climb past the basketball court through pouring rain. On the slick hillside behind Huntzel Manor, I half-expect to run into Caliban, but he has too much sense to be out in the rain.

The gate in the laurel hedge squeaks when I push it open. Kristina materializes at my side. The whites of her eyes glow in the shadows under the hedge.

"How did you get out?"

"The same way we're getting in."

I point to her dark bedroom window, then head across the yard before my nerve breaks. Rain glues my jacket to my back. I pause at the edge of the veranda to listen, but all I hear is the patter of raindrops. No lights shine within the house. Even the exterior lights are off. I can't decide if that's good news or bad.

"Have you done this before?" Maybe she's thinking about how there's no old rhododendron here.

"Not really." I try to laugh. Fail. "Catch me if I fall?"

She doesn't follow me across the veranda.

Now that it's come to it, I'm ready to rethink this idea. The pattern of protruding bricks is more widely spaced than they'd seemed in dry daylight from the window above. Each toe- and finger-hold is barely half an inch deep. The dripping water doesn't help.

Might explain why they didn't bother with security sensors on the second floor windows.

Cold rain trickles down my neck as I grab the first brick and heave myself up. My fingers are already losing sensation before I'm more than a few feet off the ground. My toes cramp. The smell of wet brick makes me want to sneeze. I can't help imagining an explosive *ahh-choo* blowing me back onto the stone veranda below.

When I finally reach Kristina's window, I rest my chin on the sill until I catch my breath. Then, hanging on for dear life with one hand, I give the window a shove with the other.

It doesn't move.

"*Fuck.*"

"What's wrong?"

Mr. Huntzel must have locked it.

I adjust my feet and stretch up as high as I can, hoping I'm wrong. With my next try, I reef with all I got. The window flies up as my toes lose their hold. I drop, chin cracking against stone. I'm not sure who squawks louder, me or Kristina. Somehow I catch the sill with my numb fingers, hang on for a second as my feet kick. I'm starting to slip when my toe finds the lintel on the living room window below.

"Are you all right?"

For a moment, I hang there and breathe. "I think I broke a tooth."

"Seriously?"

What with all the noise I'm making, SWAT should be rappelling off the roof. I pull myself up over the windowsill and fall into Kristina's room. My arms are scraped and my jaw is half-unhinged, but I'm inside.

The house feels like a ghost. Or maybe I'm the ghost, haunting empty hallways and forgotten rooms, night after night, hiding in silence from my own shadow. I shake my head and, shivering, stick my head out the window. "Come on."

What seems like a second later, she's beside me, dripping on the floor.

"You should have gone first and dropped me a rope."

She throws me a strained smile. "I'm going to find Philip."

And just like that, she's gone.

For a minute I don't know what to do. But it doesn't take much thought to figure it out. I'm in the wind. I need to grab what I can and go. The sooner I put miles between me and the detectives, the better.

I pull open Kristina's dresser drawer, then the closet. Wayne would have torn the room apart—then made me clean up after him. Mr. Huntzel didn't bother. Everything is right where I left it.

I pile my clothes into my suitcase and wrap Trisha's laptop in the *Symphonica d'Italia* sweatshirt I stole from Philip, tuck it among my skivvies. Then I loop the length of clothesline through the suitcase handle. After I lower the case down to the veranda, I give the room a final scan. Hard to believe I lived here only a couple of weeks, sleeping under the unicorn comforter, doing homework and eating pudding at the tiny desk.

Feels like a lot longer.

A sound draws my gaze to the open bedroom door, a voice maybe. Did Kristina call my name? I listen, but the sound doesn't repeat. The darkness looms like a weight. YouTube guilt squirrels through my belly. I tell myself I got her inside. That's all she asked.

Before I know what I'm doing, I'm in the hallway. A faint glow shines through the windows from streetlights outside. In the direction of Philip's room I hear a door open, but I can't make anything out in the dark.

A shiver runs through me. If I had an ounce of sense I'd be on my way to the vault. Just a few stacks of stinky green could fund my escape. Hardly enough to be missed. They say you can live cheap in Belize.

"Kristina?"

My voice is so feeble I can barely hear myself. Somewhere ahead, the door slams. Footsteps slap toward me. I shrink against the doorframe, then nearly topple over when she whams into me. "Oh, my God...oh, my God." Her hands grip my arms with frantic strength.

"What's wrong?"

"She took him." I can smell her sweat: fear cut with acid.

"Who took who?"

"Victoria." Her moist eyes pick up a gleam from the street light. "She took Philip."

Between what I've guessed and what Kristina has admitted, even I might concede Mrs. Huntzel taking Philip away ought to be a good thing. Sure, she killed Duncan—the crap she fed the cops about me driving her car confirms what Courtney already guessed—but still, she's his mom. According to legend, mothers look out for their kids.

And if I'm a good little boy, Santa will bring me a brand new bike.

"Kristina." There's too much I don't know, but I'm starting to have my guesses. "What haven't you told me?"

"There's nothing to tell." In the dim light I can see her jaw clench so tight it might crack.

This isn't my problem.

Behind me, wind and rain rush through the open window. Three steps and a fall and I'm on my way. It'll be tough, living on shoplifted pudding cups while dodging cops and hobos. I'll have to keep my eyes open and my head down every second. In other words, exactly what I've been doing my whole life.

But I can't escape the fact if I leave Kristina here in this hallway, it's Trisha on the couch all over again.

"Kristina…" Nothing good ever comes of learning other people's secrets. "…who else knows about the money?"

"What money?" There's no conviction in her voice. I wait. After a moment she sags. "I don't know. No one." The *I hope* is left unsaid, but I can fill in the blanks.

Of course it's hers. Makes sense, really. The Huntzels would keep it close at hand, in Mrs. Huntzel's office or their bedroom—maybe inside Mr. Huntzel's unused mattress. Behind a loose board in the basement vault is the choice of a lurker. Like me.

My best guess is Kristina took it from Nick or Bianca while they were caught up in Philip's violin adventures. She keeps it in the vault because she can get to it easily. Sneak in through the side door while everyone's asleep and make a withdrawal. For a girl on the run, it was safer than a bank until I showed up, the wayward orphan with his own shit to hide.

I can feel Kristina's wet gaze in the darkness. "Philip was always the special one, the one with a talent Bianca could use." Resignation seems to bleed from her pores. "I was the inconvenient afterthought. So I left."

"Just to sneak back again? With that much money, you could go anywhere."

"It's my house, too." Her words burst out in shreds. "All I wanted was to stay close to my brother. But he hates me for abandoning him."

I don't need to ask what she ran from. Not good enough, pushed aside, ignored. She can blame Bianca all she wants, but the choice belonged to her mother and father. It's like Kristina is her own kind of orphan. Her parents may not be dead, or in jail, or fugitives, but as far as she's concerned, they may as well be.

"I'm sorry." My words sound hollow, but she seems to take them for what they should mean rather than what they don't. How do I tell her she's nothing special? People run all the time. Eva Getchie ran as the house burned. Wayne ran from me. And now I'm running too.

"We should go."

She shakes her head. "I need to search the house. She might have left something behind that will tell me where she took Philip."

"And the money?"

"What about it?" Suddenly defensive.

I'm not sure how to say this, so I just say it. "Listen. I didn't take any, but the day I found it, your mom saw me coming out of the vault."

"Victoria?"

Victoria…Ludolph. Kristina's habit of referring to her parents like they're actual people is unsettling. "I didn't think she noticed anything at the time, but—"

Almost before I realize she's moving, she bolts. In an instant, she's a dozen steps ahead of me.

"Kristina! Wait!"

I chase her down the main stairs to the basement and into the utility hall. My feet skid to a stop outside the vault door, eyes drawn to a cluster of gasoline cans at the far end of the hallway.

"Kristina—"

"Shut up." Inside the vault, she's tossing Mason jars. One of them breaks at the foot of the wine rack. I have the crazy thought I should get the broom and dustpan. As I dart to her side, another jar rolls to a stop against a lumpy shape near the wall. I blink, and the shape resolves into a half-familiar figure in a wrinkled suit. In the dim light of the overhead bulb, I see dark blood pooling around the figure's heaped shoulders.

"You need to look at—"

"Shut. *Up.*"

As she tears at the bottom shelf, I hear the scrape of a shoe behind me.

"Don't be a fool, darling."

The woman in the doorway stands in shadow, but her voice is somehow familiar. We both gape as she slips a scarf off her head and steps into the vault.

Just as Kristina had feared, Bianca Santavenere followed the YouTube trail right to our damn door.

3.5: Wait

Kristina's face goes gray. For a second, I'm worried she might pass out. I put out a hand to catch her, but she shrugs me off and her gaze hardens. In the space of a heartbeat she turns back into the girl I remember from all those late nights and lunges.

She's fast, but Bianca is faster. Before Kristina can reach her, Bianca slaps her across the face. Hard. Kristina's face blossoms livid red. She falls to one knee.

"Con*trol* yourself, young lady."

"I won't let you take him back!"

Bianca sniffs dismissively. "Better me than your father, don't you think?"

"He's not my father."

"He could have been, darling. You never gave him the chance."

My blood pools somewhere below my heart. Anita said the same thing about Wayne, an impostor in a dad mask. Bianca can't be talking about Mr. Huntzel. Can she? It makes no sense. But what does make sense leaves me gulping like a goldfish out of water.

Bianca Santavenere, ex-teen actor, reality TV star, gossip site queen. Now that she's standing in front of me in real life, I see someone I never expected. Everything about her seems less exaggerated than I recall from pictures and video. Smaller nose, narrower chin—she's no taller than Kristina. Still, there's a presence to her. She's a woman used to getting what she wants.

But take away the spray tan, the designer clothes, and the attitude and what's left are the elf features of Philip and Kristina.

"This is…She's—?"

The words get tangled on my tongue. Caught up in their stare-down, they're not listening. In that moment my image of Kristina as a weird kind of orphan takes on new meaning. She's more like me than I knew. But for her the system running her life isn't some public agency. She was never property of the state, never had a caseworker—she had some personal assistant who probably worked for Bianca's publicist.

"She's your mother." It's not a question.

"Don't call her that!"

"Kristina, you're being ridiculous. You'd think you'd show a little gratitude to the woman who bore you. I gave you *life*."

"Your idea of *life* was locking me in the walk-in freezer when I broke your coke mirror—"

Bianca stumbles as if pushed from behind. Eyes bulging, Kristina crawls away from her, stops at my side. I follow her stare and see Mrs. Huntzel in the vault doorway.

"Nothing ever changes with you two, does it?" She looks from mother to daughter, her face dripping with scorn. "No entourage, Bianca? Are you afraid of a press leak you didn't plant yourself?"

The two women stand facing each other, a couple of short strides apart—well within range if Bianca decides to strike. She flexes her long fingers and I give Kristina a tug on the elbow. The vault, never large, seems to shrink around us. Mrs. Huntzel blocks our only way out, but I'd like to keep us out of the fray if all hell breaks loose. To the right and backward is our only option.

But then Mrs. Huntzel raises the gun and everyone stops. *Wouldn't even make the cut in your average first-person shooter,* I remember thinking when I found it. The gun looks much bigger than it did in her nightstand drawer. Her hand is completely still. In her place I'd be a scared kitten, but Mrs. Huntzel is a stone.

Bianca just looks pissed. She seems to inflate, oblivious to the threat lurking within Mrs. Huntzel's unsettling calm. Either she didn't register the body when she came in, or such a thing is beneath the notice of the likes of Bianca Santavenere. Too busy sneering at Mrs. Huntzel, maybe. "You think I need help dealing with the likes of you?"

In response, Mrs. Huntzel points the gun at Bianca's well-crafted chest. I brace for the shot—it's not the first time she's pulled the trigger tonight. What else could explain the still, bleeding figure dressed like a Walmart greeter behind us? Why she shot her husband is anyone's guess, but a dispute over the nylon bag full of stinky money would be motive enough.

A sound, half-snarl, draws Mrs. Huntzel's attention. I steal a glance at Kristina as she spits, "After all the help I gave you, the money—"

"Your *help* has led to this pass." Mrs. Huntzel's lips pull back from her teeth in disgust. "Our arrangement was clear."

"I wanted to be near my little brother."

"He doesn't *need* you. All he needs is me." Mrs. Huntzel's gaze lifts, as if she's inspecting the brickwork overhead. For a moment, her eyes glaze over and I wonder what she's seeing. What she's imagining. Then she lets out a breath that's almost a wistful sigh. "By the time the police sort through the rubble, if they even bother, Philip and I will be long gone."

My mind flashes to the gasoline cans I saw up the hall. A sensation like melting ice drains through me, but before I can say anything, Bianca takes a step toward Mrs. Huntzel.

"Victoria, you're being ridiculous. What Philip needs is his mother."

Mrs. Huntzel's eyes snap back to reality and her lips draw back from her teeth. "You were *never* his mother." Her voice is a hiss now. "All you did was give birth to him. I'm the one who *always* took care of him."

"Spare me the amateur dramatics, Victoria. You're a glorified babysitter."

"I'm more of a mother than you could ever be."

"You're an employee. An *ex*-employee. And isn't that what this is really all about—?"

"Shut up."

"You resent the fact that I fired you—"

"I said shut up."

"—and in a petty act of vengeance you stole *my* child!"

The gunshot explodes in the confined space of the vault.

I expect someone to fall, but no one moves. The acrid stench of burnt gunpowder sears my eyes as the gun tracks from Kristina to me, then back to Kristina again. It hangs there in Mrs. Huntzel's hand.

"Wait."

My voice sounds like it's coming out of an old radio. I raise my hand.

"You stupid bitch!" Bianca's shout tears my eyes away from the gun. "You could have killed me." Blood drips from her arm, but Bianca seems less hurt than outraged. She launches herself at Mrs. Huntzel, all flailing arms and flying spit. Kristina and I watch, stunned, as the two women grapple through the steel-framed doorway.

Kristina reacts first, managing two steps toward the door before the gun goes off again in the hallway. Someone screams. I scramble after Kristina and pull her back as another shot sounds. Then a loud, metallic shriek fills the vault. By the time I realize what it means, it's too late. I gape, helpless, as the vault door slams shut.

Kristina rushes the door, pounds on steel. "Are you going to help?"

"Kristina—"

"There has to be a way. A latch or something."

Except for a line of bolts framing the inner edge, the vault door is a smooth expanse of steel. I grab her by the shoulders, turn her to face me.

"She has gasoline." My voice is trembling. "I saw cans of it in the hall."

At first she resists me, then the horror registers on her face.

Her forehead falls against my chest. A tremor runs through her, like power in a high tension line. "Oliver, I don't suppose you have a phone." The fabric of my shirt muffles her voice.

"A long way from here." In my backpack, wherever Mrs. Petty left it.

"Mine's in my messenger bag. I think I dropped it in Philip's room." Her shaking could be a humorless laugh or the start of a sob. All I can do is hold her.

By the time the police sort through the rubble, Mrs. Huntzel said, *Philip and I will be long gone*. She's going to burn the house down, us with it. Witnesses, evidence, any traces of the Huntzels will all be reduced to ash and soot.

And there's not a damn thing we can do to stop her.

3.6: In the Vault

After a while Kristina pulls away. It's only then that she notices Mr. Huntzel.

"Oh, my God."

"Tell me about it."

In all the crazy, I guess he was easy to miss. I cross the vault and kneel next to him. He's lying in a pool of drying blood, black under the dim overhead light. A sickly wobble churns my guts as I check for a pulse at his wrist. Nothing. No sign of breathing either. I wonder if I should try CPR. I've never had the class, but I don't think it matters.

He's dead.

I slip off my jacket to cover him, but before I can, Kristina says, "See if he has a phone."

Last thing I want to do is loot a corpse, but she gets points for being practical. We're short of options.

I run the back of my hand across my mouth. His cologne stings my eyes as I pat down his suit coat and rifle his pants pockets. Nothing. He doesn't even have keys or a wallet. Mrs. Huntzel must have searched him first. A shudder ripples through me and I toss my jacket over his head and upper body. His exposed legs seem somehow more horrible than his dead face.

I turn away.

Kristina is staring blankly at the vault door.

"So. Which one of your mothers do you figure locked us in?"

At first I think she's going to jump my shit—not that I could blame her. It's a lame attempt at humor.

"I never had a mother." She offers up a sad little laugh.

I open my mouth to say I'm sorry, but she just shakes her head. "Victoria is the one with the gun. You tell me who locked us in." She eyes me cautiously. "I suppose you have a lot of questions."

One or ten. "I've figured out a few things. You stole a bajillion dollars from your father—"

"*Step*-father."

Right. *Us Weekly* mentioned a dead first husband, Pip McEntire. "—and ran away. Mrs. Huntzel was what, the nanny?"

"Philip's nanny, at least until Bianca decided Victoria had become a little too important to him and fired her. I was pretty much left to myself."

"Did your—did Mrs. Huntzel really kidnap him?"

She takes her time answering. I don't push it. Not like I have anywhere else to be.

"When I was little, Bianca would audition, but she couldn't land a role to save her life. My father was a hot shit entertainment lawyer, and through his connections, she got into reality TV. But after he died, the spotlight faded. Fewer invites were coming her way, swag parties dried up. When the Grammys dropped her from their seat-warmer list, she went on the prowl. Within a month, she turned up married to Nick Malvado. Scary tan, gold chains, and way too many bodyguards. A real estate developer, Bianca called him."

"What did you call him?"

"Everyone knew he was a drug dealer. I'm not sure what she married him for, the coke or cash." She shakes her head. "We ended up in this weird plate-glass house in Miami. It was a nightmare, but Philip was oblivious. I mean, he was eleven years old. And anyway he had his violin. Bianca was getting him on TV, mostly in Europe—not that he cared where. He loved any chance to play. But things around the house were horrid. She was using, and Nick's creeper goons kept hitting on me like I was a party favor." She releases a long, ragged breath. "Do you remember when she OD'ed?"

An image from last spring flashes through my mind—Anita mesmerized by an *E! True Hollywood Story*—and suddenly I remember why Bianca's press conference was so familiar. The segment was from the year before, after her overdose. That's what the video was all about— Bianca making a fuss about going into rehab. "*For them, I promise to get clean.*" Despite the tears, the state of Florida threatened to take the kids. I don't remember ever hearing their names.

Philip and Kristina.

But a week into rehab, the kids disappeared. The husband claimed they ran away, but no one believed that. Big investigation, lots of hand-wringing on cable news. No way could two kids simply vanish without a trace, not on their own. But the investigation went nowhere. The *E!* story ended on a question mark.

She sees the lights come on in my eyes. "The unofficial speculation was Nick dropped us in the Gulf Stream where we wouldn't be found until body parts washed up on Amity Island. What most people didn't know was I'd been gone a couple of weeks before Philip disappeared. One of Nick's men cornered me in the back hallway and tried to put his hand down my pants. When I told Bianca, she said I had no reason to complain. With my assets I could lead guys around by their dicks. I just had to put my mind to it. I was *fifteen*." She laughs bitterly. "After that, I knew I had to get away."

"And the money—?"

"Was a fucking *bonus*."

Over the years, I've known a lot of foster kids who made a break. They always turn up. Sometimes they're three states away, sometimes they're wrapped in a tarp on Pioneer Courthouse Square. It may be days, weeks—even months. But they're always found, alive or dead.

Whole 'nuther matter when you have a duffel bag full of money.

"Why did Mrs. Huntzel take Philip?"

"Nick threatened to hurt him if Bianca didn't get the money back. I don't know how Victoria found out. Maybe Philip called her—they've always been tight. All I know is I woke up one morning and there was Bianca on TV whining about her missing baby. She couldn't be bothered when the missing baby was me."

"Miami to Oregon is a long way."

"It was obvious Victoria had taken Philip. Sooner or later Nick would have found them, unless they had help hiding. I went to Ludolph. They were divorced, but I figured he'd know how to reach her. I suggested Portland."

"To this mansion you had sitting around."

"The house belonged to my dad's sister." She sighs, long and wistful. "When she died, she left it to us in trust, but title doesn't transfer until Philip turns twenty-one. I'll be twenty-five. In the meantime, a property management company looks after it. I gave Ludolph cash to spread around and he quietly arranged for Victoria to get hired as caretaker."

Give Kristina credit. The girl has her shit together. Still, something's not right. "Isn't this the first place Bianca would look?"

"My father had all kinds of property, but my aunt's estate was never part of it. There are layers upon legal layers protecting this house."

"So the Huntzels just picked up and moved across country to nanny Philip again?"

"Victoria did. Ludolph still lives back east, though he comes out pretty often. We made a deal: if they help me hide Philip until he's old enough to be on his own, they can have the house. I always figured they'd sell and split the proceeds, but whatever. In the meantime, Ludolph's job was logistics. He arranged Philip's ID and transcript so he could get into school. He's also good at finding things out."

That explains why Kristina and Mr. Huntzel met downtown. He's her henchman.

"And you don't live here because you ran away."

"That was the most important part of the deal. Victoria won't forgive me for leaving him alone with Bianca, and Philip won't forgive me because I'm why he couldn't stay. I even bought them that fucking *car* to drive around in, for all the good it did me. I'm screwed any way you look at it."

I find myself gazing at Mr. Huntzel's rumpled form. "Why did she kill him?"

"I bet he talked to Bianca. That would explain how she found us so fast." She considers for a moment. "I don't know if she called him or he called her, but either way he had to know things were unraveling. He probably thought he could make a deal."

"Mrs. Huntzel has her own plan."

"No kidding, Oliver." Her voice breaks. "No. Fucking. Kidding."

3.7: Bad as It Gets

Kristina moves to the back wall and sits, staring blankly. "I used to come here when I was little. This probably sounds silly, but I remember the house as a bright, sunny place. When grandma passed, my aunt inherited it. Dad got the house in Cannon Beach. He sold it right away—he was living in L.A. and had more than he could keep track of by then—but my aunt wanted to keep her childhood home in the family."

"How did she die?"

"A car accident when I was nine. Drunk driver." I expect her to start crying, but she just stares. "She was so beautiful and kind. Aunt Myra."

"That's a pretty name." The words feel stupid coming out of my mouth, but I don't know what else to say.

"It means 'astonishing.'" She smiles sadly and looks up toward the ceiling. Sighs. "Philip hates this house. It reminds him he lost his grand life as a violin wunderkind when Victoria took him away from Bianca. He never understood he could have lost so much more if he'd stayed." A bitter laugh escapes her throat. "She's dangerous and crazy, but she's his mom, you know?"

"Yours too."

"Would you claim her if she was your mother?"

I wouldn't claim anyone. But that's not what she's asking. She's not asking anything. She's telling. The last thing she'll ever tell anyone.

I sigh.

"I wonder what the cops will think."

She flinches a little, but then shrugs. "Does it matter?"

I guess not.

"Mrs. Huntzel knows how to mop up after herself, that's for sure." Duncan must have figured out who Philip really is because of the violin playing, so she killed him. Whatever it takes to protect Philip. "Do you know where she'll take him?"

Now Kristina throws her hands down. "Who gives a fuck? We'll be dead."

The air in the vault is stuffy. I wonder if the fire has started yet. Maybe not. There's no smoke detector in here, but there are plenty of others. Thirty-two in all. We'll hear when hell breaks loose. But by the time the ashes settle, she and Philip will be long gone with half a million dollars.

"Why are you so calm about this?"

It takes me a moment to respond. "I used to say where I come from doesn't matter."

"What do you say now?"

I've already told her more about myself than I've ever told anyone else, caught in a moment of weakness that night after Trisha came to Huntzel Manor. I wish I could make sense of it.

"When I was six, I snuck off into the woods with my father's hunting rifle."

"Something happened?"

"Yes. Something happened."

"Bad?"

My throat constricts. "Bad as it gets." I go quiet.

What I didn't know was the rifle was loaded, with a round in the chamber. I must have hooked the trigger on something, a branch in the thick undergrowth maybe, because the gun went off as I was looking down the barrel. By some miracle, the bullet missed me, crashed through the trees instead. The shot echoed, a sharp double-tap resounding through the Mount Hood foothills. Terrified, I flung the rifle into the woods as if it was an animal come to life in my hands. Didn't think about how Orville would probably want it back.

Not long after I smelled smoke. The house was burning. I ran to the front door and saw my father on the floor inside. The bullet missed me, but Orville Getchie wasn't so lucky. On its way through his brain, it knocked out teeth and his ever-present Lucky Strike. The cigarette must have caught a stack of newspapers, or maybe when he fell he knocked over the can of kerosene he kept to light the wood stove.

Near as anyone could tell, Eva didn't try to help. She left me there on the porch, left my sister in her crib—the crib I last remember draped with fire as the paramedics wheeled me away. They say I tried to get to Laura, but I don't remember that. I only remember the flames.

Orville Getchie was dumb as a post—leaving a loaded gun where a kid could get to it. Maybe he deserved what happened to him. But Laura didn't deserve what happened to her. All this time I've kept the secret of the rifle, as I've kept so much else hidden in cubbies and compartments. My shitty life is punishment for what I let happen to my sister. This moment seems inevitable.

And yet, I don't want to die.

I shudder, jam my hands into my jeans pockets. Something coarse scrapes my knuckles and I pull out the sea cookie. An interesting token—a wonder it hasn't broken. If they find me, if they find it seared into my hand, will they report the fact in the news? Will Trisha hear and know I thought of her at the end?

Kristina shivers. "I'm cold."

Not for long. Even I'm not asshole enough to say that out loud. All she wanted was to protect her brother and make amends for leaving him behind when her own fear got the better of her. Whatever I've earned, she shouldn't have to own a share of it.

"Joey?"

"Yeah."

"Remember that night when you touched me and I said I didn't like it?"

"Yeah."

"I lied."

It takes me longer than I expect to answer. "It's okay."

"I never wanted to become her, but look at me."

A vision of her green bra and panties spills through my mind, and I remember her touch through the security bars earlier this evening. Was she leading me around by my dick? Maybe, but then I think about her fierce protectiveness toward Philip and the way she spoke about her Aunt Myra.

I swallow.

"You're not her, Kristina."

I join her against the wall, wrap my arm around her shoulder. I feel inadequate to her need, but I'm who she has. And she's who I have. Perhaps that's why she cuddled up to me in the middle of the night. Hard-case Kristina.

She's me.

I'm her.

We're all orphans.

A chill creeps over me, starting at my side and moving inward.

I sit up.

"What is it?"

"A draft."

3.8: Boy Hero

Air pushes up through the drain opening next to us. The grate is inset, resting on the lip of the opening. At one time, it must have been secured with screws, but those rusted away long ago. I perch on my hands and knees and pull the grate off. From the dark shaft, I hear a trickle of water and catch a whiff of mud.

Kristina slides in beside me. "There are drains like this throughout the basement. Do you think they're connected?"

"You'd think." I shake my head. "But it would kinda defeat the purpose of the big metal door."

"The vault goes back to Prohibition when the house belonged to some old bootlegger. My grandparents added the drains later. A lot of water comes down off Mount Tabor when it rains."

I think about the smell Mr. Huntzel wanted me to find. Water isn't the only thing.

"So, what we know is there are openings in other parts of the basement and air is coming through this one."

She inspects the opening. "It's small."

No argument. The shaft is barely shoulder width across. I can't see the bottom, but the trickle sounds close. "It might be our only way out."

I slide my feet into the hole and grip the edge with my hands.

Kristina grabs my arm. "Joey, don't be crazy."

"Won't know if I don't try."

Before I can drop into the hole, she pulls me back. "I'm smaller. I'll go first."

"It's too—"

"Oliver, puh-*leeze*. Do *not* go all Boy Hero on me."

"Who was it that needed me to climb into the house first?"

"That was different. You never said you left my window unlocked. Besides, if it didn't work, the worst thing that would happen was we'd both get rained on."

She's not the one who nearly broke her jaw on the window sill. But I can tell by the look in her eyes she's in no mood for an argument. Maybe this is her way to prove to herself she's not Bianca.

"What if she spun the dial?"

She rolls her eyes. "My house, Oliver. You think I don't know the combination to my own damn vault?"

"Okay, okay. Be careful. You don't know where either one of them is."

The edge of the hole comes up to her waist. With a little wriggling, she's able to lower herself until only her head is above the rim. "There are openings at the bottom. I think one points toward the next room over."

"Is it big enough?"

"Of course!" Her grin is strained. "Here goes." With that, she slithers out of sight. An echoey grunt sounds from the bottom of the hole, but in her black outfit, she's invisible. I hear the scrape of gravel and inhale a fresh breath of pungent mud. Then, nothing.

All I can do is wait. I keep my back to Mr. Huntzel, walk to the vault door and press my ear against the cold steel. Silence. I feel weirdly alone without her. Acid rises in the back of my throat. My fingers drum metal. My pulse thrums in my hands and feet, but my chest feels as hollow as an empty barrel. After an interminable wait, I return to the drain hole.

"Kristina?" My voice barely makes it past my thickening tongue. "*Kristina?*"

I hear a distant metallic sound, so faint I wonder if I'm imagining it. The chamber is starting to feel hot. I sniff for smoke, but all I can smell is dust and my own sweat. A scrabbling sound rises from the dark shaft, like nails on concrete.

"Are you all right?" I want to shout and whisper at once. I'm as afraid Mrs. Huntzel will hear me as I am Kristina won't. After a moment she answers.

"Joey, can you hear me?" Her voice, resonating up through the drain, sounds so close I almost expect her face to materialize in the hole below me.

"Are you stuck?"

"I'm in the laundry room. I couldn't get the vault door to open."

"I thought you knew the combo."

"That's not the problem. The door won't budge. It's been so long since it was closed, either the hinges seized or something's jammed in the frame."

"Should I crawl through?"

Her hesitation is enough to tell me she thinks that's a bad idea. "If you push the door while I pull, we might be able to force it."

"Okay. Tap on the door when you want me to push."

I move back to the vault door. The steel is cold against my cheek. After what feels like hours but is probably only seconds,

I detect a faint, metallic *tink-tink-tink*. With a grunt, I throw my shoulder into the door. There's nothing to grip but a frame of smooth rivets. My feet scrabble against the concrete floor for purchase. At first, it doesn't move. After a moment, I gasp and sag against the door.

I suck in a deep breath. A glance toward Mr. Huntzel gives me strength for one more push. The vault door groans open.

Kristina pulls me through a gap barely wide enough for my narrow shoulders. I take a moment to catch my breath, then look around. There's blood all over the hall. I don't know if that's good news or bad. But we're free.

"Kristina, you're insane."

"You're out of the vault, aren't you?"

"I'm not complaining."

She gives me a feisty smile. Her face is streaked with mud, her green hair plastered against her head.

"You look like Caliban."

"I'm not sure how to take that." She offers me a tight-lipped smile. "He's a sweet fella. I hope he gets away." But then her face darkens. "I need to find Philip."

"*We* need to get out of here." I look down the hall. Mrs. Huntzel's gas cans are gone. "This place could up go any second, if it's not burning already." Only the quiet offers any reassurance. Thirty-two smoke detectors will make a helluva racket once she ignites all that gasoline.

"If she gets away with him, with all that money—"

"Worry about that after we're safe." I tug her forearm, and for a second she resists. I can almost feel the weight of the house above us. "*Please*, Kristina. You didn't crawl through that pipe just so you could die in this hallway."

She stares at me another half second, then nods. "You're right."

This time, Boy Hero takes the lead.

3.9: We All Have Secrets

We can't risk going back through the house. Kristina's door in the rec room isn't an option after Mr. Huntzel jammed the lock, and we could too easily be spotted from the open shaft of the staircase if Mrs. Huntzel is up that way sloshing gasoline around. Instead, I guide Kristina the other direction, down the utility hall past the laundry room and under the stairs. There, a narrow passage connects the basement and garage cellar. The space is moldy and dank, but mercifully free of the stink of gasoline or smoke.

I pause at the foot of the ladder that climbs up to the garage proper and cock my head, listening. All I can hear is the quiet patter of rain on the garage roof.

Kristina nudges me from behind. "What's the holdup?"

I'd like to avoid a headshot, I think, but I keep that thought to myself. With Kristina's hands on my back, I stick my nose up over the lip of the garage floor. Dim light glows at the far end of the space, silhouetting a car in the near stall—the BMW. For a second I can't believe Mrs. Huntzel abandoned her beloved Beamer, but then it clicks. Easier to escape notice in an anonymous Toyota than a high-end luxury car.

Our own escape is behind us, through a side door that faces the house. For a few short steps, we'll be in plain view of the kitchen and the front corridor outside the dining room. But a quick sprint around the corner of the garage and past the laurel hedge should lose us in darkness even if Mrs. Huntzel is still around to see.

"Come on." I hoist myself onto the concrete floor then turn to offer Kristina a hand. But she's already up and rushing past me.

"Oh, my god."

"Kristina, wait. We've got to…"

The words die on my lips as I follow her around the nose of the car. The light is coming from the interior of the Toyota, parked on the far side of of the BMW. I blink, and a figure resolves in the passenger seat.

Philip.

He sees us almost as soon as we see him. I half expect him to make a break for it, but he just sits there.

Kristina yanks the car door open and grabs his hand. "Philip, sweetie. Are you okay?"

In the backseat, I spot black nylon and catch a whiff of B.O. The duffel bag is half-buried under a heap of Philip's clothing and Mrs. Huntzel's purse. I squeeze Kristina's forearm, but his voice draws my gaze back to the front seat before I can say anything.

"Did Mom say you can come with us?"

At mention of his mother, an electric trill jumps through me. Kristina's attention is all on her brother. "Of course, honey." She's studying him now. Her hands run up and down his arms as if checking for injury. Philip seems to be trying to meet her worried gaze, but his eyes can't quite find focus.

I lean into the open car door. "Kristina." The air feels charged around us, or maybe that's just me. "If he's still here, she's still here."

"Right." A heavy breath comes out of her. "Philip, come on." She tugs his hands, gently at first, then with more strength when he resists. "Come on, Philip. Please."

His chin starts bouncing side to side. "We gotta get my my violin." His voice is plaintive and reedy, with a familiar slur.

Kristina looks at me, eyes darting and anxious. "What's wrong with him?"

"We gotta get my *violin*," he says again, more urgently. He sounds like Anita on a binge, sloppy and uninhibited.

"Shit."

"What?" she snaps.

"She drugged him." The last of his Vicodin, most likely. Probably put it in his cocoa, thought it would make him more manageable.

"Why would she do that?"

I shake my head sharply. "It doesn't matter. You found him. Now let's go."

"Just give me a minute to calm him down."

"We may not *have* a minute." I stare at the side door, watch for it to burst open. My pulse pounds inside my head, my nerves scream for me to run. But I stand there. I stand there and wait.

When Philip starts crying, I look back as his big sister takes him in her arms and pulls him close. "Shhh, honey."

"I need my violin." He sounds like a lost kitten now, helpless.

"Okay, sweetie. Okay. We'll find it." He sinks into her embrace, peaceful at last. When she looks up at me I can see what she wants me to do.

I tilt my head toward the back seat and the black nylon bag. "You can't just buy him a new violin?"

"Our father gave it to him before he died. It's special."

"Nothing is that special."

"Joey, please."

As the pressure mounts behind my eyes, I watch Philip rocking in Kristina's lap. He's so different from me—chess wiz, violin prodigy. I remember thinking Philip took for granted a certainty Trisha and I never had, but here he is—with me—and his life is about to be turned upside down again. Like me, like Trisha, like every foster I've ever known. Not property of the state maybe, but a still pawn. Still just a kid trying to stake a claim to himself.

Maybe not so different from me, after all. We each cling to something we can to call our own. A few tools, a poem. For Philip, it's his damn violin.

Ten years ago, I failed my sister Laura. Three days ago, I failed Trisha. And tonight? Philip wouldn't even be here now if I hadn't pretended to be a chess player. Without me, his life would have continued—awkward and miserable maybe, but safe. For that matter, if I could have found a single moment of trust in Trisha, maybe YouTube wouldn't have happened either.

Duncan is dead, and Mrs. Huntzel is responsible, but in a way, so am I.

I can't help Duncan now. But maybe I can make up for my piece of it.

I nod toward the backseat. "Her purse—"

Kristina dumps the purse before I can finish the thought. She hooks the set of keys on one finger and displays them triumphantly.

"Good. Now will you please get going?"

She nods, but then she takes my hand. "Joey, you know I'd go for the violin myself if I could."

"I get it. You're his sister." I make no effort to keep the anxiety out of my voice. "It's fine."

"How will I find you later?"

I think for a second. "You know Uncommon Cup, on Hawthorne?"

"Sure."

"Leave a message with Marcy there. I'll get in touch as soon as I can, assuming I don't end up a french fry." My voice hitches and I have to blink away an image of burning walls.

The way she squeezes my hand feels like it will be the last time. "Thank you, Joey."

"Don't thank me yet."

3.10: Smoke Alarm

Stillness surrounds me as I creep back to the basement. My ears strain for any sound of movement, but all I can hear is my own drumbeat pulse, my own gasping breath. The smell of gasoline is almost overpowering as I creep up the stairs, but at least it's not smoke. I wonder again, why hasn't she started the fire? Against the pressure of the silence, I edge one foot ahead of the other and force my way through the house.

Gasoline drenches the floors in the kitchen and butler's pantry, and up the first few risers of the south stairs. That tells me she's been here, which is good. I'm less likely to encounter her where she's already been. The gas also confirms who won the WWE SmackDown outside the vault. No telling where Bianca is now.

The air is clear of fumes and the carpet dry when I reach the second floor. I scurry down the dark corridor—expecting gunfire with each step—and dart into Philip's room.

Where I stall. I have no clue where he keeps the damn violin. Helpless, I stare into a degree of chaos that would make Mad Maddie stroke out. Scattered books, DVD cases, heaps of clothes, forgotten plates and bowls—and no sign of a violin.

There's no time for finesse. I tear through the room, spilling drawers, sweeping books off shelves, scattering clothes. Too loud, but I half imagine the smell of smoke already. I trip over Kristina's bag and kick it out of the way. She can damn well buy another bag. No such luck with the violin.

He needs to keep it secret, yet close enough to easily get any time he wants. In his place, I'd build a hide, but Philip never got a carpentry lesson from Mr. Rieske. The back of his closet is solid: old plaster years overdue for paint, oak floor intact, no unexpected seams. The room's baseboards aren't deep enough to hide a violin case.

Think, dumbass.

But it's no good thinking like me. When Wayne found out about my tools, he made them his—probably to sell on craigslist so he could buy a Blu-ray player to go with his new TV. But there's no Wayne in Philip's life, no Anita, or Reid, or even Mrs. Petty. Just Philip and the woman he calls mom. He might be hiding the violin from the rest of the world, but in the house it's safe.

Then it hits me.

I turn to the bed.

The sheets and blankets are wadded up at the head, same as the day I came to scrounge some clothes.

What's the violin to Philip?

It's *Stravaganza del Talento*, it's the anti-chess. It's his power, what he's best at. It's his escape.

Even among neurotypicals, Reid said, *there is no normal.* The violin is what he *loves.*

I grab a handful of the blankets and yank. As the covers untangle, the violin case tumbles out. Of course he sleeps with the damn thing.

Time to bail.

I listen at Philip's door, wishing I really did have the super hearing Trisha makes fun of. I hear nothing, but that's small comfort. I ease the door open to the stench of gasoline and a deeper silence. All I can do is make a break for it, but when I slip out of Philip's room, Mrs. Huntzel is waiting. A gas can rests on the floor at her feet, but my attention is all on the gun. The black hole in the end of the barrel freezes me.

For a moment, she looks at me like I'm a rat turd in her salad. I don't know who she was expecting as she waited outside the door, but I'm not it. Then the understanding seems to set in.

"You always were a resourceful boy."

I have no response, but she's not looking for one.

"My husband warned against bringing you into our lives." In the faint light, I can just make out the trace of a wistful smile. "I suppose I should have listened, but you know I always liked you, Joey."

No one ever says *I always liked you* unless things are about to go sideways.

"You took care of my baby when he needed you, and I'm grateful for that." She sounds resigned, but the gun in her hand tells a different story. I assume the only reason she hasn't pulled the trigger so far is fear of hitting Philip's precious instrument.

"I'll leave. We can all leave."

Her response is a sad shake of her head. "Give me the violin."

I take a step back and clutch the case to my chest. Kristina should be gone by now. I hope. "It belongs to Philip." I only have to stall long enough to be sure.

"I'll take it to him."

At that moment I hear approaching sirens.

"What have you done?" she snaps.

I can't help but smile.

She raises her arm and fires. I stumble back as the bullet shrieks…into me or past me? There's no time to think about the sudden pain along my jawline, because Mrs. Huntzel screams as flames erupt and engulf her arms and chest. Gas fumes and gunfire: not a good mix.

In horror, I crawl backward as she throws herself against the wall, howling like an animal. Her thrashing throws sparks in all directions. Then the gun goes off again. The gas can on the floor explodes and throws me down the hall. Everything goes dark.

Seconds or minutes later, the shriek of smoke detectors snaps me back to my senses. Around me, the walls are on fire, the carpet crackles, black smoke boils along the ceiling. I spot the smoldering lump of Mrs. Huntzel against the far wall and, for an awful instant, picture my sister's crib draped in flames. I shut my eyes, clench my teeth, but the piercing wail of the detectors alights every nerve, exhorting me to run.

Philip's violin is still in my arms. I roll over, crawl away from the flames, jump to my feet. Fire chases me down the hall, then leaps up to block my way through the library. It's too much. I head back the way I came. Flames climb the walls of the central staircase and leap across the treads. I start down anyway, four steps, five. Then lunge backward when something cracks overhead and shower of sparks and burning debris falls across my path. When I turn, the hallway is impassable. My only choice is down—or dead. I jump—

—and hit the top of elevator, one leg crashing through sheet metal. Fire pours down the lift cable. I throw myself backward, nearly twisting my foot off. A sharp pain knifes through my ankle as I fall. Something cushions my landing, but my breath whuffs out of me. At least I manage to hang onto the damned violin.

When I roll over and look up, Bianca stares back at me.

I yelp and crab backward. The violin case skids across the floor, but her eyes don't follow. She's propped against the bottom of the lift. Her flesh is the color of old concrete. Her designer outfit is in shreds, her shoes gone. She doesn't react when a cinder falls on her exposed forearm. Her body is what broke my fall.

I shudder and turn away. I find the violin and drag myself to the rec room door, test the wood before I reach for the doorknob. It's like touching a stove burner. The other direction, at the far end of the utility hall, the firelight is blinding. The smoke detector screams are less piercing now, or maybe my eardrums have burst.

Behind me, the central staircase collapses, burying Bianca in flames and debris. Every exit is cut off by fire. My ankle is a mess, my chin bleeding. I stand on one foot. The slate floor won't burn, even if everything else will. I hobble to the back wall near the bathroom. The plaster-coated concrete will probably be the last thing to go. Does concrete burn? Hot as it's getting, fucking steel will burn. I sag onto my ass and cradle the violin. Water floods my eyes. I can hardly breathe. "I'm sorry, Philip." I don't know what I'm apologizing for. For failing to escape with his precious instrument? For letting his secret out into the world? For not understanding who he really is. An orphan, like me. Like all of us.

I squeeze my eyes shut. See Kristina…and Trisha. I'm sorry I'll never be able to make things right with her. My head swims. I can't stop the sounds burbling up from my throat. I don't want to die like this, like my sister died. *I'm sorry, Laura.* I'm sorry for a lot of things. All I can hope is that Trisha frees herself from Mr. Vogler, and that Kristina and Philip get away. Hell, I even hope the ugly old dog got clear of this disaster—

The dog.

"Caliban." The name is a revelation in my throat.

No one knows how he comes and goes. I remember him jumping into that hole up the hill from the house, the scrabbling sounds I heard rising from the shaft when I called out for Kristina from the vault. *A lot of water comes off Mount Tabor when it rains,* she said. The drains must not connect just to each other, but to a larger system.

Is it big enough? Caliban is half my size. Kristina is near enough to me, though, and she made it. But it's one thing to match her feat, crawling through the pipe from one room to the next. It's quite another to think I can wriggle my way up the hill to the hole the damn dog uses. But I'm dead for sure if I stay where I am.

Fuck it—

Fire chases me down the utility corridor. I beat it through the first storage room door and claw at the grate covering the drain. The screws here are intact. Caliban must have another way out, a drain where the grate has rusted away. Maybe the spot where Kristina came up during the Great Vault Escape.

For half an overheated second, I wonder if I can get to it. But a *whumpf* and the crash of falling brick in the doorway cut me off from the basement maze. I look around for something to pry up the grate, but all I see are bare walls. Six months ago, I cleaned this space out and got rid of anything of possible use. The project earned me my first Huntzel hundred. Nice job, Joey!

Out of options, I thread my fingers through the bars of the grate and heave with everything I've got. I'm not sure what will give first, the screws or my shoulder sockets. A cinder lands on my neck and I scream, the sound punctuated by a sudden pop as the old screws break. Momentum throws the grate into my chin and I topple over backward. For a second I lay there, dazed. But the sight of flames boiling across the ceiling clears my head in the space of a single coughing gasp.

I kick the violin case into the hole, then drop down after it. I splash into knee-deep water, in some kind of catch basin. A pair of pipes run off in opposite directions. Pick a hand, white pawn or black. Either option is as likely as the other to end in checkmate. I grab the violin and go for the one which smells less of smoke.

The space isn't big enough for me to crawl on my hands and knees. I have to push the violin case ahead of me and wriggle on my belly, like a cork trying to squeeze back into the bottle.

Cracks in the pipe offer fingerholds I can use to pull myself along. Sharp edges tear at my arms and legs. The stench of rot threatens to bring up whatever's left of the conveyor belt sushi I ate a lifetime ago. If I get out of here, I'm going to have to soak in a vat of antibiotics for a week.

At the next catch basin, and the next, the drain shafts look up into the inferno. Falling cinders keep me moving through a tunnel that seems to go on forever. I only hear the roar of the fire and the sound of my own sobbing. As the world above burns, all I can do is thrust the violin case forward and follow what I hope is the hideous, beautiful dog's escape route. Not until I reach a basin with a third option, a pipe that slopes upward, do I dare allow myself a shred of hope. I choke on rushing water. Inhale mud. Roots and stones scrape my flesh. But somehow, I find my way through Caliban's hole in the hillside into free air.

Below me, Huntzel Manor burns. The night sky is filled with glowing ash. For a few minutes, all I can do is sit in the mud and draw exhausted breaths. But I can't afford to rest for long, not with emergency vehicles pouring into the area. I give myself another minute, then hobble down the hill to retrieve my suitcase with Trisha's laptop from the upper veranda.

Moments later, as the house collapses behind me, I limp off into the wet night.

Document Name:
Dear Trisha.docx

I'm giving this to Denise to return to you. I understand why you don't want to see me, but at least you'll have your laptop back before Cooper ropes you into the corral for a powwow, or whatever he calls it.

I did make a print-out of your poem. I hope that's okay.

I want you to know I'm sorry. I'm sorry for not being there for you. I'm sorry for not trusting you.

If you ever decide you want to talk, I'm ready to listen to whatever you need me to hear.

—Joey

4.0: Thend

I find Mrs. Petty's car in the lot outside the Department of Human Services office on SE 122nd. I haven't been here in a while, but I don't imagine things have changed much. Her cubicle is on the far side of the building with no view of the parking lot. The near side has a few meeting rooms. The blinds are drawn in most, but through one wide window I see people sitting around a long table. Little kids and adults, some kind of group session. The kids are drawing or writing. I can see through the glass front doors as well, but the way the diffuse light hits the glass makes it hard for me to make out anything inside. If Mrs. Petty is standing there looking out at her car, I'm busted.

I pull the slim-jim out of my new backpack—bought with smelly cash. Kristina tried to give me a bundle of hundreds, but all I would accept were twenties. "They'll take it away if they catch me. Besides, it's easier to deal with smaller bills." A teenage boy showing up at Home Depot with a stack of Benjamins is asking for trouble.

"You ever need any more, call me."

"Sure." We both know I never will.

I slide the metal strip of the slim-jim down between the window and the doorframe on the passenger side. I'm lucky

Mrs. Petty's underpaid and overworked; the old Impala is held together by rust. I don't have to fight too much to pop the lock. I'm in and out in seconds, take nothing, leave only one item. I lock the door and turn.

She's behind me. Of course.

"Hello, Joey."

I'm supposed to feel embarrassed or ashamed. She's supposed to be angry. Instead, she seems amused and a little sad, and I feel...I don't know what. "Hi, Mrs. Petty."

"I've been worried about you."

"No need."

"Your chin looks—"

"I'm fine." I don't want to talk about how close Mrs. Huntzel's bullet came to making me Orville's twin.

"Of that, I have no doubt." Is she being sarcastic? I can't tell. "What does the note say?"

"How do you know it's a note?"

"I don't suppose it's a cookie recipe."

I smile. A little. There's a copy of Trisha's poem, with her byline. But that's not what Mrs. Petty is asking about. "Among other things, it says I've decided to withdraw from state custody on my own initiative."

"You know I can't allow you to do that."

Here we go. "So...what then? Juvenile detention?" Or maybe Detectives Heat Vision and Man-Mountain would rather try me as an adult.

"You could always go back to the Bobbitts."

"What about the cops?"

She breathes. "The investigation has advanced in a new direction. You are no longer a person of interest."

My mouth opens and closes. "Well...Anita is a drug addict and Wayne can't get his fill of Internet porn."

Now her breathing becomes a sigh. "Joey, tell me something I don't know."

"If you know, why did you keep me there?"

"You're sixteen. You haven't finished high school. You need to be somewhere. We have a shortage of foster families."

"So you stick me with the Boobies?"

"I stick you with them because I know you'll be all right. You can handle them, and if I put you there, another spot is freed up for one of my more fragile clients."

"He changed the locks."

"I've dealt with that, I promise you." She stares off into the distance for a moment. "Listen. I know it's not the best situation. In a perfect world, the Boobies would be off the foster rolls. But in this world I need them. And they *will* provide a roof and clothes and creamed chipped beef. That gives you a chance to finish school and to grow up. You're a smart kid. I don't want to lose you."

She's never called them the Boobies in front of me. "I don't need them."

"If you agree to stay, you can continue at Katz. In January, you'll apply for early graduation. By summer, you could be getting ready for college. With your grades and background, grants and scholarships won't be a problem. But if you run, you'll never finish high school. Life on the streets sucks, Joey. Trust me." She directs a flinty gaze my way. "You certainly can't live in the ruins of the Huntzel house."

Christ. Does she know everything?

"Joey, please. If you go back to the Bobbitts, I'll support early graduation. I'll even help your bid for emancipation."

"I could get my GED in a few years."

"A year from now, you could be living in a dorm in Corvallis or Eugene."

I'm not all that surprised she's guessed my Plan. A lot of case files have crossed Mrs. Petty's desk. She knows the classes I've taken, and she knows better than anyone how determined I am to make my own way. Still, it's pissing me off that she's making sense.

"I want something."

She shakes her head, but then she laughs. "What?"

"I want you to help Trisha."

Her face goes carefully blank. "Patricia Lee? Help her with what?"

She didn't ask to be rescued, but then neither did I. Sometimes we all need a little help. Reid would have a stroke if he heard me say that.

"Her foster father."

One eyebrow rises slowly. "What are you saying?"

"What do you think?"

She's quiet for a long time, but I can see the calculation working in her eyes. "Based on what?"

"Based on her telling me, that's what." I gesture toward the printout in the car. "It's all there."

Enough of it, anyway. Mrs. Petty doesn't need to know about the Krugerrands. Trisha earned them, end of story. But she shouldn't have to keep fucking a fifty-year-old pervert.

"Thank you for telling me."

"Thank me for *telling* you? *That's* what you have to say? Screw that. You need to get after that old perv. Go in hot. Use bad language. Make him crack."

"Joey—"

"I'm serious. Don't let the fucker wiggle out."

"You like her."

"So what?" There's more snap in my voice than Mrs. Petty has ever heard from me.

"She likes you too."

My face goes hot. For a long time, she stares at me—until I feel like I'm going to melt into the ground. Then she lets out a long, slow breath.

"Joey, the situation is already being addressed."

"What?"

"The day after you ran away from the Bobbitts', she came forward about Mr. Vogler. The details of that are none of your business, but, as an aside, in her statement, she revealed where you were when Duncan got hit. Apparently she saw you sneaking into the chess room with the master key you kept hidden inside your laptop."

Obviously I have *no* secrets. "Cooper won't let me stay at Katz if he knows about that."

"Joey, we've both known about that key for months."

For the first time in my life, I have nothing to say. She seems to enjoy it.

"You're going to have to pay for a replacement laptop battery."

"Those batteries are crap." But I'm thinking about Trisha, about sitting across from her at the coffee shop next to the fish tank. About her shimmering eyes, about spending the day just looking into them. Then the amber melts into emerald and I feel confused all over again.

"Joey." Mrs. Petty puts a hand on my arm and I surprise myself by not flinching. "The Boobies. You'll go back?"

She's relentless. "Where is Trisha now?"

"She's safe."

"What does that mean?"

Now it's her turn to snap. "It means her situation has been addressed and she's working through it, and we're helping her." Then her voice softens. "I'm sure she'll be in touch when she's ready."

If she's ever ready. And if she's not, so be it. Safe is what matters. I just hope she had time to pack her things—including the contents of her hide—neatly, in suitcases, without someone looking over her shoulder. Maybe she even took my advice and faked some tears, asked for a moment alone so she could grab her loot in peace.

"I think her next foster parents should be gay."

She laughs. "You have this all figured out, don't you?"

Who the hell knows? It's obvious I've been wrong more than I've been right.

I stand there as she unlocks her crappy old car. "There's one more thing."

"You're pushing your luck."

I whistle. Caliban dashes out of the bushes at the edge of the parking lot and hip-checks me. "I have a dog now. I'm keeping him, no matter what Wayne says."

Mrs. Petty offers us a wry smile. "Are you two coming or not?"

I climb into the car, settle back as Caliban jumps up on my lap.

If we survive the drive to the Boobies, I guess I'll give it a try.

Thend

Author's Note

Many of the locations in *Property of the State* are real, including Mount Tabor Park and Pioneer Courthouse Square. Stately Huntzel Manor, alas, is not. I placed the house in a spot on the edge of Mount Tabor Park which is in fact only a hillside. Uncommon Cup and Katz Learning Annex are also made up, though Katz is modeled *very* loosely on some actual schools in the Portland area. Uncommon Cup is not unlike many of the independent coffeehouses found throughout the city, including the Rain or Shine Coffee House in Southeast Portland where much of the novel was written.

A couple of times Joey mentions SWAT. The Portland Police Bureau doesn't use the term SWAT, but rather SERT, for Special Emergency Response Team. Joey says SWAT because it's the more familiar term to most people and essentially refers to the same thing. And, in any case, despite his brushes with law enforcement, Joey hasn't had to deal with SERT himself. At least not yet.

Many characters in this book are named for people who've inspired me: writers, readers, and friends of extraordinary kindness, talent and insight. The characters are *not* based on these real life people. Rather, I've borrowed their names (first or last) as a way to show my respect, admiration, and affection. Given some of what happens in these pages, you might think I have an odd way of saying, "I like you." Nonetheless, my affection and respect are genuine and heartfelt.

This book wouldn't have happened without the critical eyes of Andy Fort, Candace Clark, Corissa Neufeldt, and Theresa Snyder. More than once they chewed through drafts and gave me the business, and the book is better because of it.

Thank you to Brett Battles for being a great friend and listening to me whine at length by phone and in person during some of the rockier moments of the writing and revising.

Huge thanks go to Ellen Larsen for loving Joey, and for guiding him and me both to the finish line.

As always, thank you to the Shark, Janet Reid, for sticking with me and helping make this book happen. It remains and honor and a privilege to be counted among the Chum.

And of course I couldn't do this without the love, support, and endless patience of my lovely and brilliant wife Jill. Thank you, sweetie!

To receive a free catalog of Poisoned Pen Press titles, please provide your name, address, and email address in one of the following ways:

Phone: 1-800-421-3976
Facsimile: 1-480-949-1707
Email: info@poisonedpenpress.com
Website: www.poisonedpenpress.com

Poisoned Pen Press
6962 E. First Ave. Ste 103
Scottsdale, AZ 85251